WITCH OUT OF WATER

A MOONSTONE BAY COZY MYSTERY

AMANDA M. LEE

WINCHESTERSHAW PUBLICATIONS

❀ Created with Vellum

1

ONE

A naked woman stood in my backyard when I took my coffee to the patio to enjoy the sunrise.

Don't worry; this story won't veer into porn territory or anything. I simply thought it merited noting because it wasn't as if I could look away from the ridiculously-toned silhouette … and I'm big on sharing the suffering when the opportunity arises.

I ran my tongue over my teeth and regarded Aurora King – she of the gleaming fins and tail when hitting the water off Moonstone Bay – with an uncertain look. I hadn't seen her in almost a week, not since she'd saved me from a madman who wanted to steal the lighthouse I found myself living in.

That's when I discovered she was a mermaid, for the record. I was in the water and trying to swim toward shore even though I was terrified of sharks (or worse yet, shark shifters) coming after me. Aurora showed up out of nowhere – naked, as is her way – and towed me to shore where the cavalry was waiting.

The man who wanted me dead so he could steal the property my grandmother had left me in her will was now gone – shot by a grandfather I never knew I'd had – and I returned to a life I couldn't quite wrap my head around. I was still struggling with the aftermath, although my panic and uncertainty lessened every day.

"Hey, Hadley." Aurora offered me a wave as she tugged on a pair of knit shorts, her bare breasts still fully on display. "Do you have a cup of that for me?"

I flicked my eyes to the coffee mug in my hand and found myself nodding before I gave the question much thought. "Sure. I'll be right back."

I returned to the lighthouse kitchen long enough to pour another mug of coffee from the percolating machine – something that felt somehow antique in this day and age – and found Aurora sitting in a lounge chair when I returned. Her hair wet, her T-shirt clinging to her in ways that made me realize she hadn't put on a bra before getting dressed, and her smile somehow mischievous rather than warm and welcoming.

"Here." I handed her the mug and sat on the lounger across the way, my heart rate picking up a notch as I debated what to say to her. It somehow seemed disingenuous to thank her for saving my life a week after the fact, but I couldn't remember thanking her that day on the beach. I had other things on my mind … like a crazed lawyer with a gun and finding out Aurora was actually a mermaid.

Yeah, I was still floundering over that one.

"You look like you have a lot on your mind, Hadley," Aurora noted after sipping her coffee. "Would you like to talk about it?"

The woman was prim and proper – as if she was a therapist trying to delve into my busy brain – and the realization did little to ease my discomfort. "I don't have a lot on my mind." I averted my gaze. "What makes you think I have a lot on my mind?"

"Because I've met you and I've yet to see you when you didn't have a lot on your mind," Aurora replied, pursing her lips as she looked me up and down. Thankfully I was smart enough to dress in simple shorts and a T-shirt for bed, so there was nothing about my pajamas she could find objectionable. "How is May?"

Oh, well, that was a loaded question. May Belladonna Potter was my grandmother. She was the reason I found myself living in Moonstone Bay. She died, left me a lighthouse on an island I'd never heard of, and sent me on the adventure of a lifetime.

I still wasn't sure if I should be grateful or annoyed about any of it.

"She's still around, although she pops in and out a lot," I answered. "She doesn't seem keen to answer questions, instead showing up in weird spots – like the kitchen or library – and spending five minutes prattling on about me and how I should drink more water before leaving the second I ask her a question about anything else."

"That sounds just like May." Aurora adopted a fond smile. "Did I tell you that she used to have coffee waiting for me on this patio at least twice a week? She always liked hearing about what was going on in the sea."

I nodded. "You told me."

"As for her not answering questions, I'm going to guess that's a multifaceted problem she's still trying to figure out. She probably thought she would have more time before explanations were necessary but then you turned into a target and figured out you had magic. That meant she had to work faster than she would've liked. I wouldn't worry about it."

I couldn't stop myself from making an exaggerated face. "You wouldn't worry about it?"

Aurora was blasé. "Nope. I wouldn't worry about it at all. I'm sure May will come around when she feels it's time."

That was another thing that bothered me. "Yeah, um, that's weird, too. I mean … May is dead. I never got to meet her in life and yet she's running around as a ghost in the lighthouse where I live. Don't you think that's weird?"

Aurora shrugged as she sipped her coffee. "Not on this island. I'm sure you find it weird, though. Have you ever asked yourself why you think that way?"

And she was back to being a therapist … and not a very good one. "I think it's weird because ghosts aren't supposed to be real."

"Says who?"

"Says … um … anyone who has ever lived in a place other than Moonstone Bay." I was uncomfortable with the conversation so I decided to change it. "What about you? Do you have any good gossip from town?"

"Oh, the town is always thick with gossip." If Aurora was annoyed at my rather clumsy transition she didn't show it. "Sunny Lee, who owns the nail salon, and Babs Houghton, who owns the laundromat, are going to war over a small park they share in the downtown area. That promises to be all kinds of fun."

I wasn't sure what to make of the tidbit. "Oh, well ... why are they fighting over a park?"

"It's not really a park. It's more like a small patio area between the laundromat and nail salon and it's used most often by people having lunch on the main drag. Other than that, it's largely ignored."

"Huh." Really, what more was I supposed to say? "So why are they fighting?" Aurora showed no signs of leaving, so I had to keep the conversation going somehow. I didn't want to talk about May, so that meant we had to talk about something else. If warring business owners intrigued Aurora, I was happy to stay on that subject. "I mean ... what's their beef with one another?"

"Oh, it's a very long feud," Aurora replied. "Those two have been going at each other for twenty years."

"And why is that?"

"Sunny used to work for Babs but decided to branch out on her own and just happened to lease the space next door to Babs," Aurora explained, her eyes lighting as she warmed to the story. "Babs was grooming Sunny to take over the laundromat without realizing that Sunny didn't want to take over that business – she told me she found it boring and hated answering questions about stain removal – and much preferred a colorful avenue ... like painting nails."

"Ah, well ... ." I really didn't care about the laundromat and nail salon going to war. "I'm sure they'll work things out."

"I'm sure they will, too," Aurora agreed. "If they don't, we're going to have a real human centipede problem on our hand, and nobody wants that."

"I ... what?"

Aurora didn't slow to respond to my obvious confusion. "And how are things between you and Galen?"

I instantly forgot about the human centipede reference and straightened in my chair. The last thing I wanted to talk about was Galen Blackwood, Moonstone Bay's sheriff and prime hunk of burning love. Okay, I added that last part. I was the only one who'd lost myself to thoughts of his burning love ... but I couldn't help myself. The man was smoking hot and caused something chemical to ignite in my brain. I couldn't explain it.

Wait ... what were we talking about again? How did we go from human centipede talk to conversing about Galen Blackwood?

When I didn't answer, Aurora arched an eyebrow and grinned. "That good, huh? Has he rendered you speechless? I seem to remember him having that effect on a lot of women over the years. Now he seems to be keeping to himself – and you – more than spreading the wealth."

Hmm. Just how much "spreading" were we talking about here? "I think you should ask Galen how he is if you want to know," I said. "I'm not his keeper."

"No, but you are dating." Aurora's eyes sparkled as she drank in my amusement and ... well, basked seemed to be the right word. She was clearly enjoying herself and basking in my discomfort. "Last time I checked, you guys have been together every night this past week."

That was a horrible lie – or at least a blatant exaggeration. "We haven't spent a night together since the kidnapping," I countered. "Once Ned was gone I wasn't in danger. There was no reason for Galen to stand guard, so he's been spending nights at his house ... or apartment." Huh. I had no idea whether Galen lived in a house or apartment. That was probably something I should know.

Instead of being surprised by my outburst, Aurora was amused. "Uh-huh. I wasn't talking about your sleeping arrangements – but thanks for the update on those all the same. I was talking about your dating arrangements. You guys have been seen at different establishments across the island every night this week."

"Oh, *that*." Hmm. There was every chance Aurora thought I was spastic. Normally I wouldn't care, but Moonstone Bay was nothing if not a hotbed of gossip and innuendo. I didn't want to be at the center of those circles. "We've been out a few times."

Aurora snorted. "You've been out every night this week. In fact, Jadis Lacosta says that you guys were walking on the beach five nights ago. She said you were holding hands and everything."

"I don't know Jadis Lacosta." That was true, and completely trivial given the conversation.

"Alana Jeffords said that four nights ago you were seen at the tiki bar on the pier and you were sharing mussels and beer."

"We didn't share beer," I said hurriedly. "We each had our own beer."

Aurora barreled forward as if she hadn't heard a word I said. "Alaric Reynolds says that he saw you guys by the cemetery one night and that Galen had spread out a picnic blanket, as if you guys wanted to be alone while watching the ghouls dance on the other side of the wall."

I sobered at mention of the cemetery. It wasn't exactly a sore spot between Galen and me – he hadn't erected the walls or enacted the curse that made those laid to rest inside get up and walk once darkness hit, after all – but it was something I had trouble accepting, so we didn't talk much about it.

"Galen wanted me to be aware of what was in the cemetery." My tone turned decidedly chilly even though I knew Aurora wasn't at fault for being curious. After all, I was the curious sort, too. I, Hadley Hunter, was known to stick my nose into other people's business whenever the chance arose. The cemetery was something I was having trouble wrapping my head around, though. "My mother is in there."

Aurora sobered at the simple statement. "I know she is. I didn't think about that when I brought it up. I'm sorry." She seemed legitimately contrite. "Galen was showing you the cemetery because he didn't want you to accidentally stumble across the zombies and see your mother without someone warning you that it was a possibility."

That was basically it in a nutshell. "He thought, for once, I should be ahead of the curve," I supplied. "He wanted to make sure I had a chance to see her because … well, because I never got to meet her before all this. He also wanted to make me aware that the creatures in the cemetery are dangerous and I shouldn't risk running around there after dark."

"They're not creatures. They're zombies." Aurora was practical. "You can say the word."

I didn't want to say the word. It made me feel like an idiot. I decided to change the subject, again. "So, there's a festival this week, right?"

Aurora blinked several times in rapid succession as she absorbed the shift in my demeanor. "Right," she said finally. "For several days, the festival will mainly cater to residents and the few stragglers hanging around between jaunts off the island. After that, it will be a huge free-for-all when all the new visitors get involved. At that point you'll wish you'd never moved to the island."

Hmm. That was interesting. "And why do you say that?"

"Because festivals are loud, annoying and we have them all the time. I mean … all the time. I don't think a month goes by without some sort of festival. They seem fun and entertaining at first, but they get old really fast, especially when you're forced to constantly deal with drunken tourists."

I wasn't an expert on Moonstone Bay – I'd lived here only a few weeks, after all – but something about that statement caught my interest. "Aren't the tourists here always drunk? I mean, you guys have, like, two stoplights and eight tiki bars."

"You're exaggerating. We have six tiki bars."

That was actually more than I'd counted my first day of touring the island. I'd seen a few more since then, but opted not to count because it gave me a headache. "Fine. You have six tiki bars. That only proves my point. The tourists here are always drunk. This is an island getaway and people go to islands so they can drink out of coconuts and imbibe before noon without getting the hairy eyeball from a boss. I don't see why the festivals would make things worse."

"Oh, you're so cute and shiny," Aurora cooed, catching me off guard. "I forget that you're not part of the regular gang and don't know how things work. No matter. You'll figure things out on your own soon enough. Everyone always does."

That sounded rather ominous. "So, you're not going to tell me why festivals are so terrible?"

Aurora merely shrugged as she stood and handed me her empty coffee mug. "Here's the thing, I don't want to taint your opinion about the island or what it has to offer because I've been warned repeatedly to keep my mouth shut."

That was news to me. "Who told you to shut your trap?"

"Galen, and he didn't use those exact words." Aurora offered me a pretty smile. She really was quite striking, which made me wonder if she and Galen had had a thing before I landed on the island. She seemed his type. Wait ... that was so not the point of the conversation right now. I had more important things to worry about.

"What words did he use?" I was honestly curious. If Galen was telling people how to act around me, there had to be a reason. I didn't know him all that well, but I recognized that fact fairly easily. "I mean ... what exactly did he say?"

If Aurora sensed danger lurking behind my reaction, she didn't show it. She was incredibly nonchalant as she shrugged. "He said that he didn't want anyone foisting his or her preconceived notions onto you. He wants you to discover what you like and don't like about Moonstone Bay on your own.

"I think he's hoping that he's the thing you like best," she continued. "He didn't come out and say it, but it's written all over his face. He's got a huge case of crush-itis."

It took me a moment to comprehend what she was saying. "You think he has a crush on me? That seems ... ridiculous ... since we're dating."

"I agree." Aurora beamed, clearly not caring if the expression irritated me. "I don't see why he's so up in arms about protecting you. He is, though, and I agreed not to complain and force you to my way of thinking when it comes to the island. He wants you to like what you legitimately like and hate what you legitimately hate … as long as the hate doesn't extend to him."

"I don't think he has to worry about that," I said absently.

Aurora barked out a laugh so loud and raucous it caused me to jolt. "I don't think he does either. It really doesn't matter, though. You'll make up your own mind about the festival. Don't let the rest of us steer your opinion."

"I'll try to keep that in mind."

"You do that." Aurora pointed herself toward the beach. "I'm heading home. I'm sure I'll see you around."

"It seems to turn out that way." Mostly because she insisted on swimming naked in front of my lighthouse.

"It certainly does," Aurora agreed, offering up a half-wave. "I'll see you soon. Toodles."

And just like that she was gone and I was left to ponder the upcoming festival. What odd new thing – or event – was Moonstone Bay about to introduce me to? It wasn't really a matter of if it would happen, but rather when things would take a turn for the weird. I was resigned because it was inevitable.

Seriously … now what?

2

TWO

I was bored at home after Aurora's departure, so after showering and changing into simple cargo shorts and a tank top, I locked the lighthouse and headed to town. Moonstone Bay is an island, so the town representatives limit the number of vehicles allowed on the relatively small landmass. Only a few people are allowed to own motor vehicles – mostly farmers, construction workers, emergency personnel and shuttle drivers – and even though I found it strange at the start I was almost getting used to walking everywhere I needed to go.

The busy downtown area wasn't far from the lighthouse. I could easily make the trek in less than five minutes. My only problem with the constant walking was dealing with the heat and humidity, which was boiling hot and dripping wet before the noon hour set in.

"I'm bored," I announced as I took a seat at the counter of my friend Lilac Meadows' rustic and cute bar.

Lilac, who was twenty-three going on sixty if you believed the way she communicated with people, arched an eyebrow as she automatically filled a glass with iced tea and shoved it across the lacquered countertop. "Well, hello to you too."

I was instantly contrite. "Sorry. That wasn't much of a greeting. How are you, Lilac? How is your day going?"

Lilac, her frizzy flaxen hair reminding me of a bad eighties perm, merely shrugged in amusement. "I'm fine, Hadley. How are you?"

"I'm bored."

"And we're right back to where we started." Lilac grinned as she plopped a lemon wedge in my iced tea and watched me slurp down a third of the glass. "You really need to start carrying a bottle of water with you when you walk around. We've been over this. If you carried water, you wouldn't be so thirsty when you get here."

"This place is five minutes from the lighthouse," I reminded her. "I shouldn't get dehydrated simply from walking for five minutes."

"Welcome to Moonstone Bay."

I rolled my eyes. "Yeah, yeah. I'll try to remember to carry water with me. I forgot to put fresh bottles in the refrigerator last night. There's nothing worse than warm water."

"I can think of a few things that are worse … like running into an electric eel shifter underwater and having to deal with the catastrophic hair ordeal that always accompanies that for the next month."

I pointedly shifted my eyes to Lilac's hair. Her curls did seem to have a mind of their own of late. That might explain a few things. "Uh-huh."

"Stop staring at me like that." Lilac snapped her fingers in my face to get my attention. "That is not what happened to me. It's just the island humidity. When it's at seventy percent I can deal. When it's at ninety percent it's as if the world is going to end. The last two weeks have been in the ninety-percent range."

I pressed my lips together to keep from laughing. Lilac was the first person on the island to offer her friendship, and I would be forever grateful to her for that fact alone. Learning the ropes on an island like Moonstone Bay – a place where zombies roam free in the cemetery and nobody cares but everyone is afraid of the Downtown Development Authority and the citations it might issue on a whim – was a tangled minefield of trouble. Lilac willingly helped me navigate that field. That made me like her and the mop resting on top of her head.

"Well, I think the curls are nice," I lied. "They give you a certain … ." I pinched my fingers together as I searched for the right word.

"They make me look like Little Orphan Annie, except I have real eyes," Lilac shot back. "I know I resemble a poodle. There's no reason to pretend otherwise."

I balked. "You don't look like a poodle." Labradoodle was more like it. "I swear."

"I'm going to take you at your word and move on from this conversation," Lilac noted. "You said you were bored when you came in. What do you plan to do about that?"

That was a very good question and I wasn't sure I had an answer. "I don't know." I held my palms out. "I've never been without a job for more than a week. I mean … never. Sure, they weren't all great jobs, but I'm at a loss about what to do with my time."

"Do you want a job?"

I'd been asking myself that for seven days straight. Once I was over my kidnapping and near murder, I'd had no choice but to think of the practical. "I don't know. Technically May Potter left me enough money that I didn't have to worry about working for the foreseeable future.

"The lighthouse is paid for and I can cover the taxes for years," I continued. "I have enough for groceries and I don't need to spend a lot of money on clothes. I don't have to work if I don't want to work."

"So don't work." Lilac was blasé as she set about making piña coladas. "If I didn't have to work, trust me, I wouldn't work. I would turn myself into a lady of leisure and spend all my time reading trashy magazines on the beach."

"But don't you think that would get old after a little bit?"

"Not really. You obviously do, though."

I did. That was only one of my problems. "I've always had something to do. My father was a big proponent of me having a job so I valued the things I could buy. He didn't want me to become jaded about money."

"I think money is the best thing to be jaded about."

"And I get that," I said. "I just can't shake the feeling that I should have a job. Aren't I lazy if I don't have a job?"

Lilac widened her eyes when I finally admitted the source of my discomfort. "Wow. Lazy, huh? I wasn't sure you'd get there. You've been beating around the bush for days regarding that subject."

"Yeah, well, I'm antsy." I found it wasn't that hard to tell Lilac the truth, and once I opened up I wanted to keep talking. "I think it would be easier for me to settle into a routine if I had a schedule to follow. Right now, I basically get up and drink coffee before coming here to drink iced tea. That can't be healthy."

"You're leaving out the part where you let Galen take you to a restaurant or bar and drink rum runners at night," Lilac teased.

I scorched her with a dark look. "You promised not to pry when it comes to Galen."

"I don't believe I uttered a promise. I believe I said I'd try to do better."

"Is this you trying to do better?"

"Trying but not succeeding." Lilac's smile was so wide it stretched across her entire face. "I think getting a job is probably a good thing even though I'd absolutely love it if I didn't have to work. I could offer you a job here, but I don't think our friendship would survive that."

I had no doubt she was right, and our friendship could not survive her being my boss. In fact, I wasn't sure if our friendship could survive more than a handful of hours a day together. I decided to keep that to myself, though. "I'm not even sure what kind of jobs are available on Moonstone Bay."

"Oh, well, I think the job selections are kind of normal." Lilac strolled to the end of the bar and handed the two women sitting there – who happened to be lost in their own little world as they bent their heads together and gossiped – glasses of iced tea before strolling back to me. "Basically there are always open waitress, cleaning and hospitality gigs. Can you do any of those things?"

That had to be a trick question. "Can I be a maid or hostess? I think I can handle it."

Lilac wagged a finger close to my nose. "Being a waitress is harder than it looks."

Whoops. She'd misunderstood me. "Oh, I understand about that. I worked my way through college as a waitress so I could have enough money to party. My father insisted he wasn't bankrolling my drinking habits."

Lilac stilled. "I thought you had an English degree."

"I do. It's essentially the most worthless degree out there. Unless I somehow luck out and get a college teaching position – which I don't want because I can't stand dealing with young people of a certain age – then I'm stuck doing jobs that have nothing to do with my degree. I should've thought better before majoring in English. I mean ... I ended up working in graphic design, for crying out loud."

"Huh." Lilac looked mystified. "I didn't even consider that. It makes sense, though."

"I've also worked as a secretary, a pizza delivery woman and a shoe saleswoman," I added. "I'm what you would call 'flexible' when finding work."

"That actually might benefit you in Moonstone Bay," Lilac noted. "I'm not sure who's hiring, but I'll keep my ear to the ground. If I were you, I'd give serious thought to what you really want to do with your time. You might be surprised what options are open to you on Moonstone Bay."

"Which options are you talking about?" A gravelly voice asked from behind me, causing me to jolt.

I swiveled on my stool and widened my eyes when I saw Galen Blackwood, he of the ridiculously glossy dark hair and sinfully blue eyes, standing behind me. He had a small smile on his face, which was hard to focus on given his broad shoulders and overall package. "Hey," I sputtered, choking a bit on my iced tea. "What are you doing here?"

Galen's mischievous grin was contagious. "Can't I simply want to stop for some iced tea?"

As if on cue, Lilac slapped a glass in his hand. "I had it ready for you and everything, big guy."

Galen snorted as I shot him a dubious look. "Or perhaps I noticed you walking downtown when I was driving through a few minutes ago and figured you were on your way here," he corrected. "I had a break in my schedule, so I thought I'd spend a few minutes with my favorite bartender." He winked at Lilac for emphasis.

"Oh, isn't he sweet as the dickens?" Lilac drawled, rolling her eyes. "I almost want to believe those flirty words. Of course, only an idiot would think he's not really here for you, Hadley, and I'm not an idiot."

My cheeks burned as I shifted to face forward while Galen took the open stool to my right. "So … you came to see me?"

Galen chuckled, legitimately amused. "You make me laugh. I love it when you get all flustered. Usually you're in the mood for fights and frolicking – yeah, I used the word 'frolicking' and I don't even care – but occasionally I catch you off guard and you turn into a blushing mess."

Was he right? Did I turn into a blushing mess when he was around? That needed to stop, and soon. "I am not blushing. The lighting is simply off in here."

"If that's your story." Galen sipped his iced tea before focusing on Lilac. "What were you talking about when I came in? I wasn't exaggerating about having only a few minutes. I have to run to the surfboard shop before lunch, so I can't spend too much time gossiping."

"We weren't talking about anything important," I replied hurriedly.

"We were talking about the possibility of Hadley getting a job," Lilac answered, ignoring the dark look I shot in her direction. "She's at a loss and bored. We were discussing what she's qualified for, and it turns out she's qualified to do quite a lot … or very little, depending on how you look at it."

I didn't bother to hide my scowl. "Thank you so much for that."

Lilac was oblivious. "You're welcome."

I risked a glance at Galen and found him smiling, his eyes patient and considering rather than full of teasing and mirth. "I just kind of want something to do with my day," I said.

"I don't think it's a bad idea," Galen supplied. "If you're bored, a job might be good. Do you have an idea of what you want to do?"

He was so pragmatic I could do nothing but shrug. "I'm just sort of thinking about it now."

"You have time to make a decision." Galen tilted his head to the side when the women at the end of the bar started talking to one another in raised voices, narrowing his eyes for a beat. When they quieted down again, he focused on me. "We can talk about it on our date tonight. I can ask around and see who is hiring. You don't have to make a decision right away, but maybe we can put together a list or something."

I snickered. "You want to put together a list? That doesn't sound very … romantic."

Galen winked as he tipped back his head and drained the rest of his iced tea. "I can make anything romantic. I promise. As for a job, I'll give it some thought and get back to you over dinner tonight." He took me by surprise when he tipped back my chin and smacked a loud kiss against my lips. "I'll pick you up around six. Is that okay?"

I dumbly nodded as my cheeks burned. Sure, the bar was mostly empty, but that was the first time he'd kissed me in public. So far, our kisses were mostly private affairs … and that was somehow comforting for me. "Sure."

"Oh, look how cute she is," Lilac trilled, her teeth showing as she grinned. "I love it when she gets all flustered like that. It takes away from that tough mainland persona she insists on carrying around, but I find it delightful."

"I do, too," Galen enthused. "In fact … ." Whatever he was about to say died on his lips as he snapped his head to the end of the bar. It was almost as if he knew something was about to happen, because the moment his eyes landed on the two women one of them threw a punch and knocked the other from her stool.

"What the … ?" Lilac was flabbergasted as she scurried around the bar.

Galen was far ahead of her. He had his hands on the brunette attacker's shoulders before she could let loose another punch. "Knock it off, Trish," he barked, shooting the blonde on the floor a warning look before pushing Trish far enough away that she couldn't continue the brawl. "What are you two fighting about?"

"It's none of your business," Trish hissed, kicking her feet as she tried to pull away from Galen. "This isn't a police matter. It's a … friendship matter."

Lilac paused close enough to my stool that she could whisper without being overheard. She was ready to dive in should Galen need help, but otherwise she remained calm and close to me. "Trish Doyle and Ashley Conner," she muttered under her breath. "They've been best friends since roughly middle school, I think. They even graduated together, which was about seven years or so ago if you're keeping count."

I wasn't, but it was a nice tidbit all the same. "Okay." I kept my eyes on the women, who were both red-faced and flustered as they glared at one another. "Apparently they've had a falling out."

"Apparently," Lilac agreed, stepping forward. "You guys know better than to fight in here. What's got you all twisted up?"

"It's none of your business," Ashley snapped, rolling to her knees and slowly getting to her feet. She checked her arm, as if looking for a mark, and then gave Trish a wide berth as she circled the table and increased the distance between them. "As for you, I think you know what I'm about to say."

"Oh, I know," Trish sneered. "You're going to say our friendship is over because I betrayed you, but in reality you betrayed me. We both know it. He knows it, too."

"Who is 'he'?" I asked innocently, earning a quelling look from Galen and a hateful stare from Trish.

"It's none of your business, newbie," Trish barked. "Don't go sticking your nose into other people's affairs. That's a surefire way to find trouble on this island." She shifted her eyes back to Ashley. "As for you, if I see you again you know what's going to happen."

"I definitely know what's going to happen," Ashley agreed, smoothing her shirt and showing her teeth … which looked a lot longer than they should, as if she were about to turn into some sort of otherworldly creature. Of course, given the heightened situation, there was every chance I was imagining that. "You're going to lose if we run into each other again."

"Oh, in your dreams." Trish rolled her eyes. "You're the one who will lose. In fact, you'd better keep your distance from him if you don't want to lose ... well, everything."

"Knock that off," Galen warned, giving Trish a good shake. "I can't stand by and listen to you toss around death threats. You know that."

I had to admire his calm veneer even as I marveled at the way the women glared at each other. In that particular moment I had no doubt that both would be willing to use their teeth to rip out the other's throat. It was a sobering – and chilling – realization.

"You don't have to worry about us," Ashley called out as she arrived at the door. She appeared calm, but I could practically feel the distress wafting off her in waves. "We won't cause trouble, will we, Trish?"

Something unsaid passed between the two women and Trish straightened. "Of course not," she answered perfunctorily. "We're done fighting. It was a quick thing and it's over now."

Galen obviously didn't believe them, but he was in a precarious position. "Steer clear of each other until you two calm down. Do you hear me?"

Trish offered a sarcastic salute. "We hear you. We'll be good, boss. We promise."

I was new to Moonstone Bay, but I clearly recognized she was lying. Galen had no reason to restrain the women, though, so he took a step back and offered them the opportunity to clear out. "I'll be watching if you don't keep your word."

Ashley licked her lips. "Like I said, you don't need to worry about us. We've got everything under control."

"Everything," Trish echoed. "We won't cause trouble. We swear it."

For some reason, I didn't believe them.

3

THREE

Galen was prompt, knocking on my door at exactly six. He was dressed in cargo shorts and a simple T-shirt, his black hair fresh from the shower and slicked back from his face as it dried. He took a long moment to study my cotton skirt and peasant blouse and offered a smile before extending his hand.

"You look nice. I like how the white top looks against your dark hair."

As far as greetings go, it was an odd one. "I … thank you."

Galen made a face. "That came out a little weirder than it sounded in my head."

"Kind of like you were on *America's Next Top Model* and gushing about my fabulous walk?"

"Pretty much."

Even though I didn't fancy myself much of a giggler I couldn't stop myself. "Thank you for saying it, though."

"I do like the way you look in the top." Galen shook his hand, as if to remind me it was still extended between us. "Are you ready to head out?"

"Sure." I was still getting used to the fact that Galen not only wanted to spend time with me but seemingly enjoyed showing me around the island. I took his hand and cast a glance over the living room, briefly wondering if May was around and watching us depart. "I'll be back later," I called out to no one in particular. "I … um … will see you then."

I pulled the door shut and locked it before shoving my keys into my small bag and turning a set of expectant eyes to Galen. He looked amused, although I couldn't exactly figure out why. "What?"

"This is Moonstone Bay. You don't have to lock your door."

"A week ago I was abducted and almost killed by a lawyer," I reminded him. "Before that a crazy man with an ax broke in while I was sleeping."

Galen's smile slipped. "Don't remind me. By the way, I've been in contact with Ned's law firm. They want to hold onto the property he acquired – especially because he didn't have any living relatives – but I've put them in contact with the DDA and told them to sort it out with those guys."

The DDA remained the one mystical source of power I couldn't quite understand in Moonstone Bay. Sure, you might think I'd be more upset to learn I was a witch – yeah, that's totally true – or that Galen was a wolf shifter (totally true and kind of hot), but the fact that everyone in Moonstone Bay feared the DDA somehow twisted me up more.

"Exactly how much property did Ned Baxter manage to amass thanks to murdering little old ladies who lived by themselves?"

Galen shrugged. "First, I know you don't know your grandmother very well, but she's going to take that 'little old lady' comment as a direct insult. Second, he had a lot of deals in the works. The ones that weren't finished will revert back to the seller, which happens to be most of them. There were two or three he managed to shove through, though, and that's going to cause issues."

"And this DDA that you're so afraid of but I've never managed to see up close and personal, you think they'll be able to fix everything so that it's as if Ned never went on a killing spree?"

Galen was blasé as he fell into step next to me, keeping my hand in his as we headed toward the main drag. "I think that the DDA is better equipped to deal with the fallout than I am. No one knew what Ned was up to until it was too late. As for pretending Ned never went on a killing spree, that will never happen because you're here and you're only here because Ned killed May."

He had a point. "Would you prefer May back or me here?" I asked the question before I thought better of it. Putting Galen on the spot seemed somehow unfair. How could he possibly answer that question?

"I would prefer not answering that," Galen replied without hesitation. "Either way I'll look like an ass. I loved May – she was a good woman – but I kind of like having you here. It's a toss-up."

I smirked. "I'm sorry. That was unfair to ask."

"Not unfair, just … impossible to answer." Galen squeezed my hand as the now-familiar lights from downtown filled the vista stretching in front of us. "So, this is your first Moonstone Bay festival. I think you're in for some fun. What do you want to do first?"

The conversational shift threw me for a loop. "Oh, um … whatever you want is fine."

Galen's smile slipped. "You're not one of those women who says, 'I don't care where we eat' and then pitches a fit when I pick a location you don't like, are you?"

I was offended. "No. If I'm in the mood for something to eat I'll tell you. I wasn't saying that to be a typical woman."

"Fair enough. Why did you say it?"

I saw no reason to lie. "Because Aurora made it sound like the last place I would want to hang out was a Moonstone Bay festival."

"When did you hang with Aurora?"

"She stopped by for coffee this morning after her naked swim."

"Ah." Galen didn't seem particularly perturbed by the news. "I asked her not to disparage things like the festival in front of you. She must have forgotten."

He wasn't ashamed to admit it, so I saw no reason to ignore the potential conversational bedlam hanging over us. "And why did you tell her to watch what she said around me again?"

Galen held out his free hand to usher me onto the sidewalk in front of him and then matched my pace. "I didn't ask her to watch what she said around you as much as I pleaded with her not to give you preconceived notions about Moonstone Bay as a whole. There's a lot about this place you don't yet understand."

"Do you honestly think I don't know that?" I wanted to laugh at his earnest expression. "I figured out Moonstone Bay was different the first time I saw Aurora swimming naked in the surf ... and that was before I saw you turn into a wolf."

Galen pursed his lips. "I don't remember you taking that well. In fact, if I remember correctly there was a lot of screeching and whispered threats about me keeping that a secret that first night."

"That's not what happened."

"It's close to what happened."

"Not really." I moved to pull my hand away, but Galen didn't release my fingers. "I don't screech."

Galen snorted. "Right. I must have imagined that. It doesn't matter. Let's talk about something else. Let's talk about the festival."

"Okay, let's talk about the festival." I was gung-ho to talk about whatever he wanted to talk about ... as long as it wasn't my perceived screeching. "What should I expect from this happy Moonstone Bay event?"

"Well, I guess that depends on your favorite festival food. How do you feel about cotton candy?"

"It's okay but not a favorite."

"Caramel apples?"

"Not a big fan."

"Elephant ears?"

"I would roll around naked in the dough and eat them for dessert for the rest of my life."

"I knew there was a reason I was attracted to you." Galen's grin was charming as he directed me toward the front gate of the festival. The closer we got, the more I could admire the rides and bright lights. "I'm a big fan of carnival food. I like kebabs ... and hot dogs ... and burgers. There's even a food truck that serves fried green tomatoes if you're interested in that type of thing."

I perked up considerably. "Really? I love fried green tomato sandwiches."

"That just goes to prove we're even better matched than I originally thought."

He was cute, but sometimes I got the distinct impression that he was trying too hard. "You don't have to lay it on so thick," I supplied. "I know you're enjoying the dating thing we're doing as much as me. It's still new to both of us, though. You don't need to constantly ply me with compliments to get me to keep dating you ... at least not right now. That might change if you keep bringing up screeching that never happened."

"Ha, ha." Galen flicked my ear with his free hand. "I don't mean to bury you in an avalanche of compliments. I'd be lying if I said I wasn't worried about you from time to time, though. This place is new and you're still getting used to things you might not be ready to understand."

"And you're fearful I'll decide that it's not for me and take off with no warning," I mused. "I get it."

"I don't want you to take off," Galen agreed. "You belong here. I don't think you realize that yet, but given some time, I think that's the one conclusion you won't be able to ignore."

"Well, I'm willing to look at it through open and accepting eyes if you promise to stop telling people how they should react around me. I mean, for the record, I'm not going to start hating festivals simply because Aurora tells me they're a pain in the butt. I can form an opinion of my own."

Galen smirked. "I'm more than aware of that. I apologize for telling people to keep their opinions to themselves. I simply didn't want to overwhelm you."

"A festival won't overwhelm me." I meant it. "In fact, I happen to love a good festival."

Galen grinned as he tugged on my hand and directed me to the left. "Well, in that case, how do you feel about visiting the House of Mirrors first?"

"I could handle that. But I want some sugar first."

Galen's smile turned wolfish. "I like sugar, too."

"Ugh. You've got a dirty mind."

"That's just one thing you'll have to get used to."

"I think I'm up to the task."

"**HERE YOU GO,** honey. Don't say I never gave you anything."

I tried to hold my smugness to a tolerable level as I handed Galen a stuffed bear with minimal charisma and a lopsided smile an hour later. Galen took the animal, shaking his head as he studied the pathetic creature that was harder and lumpier than most plush toys should be.

"This did not work out as I thought it would," Galen admitted after a beat, his expression unreadable as he studied the bear. "Most of the time, when it comes to a festival, I'm the one who wins a bear and wows my date. It doesn't often happen in reverse. In fact, it's never happened in reverse."

I didn't know what to make of the admission. "Just how many women have you tried to win stuffed animals for?"

Instead of being abashed, Galen shrugged. "A few. I like to think of myself as the athletic sort. If you must know, though, I haven't won a stuffed animal for a woman in ages, so you have nothing to worry about."

I knew it was unnecessary to poke him, yet I couldn't stop myself. "That streak is technically still intact."

Galen scowled, which only served to make him more appealing for some reason. "Yeah, well, I don't understand why you couldn't simply let me win the stuffed animal on my own."

"You threw away twenty bucks without making any headway."

"I would've won eventually."

"Yes, well, I used to work for an indoor carnival outfit when I was in high school. I know all the tricks of the trade."

Galen furrowed his brow. "What tricks? You throw darts at a balloon. There's no trick involved with that."

I patted the top of his head because I couldn't resist his adorable expression. "You're so cute."

Galen caught my hand and snagged my gaze. "I'm serious. How can there be a trick to throwing darts?"

"How can you ask that after I won you a bear and you tossed away twenty bucks winning me nothing?"

Galen's cheeks flushed, forcing me to bite my bottom lip to keep from laughing. He looked caught, as if he wanted to learn while at the same time holding on to his stereotypical manhood. I was curious which would win out. Ultimately, his curiosity couldn't be denied.

"Okay, I'll play. How do you win the dart game?"

I smiled in triumph … and also relief. Galen was a man, but he was one who wanted knowledge more than bragging rights. That was something I could work with. "Well, for starters, you need to arc up." I gestured with my hands for emphasis. "The darts are dull for two reasons, one of which is that people can't be trusted not to poke out their own eyes."

"I can see that."

"The other is that most people aim directly at the balloons," I added. "You don't work up enough velocity at that angle to pop the balloon. If you arc up, gravity helps and gives you enough force to pop it."

Galen glanced back at the game, his lips curving down when a teenager with a puffed-out chest threw a dart directly at a balloon only to watch it bounce to the side and hit the ground behind the counter with a dull thud. "Huh. I think you might be right."

"You'll find sooner or later that I'm always right."

Galen chuckled and shook his head as he lodged the bear under his arm and linked the fingers of his free hand with mine before turning me away from the game. "I'm always up for new adventures so I'm going to take this in stride."

"Just think of it as a fond memory."

"I'm always looking for fond memories." Galen nodded his head at two young women who giggled and whispered to one another as we passed, pointing me toward the far tent in his efforts for us to escape the crowd. "Ladies."

I waited until we were out of earshot to press the issue. "You have quite the effect on women, don't you?"

"Those weren't women. They were teenagers."

"They looked old enough to drink."

"They're sixteen and seventeen. They're the Hamblin sisters. They look older, but they're not."

"Oh." I was understandably taken aback. "I guess that's okay then. You probably have teenagers all over the place who develop crushes on you."

"Both boys and girls. I find it flattering and creepy."

I decided on a pragmatic tack. "Well … things could be worse. No one could find you attractive because of your pathetic dart-throwing skills."

"Good point." Galen pressed his hand to the small of my back and prodded me toward an empty picnic table between the fortune-teller's tent and what looked to be some sort of weird beer tent. I couldn't quite decide what was going on under the second tent, but I was intrigued. "Let's take a load off for a little bit."

"Okay." I sat and watched as Galen rested the sad bear on the picnic table before sliding onto the bench beside me. It felt a little odd for us to be on the same side, yet I appreciated his closeness all the same. "You said earlier that you were going to tell me about some of the people in town. You've yet to do that."

"I know, and I've been giving it some serious thought," Galen said, causing a warm jolt of energy to course down my spine when he slipped a strand of hair behind my ear. "On one hand, I don't want you feeling left out when those around you start gossiping. On the other, I kind of think you'll miss out if you don't meet everyone on your own. It's quite the pickle."

"I don't know what to think about a guy who uses the word 'pickle' like that."

"Duly noted." Galen wasn't bothered at my continuous poking.

"Still, I think you might benefit from meeting people on your own timetable. If I introduce you, I'll be influencing your opinion whether I want to or not. If you meet the townsfolk on your own, you'll be able to form your own opinion."

"And we're back to this, huh?" I didn't know whether to be amused or irritated. I settled on amused because I wasn't in the mood for a fight. "I'm fine with meeting people on my own. I'm not going to pretend I don't find it weird that you want to shield me from everyone else's opinions, but I've decided to let it go."

Galen's eyes lit with amusement. "Good for you. That's very magnanimous."

I snorted. "I don't know about that. I'm simply having too good of a time to let something so trite distract me. I reserve the right to fight over it again when it's not so hot and I'm not so sweaty."

Galen leaned closer, so close, in fact, that I could feel his breath on my exposed collarbone. "It's always hot here. You should probably get used to being sweaty."

His playful words caused the energy bolt to return. "Really? How did I know you would say something like that?"

"I think you're getting to know me on a personal level."

"I think so, too."

"I can't help being glad about that." I could practically feel Galen's heart beating through his skin as his arm touched mine. "I like you getting to know me."

I swallowed hard as I tried to find my voice. "Well … ."

I thought he was going to finish leaning in and kiss me – something that both excited and terrified me – but instead he darted his eyes to the right and furrowed his brow. I was so lost in the moment it took me a moment to realize Galen was no longer looking at me. When that realization finally set in, I couldn't help being disappointed.

"Did you find something more interesting?"

Galen carefully shook his head as he slowly stood. "I … don't know."

I tried not to be offended. "Well, I guess I won't take that personally."

"It's not that," Galen said. "It's … that."

I was confused. "What?"

"That." Galen extended a finger and pointed toward the side of the tent.

I followed his finger with my eyes, taking a moment to allow my gaze to adjust to the gloom, and sucked in a breath when I realized what I was looking at. "Oh, my … are those feet?"

Galen nodded as he stalked in their direction. "Yeah, and I'm guessing there's a body attached. Stay close, Hadley. I don't like the looks of this at all."

4

FOUR

Galen's face was grave when he found me back at the picnic table twenty minutes later. I stayed with him after the initial discovery – long enough for him to confirm the individual on the ground was dead – and then I gave him room to work. He was the sheriff, after all. He had a job to do. I didn't want him to feel as if I was crowding him.

"Hey." Galen absently trailed his fingers over my back as he sat on the bench next to me, his eyebrows hopping when he got a gander of the huge blue slush I was drinking. "Are you trying to overdose on sugar?"

I shrugged and stuck out my tongue so he could see the blue hue. "It cools me off, which I think is going to be unnecessary now that you've found a dead body. That cools me off, too … just in a different way."

"Yes, well … ." Galen's smile was rueful and I could read the uncertainty and disappointment behind his forced smile.

"You don't have to worry about it." I squeezed his wrist to offer what little comfort I could. "I know this isn't how you saw our date going. I don't blame you for having to do your job or anything."

"I know. It's still ... disappointing." Galen tilted his head back, staring at the sky as he rolled his neck. "I was kind of hoping that I'd be able to talk you into resuming sleepovers tonight, but I think I'll have to back off that thanks to the knife wound in Trish Doyle's neck."

There was so much about that statement I wanted to press him on that I didn't know where to start. "It's too soon to have sleepovers." I meant it. "I thought we agreed to get to know one another first."

"I didn't say the sleepovers required sex."

I rolled my eyes. "Please. I'm not new."

Galen managed a grin, but it didn't make it all the way to his eyes. "I'm fine waiting. I was simply messing with you." He sobered after a beat. "I was just teasing you. I don't want you to think I was pressuring you. That was a stupid thing to say."

"I prefer it when I'm the one who verbally beats you up," I chided. "I don't like it when you do it. I know you were joking. Let it go."

"As long as you know." Galen exhaled heavily as he rubbed the back of his neck. "I'm pretty sure she either died or was severely injured here. I can smell the blood on the ground. The blow was quick and efficient and the knife is still lodged in the soft tissue. I can't pull it out until the medical examiner is done and I doubt that will be until tomorrow."

He was matter-of-fact and I couldn't hide my surprise that he was sharing sensitive case information. "Why are you telling me?"

"Because you were with me when I found her and I think you deserve to know."

"I'm not a police officer."

"No, but you are ... intuitive." Galen pressed his lips together as he debated ... something. Finally he merely shrugged. "I don't know how else to tell you this ... and May would probably be angry that I'm considering it at all ... but your grandmother used to help with my investigations occasionally. I'm wondering if you might be in a position to help."

I was understandably dubious. "My elderly grandmother helped you solve murder cases?"

"She's going to pitch a fit if you call her 'elderly,'" Galen noted. "I'm serious. She won't like that one bit."

"Well, if she ever shows up and sticks around for longer than five minutes I'll take that into consideration." I rubbed my cheek as I studied Galen's serious face. "How exactly did my grandmother help you with investigations?"

"She was a witch. You're a witch. I thought maybe you shared a few powers."

I glanced around, worriedly scanning the nearby faces to see if anyone heard. "Say that a little louder," I grumbled. "I don't think the guy over there shoving blood samples into test tubes heard you."

The man in question, a blond with a charming smile, lifted his chin and started shaking his head. "I heard him. It's fine. I already knew."

I murdered Galen with a dark look, but he was already raising his hands when I swiveled. "Did you hear that? He already knew."

"I'm sorry. I should've thought about that before I said it." The words tumbled out of Galen's mouth. "I know you're keen to keep that under wraps, big on privacy and all that."

"Even though everyone already knows," the tech called out.

"Thank you, Dave," Galen snapped, his eyes flashing. "Don't you have something you're supposed to be doing … like working on the body?"

"I'm collecting soil samples." Dave was somber as he stood. "The blood spread pretty far from where the body is. I'm not an investigator, but to me that seems to indicate she was alive and bleeding out long enough for the blood to run down the hill and pool up here or … well … ."

"Or she was initially stabbed down there and dragged up the hill," Galen finished, his expression thoughtful. "Which one do you think makes more sense?"

"I'm not the investigator," Dave replied. "I'm a lowly lab tech. Why not have your girlfriend touch the body and answer that question for you?"

I balked at the suggestion, jerking my shoulders. "Excuse me?"

Galen let loose an exaggerated sigh and pinned Dave with a dark glare. "There's a reason people say you talk too much. You know what that reason is, right?"

"I'm fine with it." Dave was blasé as he straightened his shoulders. "I'll run the blood samples. I might be able to tell you which scenario is more likely, but I'm not sure it truly matters. A knife in the throat tends to suggest a crime of passion."

"Especially when the knife is left behind," Galen murmured as he stared at the medical examiner, a lithe blonde who wore a short skirt and carried a clipboard in her glove-covered hands. "I'll talk to Darlene before she leaves and ask what she thinks."

"She's going to say what she always says," Dave countered.

"Wait for the evidence," Galen and Dave said in unison, adopting mocking female tones.

"Well, maybe she has a reason for saying that," I supplied, sipping my slush as I stared at the woman in question. "She obviously seems very diligent. She's all dressed up and came to work anyway."

"Darlene is a consummate professional," Galen said. "She's been in the medical examiner's office for a long time. I'm glad she's the one on this case. She's easy to work with."

I stared at the woman's long legs. "Yeah. I bet." I realized I was being envious – and not for a good reason – and forced myself from my reverie. "So, you said it was Trish Doyle. The same Trish we saw melt down with her buddy in Lilac's bar this afternoon?"

"That would be the one," Galen agreed, grabbing the slush from my hand and taking a sip without asking. "I can't believe Ashley would do this, but … I also saw how angry they were with one another earlier. They wanted to throw down."

"Trish Doyle, huh?" Dave knit his eyebrows. "I didn't realize it was her until you mentioned it. She was behind me by a year or two in high school. I always thought she was a bit … ."

"Fiery?" Galen suggested.

"I was going to say oversexed," Dave replied without hesitation. "I know it's wrong to speak ill of the dead, but that chick was always looking for someone to nail … or rather, someone to nail her. I think she slept with half the town … including you, if I'm not mistaken."

My stomach twisted as I pressed my lips together and slid him a sidelong look. I wasn't exactly jealous, but I wasn't thrilled with the revelation either. I couldn't put a name to what I was feeling.

Galen scowled when he saw my expression. "Thanks for that, Dave."

Dave was oblivious. "No problem. I'm going to talk to Darlene and then probably head back to the lab. I'll send you a report as soon as I have anything."

Galen was beyond listening to Dave, instead focused on me. "It was a long time ago."

I held up my hand to cut him off. "You don't owe me an explanation." That was true. "You're a big boy. You've been an adult for a long time. I've seen how you look without a shirt. I'm not exactly surprised you have a past that involves multiple women."

I was, however, surprised he had a past with this particular woman. While pretty, she seemed somehow angry and defiant to the point I had a hard time picturing Galen rolling around naked with her. That was something I wanted to keep to myself, though, and think about long and hard later.

"Oh, don't phrase it like that." Galen made a face. "We were both young and dumb … and there was a bonfire. It hardly matters. It was long before I knew anything about you."

For some reason his insistence on explaining himself filled me with mirth. "Good to know." I patted his arm before turning my full attention to Trish's body. I tried to avoid staring at it from the start, but now it was as if I couldn't look away. "She looks as if she took a beating before she died. I don't think the knife wound is the only injury you'll find."

"I agree."

"What were Dave and you talking about?" I asked after a beat. "What could May do that you obviously want me to try?"

Galen heaved out a sigh. "I was sort of hoping you would forget I brought that up. I feel kind of guilty, and I'm not sure this is the time to talk about this."

"Well, I'm not sure now is the time to talk about this either, but it doesn't seem we have much choice." I forced myself to remain calm as I met his gaze. "What could May do?"

Galen almost looked contrite as he regarded me. "Sometimes – and it wasn't something she could do every time – but sometimes May could touch a victim and … um … see what happened to them in the last minutes of their lives."

The revelation caught me off guard. "Seriously?"

Galen nodded, conflicted. "I was hoping maybe you could do the same, but … if you're not ready … ." He left it hanging.

I swallowed hard as I stared at the body, a myriad of emotions and feelings rushing through me as I tried to identify one thought to cling to. If I could focus on one thing I would know how to answer … at least I believed that was true. "Oh, well … ."

"Don't twist yourself up," Galen said hurriedly, holding up a hand. "It's too much to ask. You just found out you're … ."

"A witch. You can say it."

"Special," Galen clarified. "You just found out you're special. The rest of it was far too much to ask."

I wasn't sure I agreed. "I can try. I mean … if you really want … I can try."

Galen momentarily looked caught and then shook his head. "No. This is my job. It's not your responsibility. Maybe down the line, after you've settled a bit, but for now I think you should just be you."

I couldn't help being relieved. "Are you sure?"

"I'm sure." Galen smiled as he stroked his hand down the back of my head and handed me the slush. "Finish with your sugar. I have to … ." Whatever he was about to say died on his lips as he narrowed his eyes and looked at a point over my left shoulder.

I swiveled quickly to see what he was staring at and my eyebrows hopped when I caught sight of one of his deputies dragging a swearing and spitting Ashley Conner with him.

"I found her, sir," the deputy announced, pride evident as he puffed out his chest. "She was in the beer tent doing the limbo."

For some reason, I found the thought of that so surreal I had to chew on the inside of my cheek to keep from laughing.

"Thank you for that, Roscoe."

My mirth shifted to confusion. "You have a deputy named Roscoe? Like on *The Dukes of Hazzard?*"

Now it was Roscoe's turn to scowl. "It's not at all like *The Dukes of Hazzard*. I mean ... sheesh. Does this look like Kansas to you?"

"Georgia," I automatically corrected. "Hazzard County was in Georgia."

Galen cocked an eyebrow. "Is there something you want to tell me?"

I shrugged. "Fast cars turn me on."

"Remind me to host a *Fast and Furious* movie night," he muttered, shaking his head before focusing on Ashley. "Do you know why you're here?"

"I think I'm here because your girlfriend doesn't put out and you want a real woman," Ashley spat, causing my cheeks to color.

Galen remained calm. "That's not why you're here. You're here because of that." He pointed toward Darlene toiling over Trish's body. "Do you have anything you want to say about that?"

I didn't consider myself an expert on reading people – lord knows I made more mistakes than I could count in that department over the years – but the look on Ashley's face was so profound that I would've swore on a stack of bibles right then and there that she was innocent and had no idea the woman she called "friend" up until a few hours before was dead.

"Is that Trish?" Ashley's hair whipped from side to side as she glanced between the body and Galen. "Seriously, is that Trish?"

Galen nodded. "That's her."

"Well, why aren't you transporting her to the hospital?" Ashley barked. "Why aren't you helping her? I mean ... she doesn't look good. I'm going to make sure she knows you just left her there looking like that and she'll sue you."

Galen was calm as he slowly got to his feet and moved closer to Ashley. I studied his face for a sign of what he was feeling, but he was ridiculously hard to read. "She's not going to get better. She's already gone."

"What? No." Ashley furrowed her brow as she studied her friend's body. "That can't be right. I … no. You're wrong! Either this is a dream or you're wrong!"

"I definitely wish it were a dream," Galen said. "I also wish I was wrong. But I'm not. Trish is dead. She died sometime tonight, although it will be a little bit before we have an exact time of death. I'm sure you understand why I dragged you here."

"I … ." Ashley worked her jaw. "You think I did it."

"I think you and Trish exchanged harsh words this afternoon," Galen clarified. "I think you two were fighting about something. I want to know what that something was. In fact, I want to know who that someone was you were referring to in the middle of the argument."

Ashley wasn't quite ready to give up her secret. "How do you know we were fighting about a guy?"

"Because you kept referring to 'him' and 'he,'" Galen replied without hesitation. "I'm not an idiot. You guys were fighting over a man. I want to know which man … and I also want you to confirm your whereabouts since I last saw you at the bar."

Ashley was clearly caught off guard by Galen's matter-of-fact nature. "You think I murdered Trish! I couldn't. I was angry with her, sure, but I would never kill her."

"I didn't say I thought you murdered her." Galen was careful, remaining calm even as Ashley's demeanor fired with fury. "I simply want to know who you were fighting over and where you were this evening. We'll start there."

"I was here all night," Ashley snapped. "I was in the beer tent … and maybe outside one of the food trucks for a bit. A bunch of people saw me here. You're not going to pin this on me."

"We'll work hard to confirm your alibi."

"As for who we were fighting over, it seems stupid now, but … it was Booker."

The revelation stole my breath. *Booker?* The same Booker who was hurt when a murdering lawyer kidnapped me? The same Booker who did work around my house? The same Booker who helped me uncover a family secret? That couldn't be right.

"Not my Booker," I said automatically, earning a surprised look from Galen.

"Your Booker?"

Uh-oh. I sensed trouble brewing. "You know what I mean," I said hurriedly. "He helped me." I swallowed hard. "He got seriously hurt helping me."

Galen's expression softened, but only a little. "I understand what you mean. But you have to understand that Booker is much more than that."

"Much, much more," Ashley agreed, taking on a dreamy expression.

"Ugh." Galen rolled his eyes. "Let me guess, you and Trish were both spending time with Booker and he didn't bother to tell either of you he was playing the field. Am I close?"

Ashley returned to reality and shrugged. "He liked me more. Trish simply couldn't deal with it."

"Criminy." Galen pinched the bridge of his nose. "All I wanted was a quiet night with my girlfriend. Is that too much to ask?"

That was a loaded question. "Since when do you refer to me as your girlfriend?"

Whatever bravado remained withered as Galen shook his head. "Of course you would latch on to that one word. I should've seen that coming."

"You definitely should have," Dave agreed as he passed behind Galen and made a clucking sound with his tongue. "You've dated enough women to know that was a stupid thing to say."

Galen sighed. "Live and learn."

Live and learn indeed.

5

FIVE

May was in the kitchen when Galen dropped me off. He wasn't so distracted by Trish's murder that he didn't spend a full five minutes kissing me goodnight, which left me breathless and a little disheveled when I walked into the house.

May looked amused by my flushed cheeks and messy hair. "Hello, dear. How was your date?"

The question caught me off guard, as did the mug of tea that May magically had waiting for me on the counter even though she didn't have corporeal hands. I was still trying to figure out how she managed to physically move objects. "I ... it was okay."

"Just okay?" May's expression was speculative. "It looks as if things went better than okay."

I kicked off my sandals and left them by the front door before moving into the kitchen. Even though I wasn't in the mood for a hot beverage, I sipped the tea as I got comfortable on a stool and regarded my dead grandmother. "It started out great. It ended great. There was a spot in the middle that wasn't so great."

"Oh, that's too bad," May tsked. "What happened in the middle of the date? Did Galen get handsy? I only ask because he's a bit notorious as a lothario."

That was the last thing I wanted to hear. "No. He didn't get handsy."

"So, what's the problem?"

"We discovered a dead body and he had to work."

"Oh." May turned serious. "Who died?"

"Trish Doyle?"

"Maureen Doyle's girl?"

I shrugged. "I have no idea. She was brunette and pretty, looked to be in her mid-twenties. I never met her. I saw her in Lilac's bar fighting with a woman named Ashley Conner earlier today. I think Ashley is Galen's prime suspect."

"That would be the girl I was thinking of. How did Trish die?"

"She was stabbed in the neck and dumped between two tents at the festival. Apparently she lost a lot of blood."

"That's a lovely picture." May made a face. "It's also a hard way to go."

"It is," I agreed, sipping the tea. I wanted to ask May about what Galen related earlier, but I was uncomfortable broaching the subject. Finally I knew I had no choice. "Did you really touch dead bodies and tell Galen how they died?"

The question clearly caught May off guard. "I … well, yes."

"How did you know?"

"I could see visions from right before they died. When something traumatic happens, it sticks with a body for a bit. I couldn't always make it happen, but when I could I tried to be helpful."

"That's pretty much what Galen said." I sipped again. "How did you figure out you could do that?"

"I touched a body at the funeral home once," May replied. "Edna Wharton. Everyone thought she fell down the stairs, but when I touched her I realized her longtime maid shoved her. Granted, Edna was a real pill and mean to everyone, so she might've had it coming. I often wondered why the maid didn't quit and find something else to do. I told Galen what I saw, he questioned the maid and she owned up to what happened. After that … Galen called me occasionally when he needed help on a case. I went because I figured it was my duty."

"How often was that? I mean … how often does Moonstone Bay have murders?"

"You'd think it would be a rare occurrence given the island's size, but that's not the case." May's smile was sympathetic. "Did you touch Trish?"

I shook my head. "Galen changed his mind about asking me. He said that he didn't want to push me before I was ready, and said he'd handle things himself."

"That seems gallant."

"Yeah, well … ." For lack of anything better to do, I drained the rest of the tea. "I kind of feel guilty because I didn't insist on touching her. If I could provide answers I can't help but feel I should."

"And I think it's a waste of time to get worked up over things like this. You might still be able to help. You can't go back in time and change what happened to Trish, so ultimately it doesn't matter all that much that you didn't touch her. I'd focus on that rather than what you appear to see as a lack of courage."

"I know I can't bring her back. That doesn't mean I can't help find her murderer."

"Galen may be young, but he's good at his job. He'll figure it out."

"I guess." There was nothing left to drink so I tapped my fingers on the counter. "Trish and Ashley were in Lilac's bar earlier. They were getting along for the most part, seemed to be gossiping and having a typical outing between friends. Then they turned on each other out of nowhere and started fighting. That's not normal, even in Moonstone Bay, right?"

May chuckled, genuinely amused. "I'd say not. Do you know what they were fighting about?"

"A man. They never said who at the bar. They promised to stop fighting if Galen let them go, but it was obvious they didn't mean it. When Galen had Ashley brought to the scene tonight, she seemed legitimately surprised that Trish was dead. She actually seemed upset, too."

"Perhaps she had nothing to do with it," May suggested. "Maybe it was a coincidence that they fought and that Trish later died. I certainly hope that's the case, but I've never considered Ashley Conner the violent sort."

"Galen asked who they were fighting about."

May arched an expectant eyebrow. "And?"

"She said it was Booker."

Instead of being surprised, May choked out a laugh. "Ah, well, the boy does have a way with women."

"I've never seen Booker with a woman."

"You've been here two weeks."

"Yeah, but ... he didn't hit on me or anything." I had no idea why I said it. I realized even as the words escaped that it made me seem petty, as if I wanted Booker to hit on me. That wasn't true. I simply couldn't wrap my head around the enigmatic jack-of-all-trades and what he offered the island. He was definitely more than he appeared to be, and yet two women fighting over him seemed to indicate he was somehow less than what I expected. I couldn't explain it. "I don't want him to hit on me," I added hurriedly. "I just never pegged him as a ladies' man."

"Booker is so many different things I lost count years ago," May supplied. "He is a vital part of the Moonstone Bay team, even though he fights that notion."

What was that supposed to mean?

"He's also got a way about him that serves as catnip for women," May continued. "He doesn't have to put any effort into the seduction. The women go to him."

"And he lets them?"

"He ... enjoys various forms of entertainment."

I didn't miss the fact that May was purposely vague. "If everyone on this island is some sort of magical misfit who belongs on the paranormal spectrum, that means the same is true of Booker. What is he?"

"He's many things."

"That's not really an answer."

May flicked her eyes to the corner and, as if on cue, the antique grandfather clock positioned there struck midnight. "Oh, will you look at the time? You need your beauty rest."

"I'll sleep after you answer the question."

"Later."

"But … ." I didn't get a chance to finish my interrogation because May winked out of existence and disappeared from my kitchen, leaving me more agitated than when she'd appeared. "This isn't over," I called out, irritation weighing down my shoulders. "I'm not done asking you about Booker no matter what game you're playing."

May didn't respond or reappear. Typical.

"This place is just one thing after another," I complained as I flicked off the downstairs light and headed for the stairs. "Only a crazy person would choose to live here."

That said a lot about me, of course, but I meant it all the same. "I think I'm turning into a loon."

"It's a family trait, dear," May's voice whispered as I hit the second-floor landing. "You'll get used to it. You might even see it as a good thing."

I doubted that. "You're not going to tell me about Booker, are you?"

"Goodnight."

"That's what I thought."

WITH NOTHING BETTER TO do with my morning – I still had no idea what sort of job I wanted or what I was even qualified for on Moonstone Bay – I headed toward the beach the next day.

I packed a bag full of bottles of water, sunscreen and a book, and walked down the sandy beach until I hit the public access point near the main docks. It was early in the week for tourists, which left the beach almost empty.

In truth, I hoped I'd stumble across Booker. I knew he'd been working on various projects at the tourist center at the edge of the beach and was hoping that he'd continue today. I didn't even have to go through the pretense of spreading out a towel and opening a book because I recognized Booker's ancient van right away.

I found him at the front of the building, scraping letters from the window. He didn't look particularly hot or perturbed. He didn't look as if he thought the job was beneath him. He didn't look especially engaged in the task either.

His handsome face lit up when he saw who was coming to visit. "Hey, Hadley! I haven't seen you in a bit. How you doing?"

That seemed an odd question because he was the one who'd been hurt saving me. "I was just about to ask you that."

"I'm fine."

"I'm fine, too."

Booker's grin widened. "I guess we're both fine then." He stopped what he was doing long enough to dig in the bag by his feet, coming back with a hefty bottle of water. His eyes roamed my face, seemingly intent on whatever he found there, but he didn't ask me any odd or invasive questions. "I heard you were at your first festival last night," he said finally. "Did you have fun?"

That was the last question I expected. "It was … fine." I wasn't sure how to answer. "Given what Aurora told me yesterday morning, I expected some weird festival shenanigans or something. But it was a normal festival."

"I'd argue that nothing is ever normal on Moonstone Bay."

"Okay, let me rephrase that." I sucked in a breath as I debated what I wanted to say. "The festival had food trucks, games and a lot of people having a good time. That's how festivals are in most places, so it didn't seem strange or different to me."

Booker chuckled. "I guess that's fair enough." He took another swig of water. "Still, I heard Galen got called away to investigate a murder. I'm sorry your date got cut short."

Hmm. He was giving me an opening. It seemed almost too easy. "We had a good time until then. He promised to take me back. I think interrupted outings are a constant possibility when dating someone in law enforcement."

"That's a healthy attitude to maintain."

"And I think you were dating the woman who died." The words slipped out before I could give much thought to the intelligence associated with uttering them. It was as if I couldn't control my own tongue and something inside took over … and issued a very rude proclamation. "I mean … um … ."

Booker's expression was hard to read. He tilted his head to the side, pursed his lips, and said absolutely nothing. To me, that was worse than saying something stupid.

"I know you probably think it's none of my business," I started.

"It is none of your business."

"Probably not, but I can't help being curious. I didn't know the dead woman – Trish Doyle – but I interacted with her earlier in the day because she got in a fight with another woman at Lilac's bar. Ashley Conner. I believe you know her, too."

"Moonstone Bay is a small island," Booker shrugged. "I know almost everyone on the island."

"Yes, but both those women said you were dating them."

"And you believe them?"

The question caught me off guard. "I … well … they were fighting. Galen said they were friends, but they were fighting over you. That seems to suggest they felt they had something legitimate to fight about."

"That's some fine deductive reasoning." Booker took another drink of water before returning the bottle to his bag. "As for my dating life, I wasn't aware you had such an interest in it."

"I don't." I hated being on the defensive, but I felt that way now. "I just … didn't realize you were actively dating."

Booker chuckled, seemingly amused. "You are a trip. Has anyone ever told you that?"

Surprisingly enough, multiple people had told me that. "I know it's none of my business. You can tell me to stuff my questions if you want. I just kind of want to know the answer. I haven't seen many dead bodies in my life and it was strange to know that I saw Trish hours before she turned up dead at the festival."

"I can see how that would be traumatic." Booker dragged a hand through his dark hair. "I'm not sure I should say anything. I'm worried it would encourage you to stick your nose in my business."

"I don't want to stick my nose in your business." That was mostly true. "I can't help thinking of you as a friend, though. When my friends are in trouble, I want to help. I have to think that dating two women at the same time – and the death of one of those women – suggests trouble."

"Ah." Booker didn't look convinced. "So, your reasons for poking into my personal life are altruistic. That's what you're saying, right?"

He was backing me into a corner. I recognized the signs but couldn't figure a way out. "I'm saying that I want to help if you need it." That was also the truth. "I didn't realize you were even dating. If you want me to butt out, all you need to do is say so.

"The thing is, you got hurt while visiting my house," I continued. "I was worried about you. Of course, right before that I was worried you might be a killer, so that actually makes my guilt double the size it would normally be because I feel bad about suspecting you. I want to help if I can."

Booker chuckled, making a clicking sound with his tongue as he shook his head. "You make me laugh so hard. As for suspecting me that day at the lighthouse, that was smart. May had warned you danger was coming and I was the next person you saw. You would've been stupid to react differently."

"But you were innocent."

"I could've been guilty. You had to save yourself." Booker rested his hands on his hips and licked his lips. "You don't have to worry about me. I've been taking care of myself for a very long time. Yes, I might have been spending time with Trish and Ashley at the same time. That doesn't mean I'm a murderer, and it doesn't mean either relationship was even close to a dating scenario."

I balked. "I didn't think you were a murderer. That's not what I was saying."

"I know."

"I don't understand why you'd date two women at once. That doesn't seem very … nice."

Booker shrugged. "What can I say? Women love me. I don't know how to explain it."

I narrowed my eyes. That was almost the exact thing May had said the previous evening. It didn't feel like a coincidence and yet I didn't see how it could be anything but. "So, basically you're telling me to butt out … but in a nicer way."

Booker grinned and bobbed his head. "Basically." He moved his scraper back to the window, his eyes focused on the task he worked at before I joined him. "You don't have to worry about me, Hadley. I can take care of myself. You should spend more time worrying about yourself and less time focusing on me."

That was a dismissal if ever I'd heard one. "Okay, well, I guess I'll get going."

"You probably should do that," Booker agreed. "Worrying about me seems a foolish way to spend your time. Focus on the good things. Let everything else go."

That was it? He wasn't going to tell me anything else? I shouldn't have been surprised … or irritated … but I was both. "Okay, well, I guess I'll see you around."

Booker offered up a playful wink. "It certainly seems to work out that way."

And just like that I was on my own with no answers in sight. I didn't like it one bit.

6

SIX

I had multiple questions, no answers and a curiosity streak a mile wide. I also knew only one person who was likely to share. That propelled me to pick up sandwiches and pasta salad from the grocery store to surprise Galen with lunch at the station shortly before noon.

The woman sitting behind the counter was unfamiliar to me. She was pretty – in a very severe and formal way – and she looked to be pushing fifty. For some reason, given all the stories I was starting to hear about Galen's dating proclivities, I couldn't help being relieved that she was probably out of his dating age window.

"Can I help you?"

"My name is Hadley Hunter." I felt stupid now that I was forced to explain myself. "I … um … was hoping to see Galen."

"Sheriff Blackwood is on the phone."

"Right. Well … I can wait."

The woman stared me down for a long moment. "Fine. There are chairs over there." She vaguely gestured toward the small lobby at the front of the building. "I'll inform him you're here."

"That would be great."

I took the first seat at the edge of the lobby and nervously perched the grocery bag on my lap. I was uncomfortable with the way the secretary kept looking at me. She picked up a phone and murmured something that I couldn't hear and then continued to stare. I was relieved when I heard a door open down the hallway behind her a few minutes later and Galen appeared in the space over her shoulder.

"Hadley? What's wrong?" He strode directly to me, his face a mask of worry. "Did something happen?"

The question caused guilt to roll through my stomach. "I … well … no. I just decided to stop by and bring you lunch." I held up the bag as proof. "I thought you might be busy and I didn't want you to miss a meal."

That sounded believable, right? I worried it sounded too forced.

Galen's expression was hard to read as his shoulders slouched and he studied my face. "I see." He didn't say anything else, instead snagging the bag from my hand and looking inside. "Corned beef and Swiss. One of my favorites."

I knew that from dining out with him. "You need your strength if you're going to solve a murder."

"Uh-huh." Galen didn't look convinced. "Well, this is a nice surprise." He forced a smile and gestured for me to stand. "Come on. We have a table in the break room. We can eat there."

"Great." I flashed the secretary a haughty smile as I trailed behind him, internally cheering when she rolled her eyes. "It was nice to meet you."

"We didn't really meet," the woman drawled.

"Oh, I'm sorry." Galen stilled next to her desk. "Hadley, this is Rose DeWitt. She works the front desk here sometimes. She's not a regular or anything, but she fills in when I have a gap in my schedule. Rose, this is Hadley Hunter. She owns the lighthouse now. She's May Potter's granddaughter."

Rose's expression didn't change. "I was fine not being introduced."

I narrowed my eyes. "Well, I was fine not being introduced, too."

Galen exhaled heavily and pressed his hand to the small of my back as he ushered me toward the hallway. "Let's not turn this into a thing, shall we? There's no reason to get all … feisty."

"I don't believe that word has ever been used to describe me," Rose supplied evenly.

I could believe that. The woman was cold to the bone. "How sad for you," I muttered.

"Come on. Let's have lunch." Galen kept his hand on my back as he directed me down the hallway, not stopping until we entered a tiny room that featured one counter and two small tables. It was deserted, which somehow made me breathe easier. "This is a nice surprise."

Galen grabbed two sodas from the tiny refrigerator lodged between the cabinet doors and plopped them on the table before sitting next to me. I could tell he had a lot of questions – most of which I wasn't ready to answer – but he wisely decided to get the pleasantries out of the way before diving in.

"How did you sleep last night?"

"Oh, well ... ." I broke off and furrowed my brow. "May was waiting for me when I got home. She had tea brewed and everything."

"That's nice."

I could think of a few other words to describe it. "I think it's weird. I've never had a hands-on grandmother before. Now I have one who is a ghost. She makes tea, asks questions and then disappears before answering anything I want to ask her. It's ... frustrating."

Galen chuckled. "May was always like that. She only talked about what she wanted to talk about. You'll get used to it."

"Well, she said that she wasn't surprised Booker was dating both girls and that he's known as something of a ladies' man, that women are somehow magically drawn to him."

Galen unwrapped his sandwich, his expression never shifting. "That's probably a fair assessment."

"Do you want to know what's funny? I tracked down Booker today and he said almost the exact same thing. I mean ... he used the same words and everything."

Galen paused before he bit into his sandwich. "You tracked down Booker?"

"It wasn't hard. He was at the tourism center on the beach. He was scraping letters."

"Well … ." Galen looked to be at a loss.

"I told him I thought it was weird he was dating two women at once. All he said was that he was popular and women love him."

"That sounds like Booker." Galen wrinkled his nose. "How much time did you spend with him?"

"Not much. He was dismissive and not overly chatty."

"He might think his personal life is none of your business."

"It's not." I understood that, even if I didn't like it. "I still find the fact that he was dating two women at once disturbing."

"And I find the fact that you're fixated on that little detail frustrating," Galen admitted. "It makes me nervous that you're so invested in what Booker is doing with his personal life."

The admission threw me for a loop. "Why are you nervous? I … that's ridiculous. You have nothing to be nervous about."

"Good."

"I'm not interested in Booker," I added. "I'm interested in finding out why he's dating two women, one of whom turned up dead, and he doesn't even seem to care."

Galen bit into his sandwich, his expression thoughtful. He didn't speak again until after he swallowed. "I can't give you answers. I don't have insight into Booker's dating habits. We're not that close."

"Yeah, well … ." I decided to let it go and change the subject. "Do you have any new information on Trish Doyle's death?"

"I do." Galen bobbed his head. "Ashley Conner is in custody because her alibi didn't check out. People remember seeing her at the festival early and late, but there are two hours in there she can't account for. Trish died in that timeframe."

That was disturbing news. I pictured Ashley's face from the night before. "She seemed legitimately surprised when she saw Trish's body."

"She did. Of course, that could've been an act."

"Do you believe it was an act?"

"I believe … ." Galen broke off, as if searching for the correct phrasing. "I believe that she was genuinely upset. Whether she was upset because she killed Trish and felt guilty or was simply surprised, I can't say. Right now, though, she has motive and means."

"How does she have means?"

"She was hanging around and can't account for her time. She had access to knives and although we haven't tracked that specific one it's possible it belongs to her."

"That doesn't seem like reason enough to arrest her."

"I don't know what you want me to say, Hadley." Galen's demeanor was stern. "She'd threatened the victim hours before Trish turned up dead. She has no alibi. She's being held here for the time being."

He was firm and yet I struggled to wrap my head around what he was saying. "Are you going to charge her?"

"That's up to the prosecutor's office."

"When will they decide?"

"When they decide." Galen bit into his sandwich and stared as he chewed. I was uncomfortable with his scrutiny. "Can I ask why you're so invested in this?"

I shrugged as I tugged the lid off the pasta salad. "I don't know. I just feel ... engaged ... in the process. If you expect me to explain, I can't. I just want to know what happened to her and why."

"Is it because you saw the fight in Lilac's bar?"

"I ... don't know."

"Is it because you were with me when the body was discovered?"

"I just told you I don't know." My temper came out to play. "I can't explain it. I don't expect you to understand. I just ... want to know what happened to her."

Galen used a napkin to wipe the corners of his mouth, tilting his head to the side as he considered my morose countenance. "Fine. I'll keep you updated on the investigation. You might not like what that entails, but it's the best I can do."

I didn't expect to get a promise like that out of him, so I was happy to take it. "Thank you."

"You're welcome. Now, can we enjoy this wonderful lunch you obviously slaved over all morning? I think we've both earned it."

I made a face as he smirked. "There's no need to get snarky. We both know I'm not the type to slave over a stove … well, ever."

"That's okay." Galen patted my hand. "You're a great shopper. In fact … ." He trailed off and snapped his head in the direction of the lobby. I didn't hear anything, so I was confused by the shift in his expression.

I was instantly on alert. "What's going on?"

"Stay here." Galen was on his feet and striding down the hallway before I had registered the loud voices in the lobby.

Even though he ordered me to stay behind, I scampered after him. I wasn't keen on being separated in case something big went down and my natural busybody tendencies didn't allow me to ignore potential investigation information should it arise.

By the time I got to the lobby Galen had positioned himself between two men – both of whom looked to be in their fifties – as they were sniping at each other as Moonstone Bay's sheriff worked overtime to calm them.

"This is not the place for this," Galen snapped, his eyes briefly landing on me. "I thought I told you to stay in the cafeteria."

I held my hands palms up, my shoulders hopping. "I wanted to serve as backup in case you needed it."

Galen offered a "whatever" face. "Right. You stay over there and don't get in the middle of this. I mean it. Rose, call for backup."

Rose didn't look eager to jump to attention and follow Galen's orders. "I already did. Your backup should be here shortly."

"Great." Galen slowly turned his attention back to the arguing men. I couldn't make out much of what they were shouting, but there seemed to be a lot of "kiss my ass" and "I hope you die a terrible death" statements.

"You guys knock this off now!" Galen bellowed, causing both men to snap their mouths shut and widen their eyes.

Galen tentatively lowered his hands but remained alert should the fight resume. "That's better."

"Speak for yourself, Galen," one of the men hissed. "Nothing is better. My daughter is dead and you have the audacity to say things are better? What kind of sheriff are you?"

My eyebrows hopped as I realized one of the men, the schlubby one to the right with a pronounced bald spot and an ill-fitting shirt, was clearly Trish Doyle's father.

"And I told you last night, Gus, that I was sorry for your loss and have every intention of finding out what happened to Trish." Galen's voice turned softer, although the edge remained. "I really am sorry about what happened to Trish, and I know things aren't better for you. That was a poor choice of words."

"And what about me?" the other man challenged. "Do you think things are better for me?"

"No one cares how things are for you, Henry," Gus growled as he used a handkerchief to mop his sweaty brow. "In fact, if you never spoke again we'd all be happy."

"Says you," Henry fired back.

"You think people want to hear you talk?"

"No, I think people want to hear you shut up. Permanently." Henry threw himself at Gus, intent on great bodily harm to his face, but Galen was ready and stopped him before he could carry out the attack.

"Knock this off right now," Galen hissed. "This is not a respectful and mature way to handle a beef."

Gus let loose a "well, duh" eye roll that caused my stomach to flip. "Really? Do you think we don't know that? How stupid do you think we are?"

I was absolutely flummoxed by the display of ill-tempered testosterone. Rose must have read the confusion on my face because she decided to explain things.

"That's Henry Conner," she whispered. "He's Ashley's father. He's been in a longstanding feud with Gus since ... well, I think it was at least the late eighties. I'm not really clear on the timeline."

I wasn't Rose's biggest fan, but I was thankful for the gossip. Galen clearly had his hands full and couldn't indulge my nosy side. "So, they've been fighting for years and now one of their daughters has been arrested for murdering the other's daughter? That can't be good."

"Way to state the obvious."

I frowned. "I was merely making an observation."

"Yeah, yeah, yeah. You need to be quiet so I can hear the fight. This is going to be the talk of the festival later and it's not often I have a ringside seat for these things."

"Well, at least you have your priorities in order."

"Says the woman who tried to sweet talk her honey with lunch in exchange for information she shouldn't be privy to," Rose drawled.

I wanted to argue the point but she wasn't wrong. Instead, I focused on Gus and Henry and pretended I didn't feel guilty for being called to the mat due to my despicable behavior.

"My daughter is dead," Gus screeched. "My sweet little girl, the light of my life, is dead. This ... animal ... is to blame. I want him arrested."

Despite the difficult situation, Galen remained in control. "Henry didn't kill Trish. He was at the Elks lodge. I checked his alibi. It holds up."

Gus was flustered. "I'm not saying he killed her himself. He armed that two-bit hooker of a daughter he's so proud of and had her kill my Trish. That's the only explanation."

Henry was positively apoplectic. "I did no such thing. My Ashley is an angel. She would never hurt anyone. That's not how she is. Besides, your daughter was notorious around town for sleeping with anyone – including married men. The list of people who would want to do her harm has to be long and sundry."

"You take that back!" Gus growled.

"Never! My daughter is innocent. She's been locked up and it's a miscarriage of justice. I'm going to call Johnnie Cochran."

"I think Johnnie Cochran is dead," I offered helpfully, earning a withering look from Galen.

"That did it." Galen had had enough. "Hadley, I want to thank you very much for the lunchtime surprise, but I'm going to have to end my break early. As you can see, I have my hands full here."

I instinctively straightened. "Right."

Galen waited a beat. When I didn't move, he sighed. "That means you have to leave, darling. I need to focus on Gus and Henry. I can't do that when I'm worried you might accidentally get hurt while trying to eavesdrop … or do whatever other wacky thing that busy brain of yours comes up with."

I was pretty sure that was an insult, but I could hardly blame him. He did have work to do. "Okay, well … I guess I'll see you later." I edged toward the door. "Let me know how much later if you get a chance."

Galen kept a firm grip on the fronts of both men's shirts to make sure they didn't make a break for it. "I will call you as soon as I can. Just … go."

"Don't forget me." It took everything I had to drag my eyes from the scene. "I won't be waiting by the phone or anything, but don't forget to call anyway."

Galen sighed. "Get out."

I wrinkled my nose. "We're going to talk about your attitude later."

"We definitely are."

7

SEVEN

I wanted to be agitated with Galen for kicking me out of his office, but I couldn't pull it off. He had a job to do and I was in the way. He wasn't wrong to question my interest in the case. I couldn't explain even to myself why I was so desperate to find answers. I couldn't explain to him why it was so important when I didn't fully understand myself.

I was agitated and restless, so I needed to entertain myself for a few hours. Doing it at Lilac's bar wasn't enticing and I'd already spent time with Booker – the only other person on the island I really knew to any degree – so I had a decision to make. Ultimately, I found one of the three cabs Moonstone Bay boasted on the main drag and paid the driver – a delightful man named Aaron – to drop me on my grandfather's doorstep.

Oh, yeah, I have a grandfather. I didn't know he existed until a few days after I'd landed on Moonstone Bay. Apparently he and May divorced decades before I arrived ... but that didn't stop them from having sex on a regular basis. I was fairly traumatized by that little detail. I got over it quickly when my grandfather shot a homicidal lawyer to protect me.

Our relationship was a work in progress.

If Wesley Durham – I had trouble calling him "Grandpa" – was surprised to see a cab dropping me off, he didn't show it. He wandered from the nearby barn and arched an eyebrow when he realized who was visiting.

"Hello, Hadley."

"Mr. Durham." I straightened my shoulders. "I ... um ... thought I would drop by for a visit." I felt inexplicably stupid as I regarded him.

For his part, he seemed more amused than I felt. "You don't have to call me 'Mr. Durham.' You know that, right?"

I shrugged, noncommittal. "I don't know what else to call you."

"It's too soon for something cutesy. I agree with you there."

I pressed my lips together to keep from laughing. Wesley was a rough and tumble guy with a gritty personality. I wasn't sure I'd ever be able to think of him in a cutesy manner.

"How about you call me Wesley for now?" he suggested after a moment. "I only allow bankers and grifters to call me 'Mr. Durham,' so we need to compromise."

It felt weird to call my grandfather 'Wesley,' but I didn't see where I had many options. "Okay. Wesley it is."

"Good." He tilted his head to the side as he looked me up and down. "You're kind of wound up, huh? What have you been doing with your day?"

The observation caught me off guard. "Oh, well ... ."

"Hold up." Wesley held up a hand to quiet me. "If we're going to have us a visit we should probably do it proper-like. That means you need something to drink and I need to take a break and put on my entertaining cap."

"You have an entertaining cap?"

Wesley shrugged. "I'm trying here. Can you not give me too much grief?"

That seemed a fair request. "Okay. No grief."

"Take a seat on the porch." He pointed. "I'll join you directly."

WESLEY TOOK ONLY twenty minutes to put together a pitcher of tea and change his clothes. When he joined me in the sitting area on his wrap-around porch, I was much more settled than when I'd arrived.

"I don't have lemon for the tea." Wesley screwed up his face as he stared at the tray he delivered to the center of the table. "I'll try to remember that for next time."

"I don't need lemon." I forced a smile for his benefit as I grabbed a glass and drank half of it down. "See. The tea is great without lemon."

Wesley arched an eyebrow as he sat on the rustic bench and leaned back so he could give me a long once over. "You look a little manic."

That was an interesting observation. "You barely know me. How can you recognize that?"

"Your mother had the same look about her at times. I grew to hate it when she looked manic."

My stomach twisted at mention of my mother. That's when I realized I had a mountain of things I wanted to discuss with Wesley. I probably should've made this trip sooner.

"I saw her," I volunteered, choosing my words carefully. "Mom, I mean. She's in the cemetery. She gets up and wanders around after dark."

Wesley's expression didn't shift. "I know. I've seen her a time or two myself."

"I didn't think you were much for visiting town."

"I visited May when I could over the years. I visited your mother, too, even though that was … different."

He looked so sad my heart went out to him. "When Galen showed me what was going on in the cemetery I was kind of upset. At least … I think I was upset."

"It's good Galen went with you." Wesley's tone was unnaturally gruff. "If he's going to court you he should be standing by you through the hard stuff."

I couldn't ever remember hearing that term in real life, which forced me to arch an amused eyebrow. "Courting? I feel as if I've been transported to *Little House on the Prairie* times. I'm not sure that's exactly what we're doing."

"Really?" Wesley pursed his lips. "My understanding is that you've been out practically every night since ... well, since you were taken. You've been seen at tiki bars ... and on beach walks ... and even just laughing at the lighthouse. In all that time, you've been seen holding hands and kissing. If that's not courting, what is it?"

I was flabbergasted. "Do you have spies watching me?"

Wesley shook his head. "I have workers who live in town. They go to bars and restaurants. You haven't exactly been discreet."

"I guess." I rubbed the back of my neck, uncomfortable. "We're dating. It's not serious or anything."

"Oh, you're cute." Wesley's lips curved as he shook his head. "If Galen is bothering to see you and only you – and to do it every night – it's serious. The boy has a reputation for being good at his job and bad with female hearts."

"Meaning?"

"Meaning women go gaga for him and he loses interest after one date," Wesley replied. "Apparently, if the gossip I'm hearing from my men is true, you're different."

"We've only been dating for a week," I pointed out. "I think it's a little soon to assume I'm different."

"No, you're different." Wesley clearly wasn't in the mood to argue. "I can see it. I could see it that day on the beach. He was worried about you above all else. He barely paid any attention to me despite the fact that I'd shot a man."

Speaking of that .... "Yeah, um, I didn't really get a chance to thank you for that." I scratched my cheek, uncomfortable. "Everything happened so fast that day. You saved me and I never thanked you. That was rude."

Wesley's eyes were hard to read. "Aurora saved you," he countered after a beat. "She got you back to shore, which was the biggest hurdle. After that, Galen protected you. He made sure you were safe and taken care of. I owe him for that."

"You shot Ned Baxter."

"I did." Wesley bobbed his head. "I wish I could say my motivations for that were altruistic. It wasn't just about saving you, though. Part of it was because of that. The other part, well, it was because of something else."

Realization dawned. "May. You were getting revenge for May."

Wesley shrugged. "Ned killed May. He poisoned her. We may never know how long she would've lived otherwise. He had what I dished out coming to him. I'm not sorry."

"Did you think I expected you to be sorry?"

"I don't know." Wesley mustered a smile. "I don't know you all that well yet. In some respects you remind me of your mother. In others, you're different. I know better than to try to make you into someone you're not. You're a person of your own making. I'm fine with that."

"You haven't visited."

Wesley sighed. "No, I haven't. I thought about it but ... I wasn't ready."

"May is at the lighthouse," I reminded him. "You obviously miss her, and she's there. You could visit, spend time together. You don't need to even see me if you don't want to."

"Ugh." Wesley made a disgusted sound in the back of his throat as he leaned back and regarded me with flat eyes. "Girl, I can already tell you're going to be work."

"Are you going to say I got that from my mother?"

"I'm going to say you're that way because you're a female," he clarified. "I've yet to meet a female who isn't work."

I was amused despite myself. "I think most women feel the same way about men."

"Probably. In any case, I didn't visit for several reasons." Wesley poured himself a glass of iced tea before continuing. "The first reason is that I didn't want to interrupt you and Galen. It was obvious that day on the beach that you and he were going to ... um ... become close."

I could tell Wesley was uncomfortable with the relationship, to the point that even talking about it threatened to make him run screaming into the night. "We're just dating. It's new … and not something to get worked up about."

"I can't help it. You're my granddaughter even if I don't know you all that well. You'll have to forgive me for wanting to wrap you up and shoot any boy who comes sniffing around. That's a grandfather's job."

"Even though I'm an adult?"

Wesley shrugged, his eyes lit with amusement. "I can't help it. I want to protect you. That's something we'll both have to get used to."

"Fair enough." I'd never had a grandfather who actually cared about what I did with my day, who I spent my time with. My father's father was a gruff man who spent all his time hunting and fishing. I wasn't even sure he knew my name let alone cared about the boys I dated. "Still, you could've stopped by the lighthouse. I was worried you didn't want to see me for some reason and … well, I didn't like it."

"You could've come out here, too."

"Yeah, I guess. The thing is … I don't have a car. I don't even have a bicycle. I might be able to ride a bicycle out here, but I'm not sure I wouldn't fall over and die in a ditch due to the heat. There are three cabs on the island as far as I can tell, but finding them isn't easy and it cost me fifty bucks with tip to ride one way out here. So, I don't mind visiting, but … I'm going to have to figure out a better way to do it."

Wesley's mouth dropped open. "That shyster charged you fifty bucks to ride a few miles out of town?"

I held my hands palms out and shrugged. "He kind of had me over a barrel."

"I guess so." Wesley's agitation was palpable as he shifted on the bench. "I should've considered that. I didn't … and I'm sorry. We'll figure something out about the visits. I agree that riding a bicycle out here isn't necessarily a good idea. You're not used to the humidity and if I'm not expecting you … well, you really could die in a ditch."

"And no one wants that." I offered him a cheeky smile. "You could visit me occasionally. I mean … you don't have to do it on a regular basis or anything, but if you ever get a mind to do it, well, you're welcome to drop in."

Wesley's smile was kind. "Girl, I have no problem visiting you. My problem is with seeing May. Er, actually, it's seeing that lighthouse without May being alive and buzzing about. I know it's hard to explain, but I'm not quite ready yet. It will happen eventually, but for now … ."

"Oh." I felt inexplicably sorry for him. He seemed alone in a very big world. "I didn't think about that. I'm sorry."

"It's not your worry." Wesley awkwardly patted my hand. "We'll figure it out. This is new for both of us."

"Yeah, but … it's probably harder for you. I have so much going on it seems as if my head is spinning most days. It's harder for you because nothing is spinning. The world is quieter for you without May, so time feels as if it's slowing."

"That was a very profound sentiment." Wesley smirked. "Tell me what's got your head spinning. Is it Galen? If so, I'll have a talk with the boy. I've been meaning to track him down anyway."

That sounded ominous. "You don't have to track him down. He's been nothing but a gentleman … and I can take care of myself."

"Yes, well, that's a grandfather's prerogative and you'll have to get used to it." Wesley's kind eyes twinkled. "Other than Galen Blackwood, tell me what has your head spinning."

I related the events of the past two days, wrapping up with the intense fight between Gus and Henry in the police department. "I know I'm new to Moonstone Bay and don't fully understand all the relationships, but that seemed a bad deal."

"It is a bad deal." Wesley stroked his chin, thoughtful. "That whole situation has been a powder keg for years. I'm surprised it didn't blow before this."

"It seems to me that Gus and Henry disliked each other long before Trish Doyle turned up dead," I noted. "Do they have a feud going or something?"

Wesley chuckled. "Oh, you really are cute. A feud. I want to laugh at how naïve you are, but that's not exactly the worst word to use when talking about Gus and Henry's relationship. They are, in fact, mired in a feud."

"Why?"

"There are so many reasons I'm not even sure I can keep track. For starters, I believe their fathers were rival real estate agents and constantly going at one another."

"I can't exactly imagine real estate agents threatening to go all gangster on one another," I mused. "Did they threaten each other with signs? Did they start a race to the bottom with escrow numbers?"

Wesley snorted. "That sense of humor you have is funny."

"Did I get that from my mother, too?"

"No. From me." Wesley's smile was so wide it almost split his face. "I've never been tight with Gus or Henry. I'm not privy to the inner workings of their relationship. I simply know they've never gotten along and they tried to teach their daughters to follow suit."

I searched my memory of Ashley and Trish's interaction before the latter turned up dead. "I saw them yesterday. I mean … before Galen stumbled across Trish's body. I saw Ashley and Trish. I assumed they were old friends the way they had their heads bent together and were laughing. Maybe I misread the situation."

"I don't think you did. I'm not up on town gossip and even I heard the story about how Trish and Ashley decided to be friends to spite their fathers. They didn't want to keep the war going so they started hanging out with one another. It drove their fathers crazy, but it's my understanding that it grew into a real friendship."

"They started yelling at each other after that," I remembered. "They almost got into a fight. Galen broke it up. They were threatening to kill one another."

"Do you know what they were fighting about?"

"Ashley said they were fighting about Booker."

Wesley didn't appear surprised by my answer. "Oh, well. That boy has broken more hearts than Galen. I guess I can't be surprised about that."

I wanted to shake Wesley until answers popped out about both Galen and Booker's dating habits. That didn't seem wise or polite, though, so I battled back the inclination. "I think the whole thing sounds crazy."

"Welcome to Moonstone Bay." Wesley winked. "This entire island is wacky, kid. You need to get used to that."

"I know, but … I was there when Trish's body was discovered. I kind of want to know why she died."

"I'm sure Galen will figure it out."

"I'm sure he will, too." I meant it. "Can you tell me more about Gus and Henry's feud? I feel as if I'm missing something when it comes to that whole story."

Wesley stared at me for a long beat before exhaling heavily and nodding. "I guess I can do that. This curiosity thing you've got going for you, that you got from your grandmother. It's an annoying quirk."

I honestly didn't care. "I can live with that. Tell me what you know."

"Well, it started a long time ago. As I remember, it had something to do with a woman."

Ah, that's how all the best feuds started. "I'm not surprised. Lay it on me."

8

EIGHT

Wesley dropped me back in town, admonishing me to call should I want to visit again. Then he asked a guy I didn't recognize, who happened to be walking on the sidewalk in front of Lilac's bar, if he knew where the taxi drivers were spending their afternoons these days. I had a feeling the driver who charged me fifty bucks to visit my grandfather was about to get an earful.

I offered Wesley a smile, internally glowing when he returned it, and then made my way into Lilac's bar. My afternoon with Wesley allowed me time to come up with a plan and, unfortunately for her, Lilac was key to that plan.

"Hey, girl." Lilac breezed past me, two beers in her hands, and headed toward a corner table. I kept moving to the bar, taking what was rapidly becoming my regular stool before Lilac returned to her usual spot behind the counter. "What will it be?"

"Iced tea is fine."

Lilac flicked her eyes to the clock on the wall. "It's almost five o'clock. You can drink without your mainland sensibilities guilting you if you're so inclined."

She wasn't wrong. Still, I wasn't ready for alcohol just yet. "Iced tea is fine for now."

"You got it." Lilac filled a glass and handed it to me. "Where have you been all day? Galen stopped in looking for you about two hours ago. I'm not sure he believed me when I said I didn't know where you were."

Hmm. That was interesting. "Did he seem upset?"

Lilac's eyebrows winged up. "As compared to what? He seemed normal to me."

I didn't know whether that was good or bad. "Did he look as if he wanted to strangle me? Maybe he wanted to get in a good kick instead. I think that's what I'm getting at."

Instead of reacting with worry, Lilac snorted. "Oh, now things are getting interesting. What did you do to make Galen want to strangle you? Wait ... do I want to know?" Lilac tilted her head to the side, considering. "Oh, who am I kidding? I totally want to know. I can't believe I haven't heard this bit of gossip yet."

I risked a glance around the bar and was thankful that the other patrons were in booths along the back wall. I was the only one at the counter, which allowed me to talk freely. That was also a good thing if I wanted to enact my plan.

"I didn't technically do anything wrong."

Lilac bobbed her head. "It's always good to lead with a denial."

"I just ... well, I might have picked up lunch at the grocery store and surprised Galen with it at the station."

Lilac's face remained expressionless. "If that's the height of your gossip I'm going to be really disappointed."

I sighed. "I wanted to feel him out for information," I admitted. "I'm dying to know what happened to Trish Doyle, so I took him lunch as an excuse to question him."

Lilac's lips curved down. "You are the worst manipulator ever. That's not a fun story. I was expecting so much more. I'm disappointed ... to say the least."

I tried not to take the comment as an insult, but it was difficult. "I was totally on top of my manipulation game," I argued. "We were having a great time. He was opening up. Ashley Conner is in custody, by the way, although she hasn't been charged yet. Then something happened to derail things."

"I'm waiting with bated breath."

I didn't like her tone. "Trish Doyle's father came into the station and picked a fight with Ashley Conner's father. Galen had to physically break them up. He kind of ordered me out of the station so he could deal with them."

Lilac blinked several times in rapid succession. "Huh."

"That's all you have to say?"

Lilac shrugged. "I'm not sure what else there is to say. I didn't hear anything in that story that would suggest Galen was angry with you. In fact, I'm betting he was more resigned than anything. As for Henry and Gus, that's no surprise. They've been one argument away from blowing each other's brains out for as long as I've known them."

She was so blasé I couldn't help but wonder if I was looking in the wrong spot for investigation inspiration. "Well, I'm glad Galen isn't angry with me."

"I don't think he's likely to get angry with you for a bit. You're still in the honeymoon phase of your relationship. It's all longing looks, linked fingers and long kisses that promise more down the line."

I was dumbfounded. "That was a little … ."

"Romantic?"

"I was going to say Lifetime television for women."

"Fair enough." Lilac shrugged. "But he didn't seem angry, and I can always read Galen. In fact, he seemed more worried than anything else. He said you weren't at the lighthouse and May said you hadn't been back."

"Oh, so May is talking to him but not me, huh?" I shouldn't have been surprised, but I was agitated all the same. "Why is that so … May?"

"I have no answer for you." Lilac dropped a lemon wedge in my iced tea. "Where did you go?"

"I went out to see Wesley."

"Oh." My answer obviously took her by surprise. "What did Wesley have to say?"

"Not much." That was the truth. "We talked about a few different things. We didn't have a chance to talk after ... well, after he shot Ned Baxter."

"I didn't even think about that." Lilac turned sympathetic. "Have you been upset about that?"

"I've been confused about that," I clarified. "I thought he didn't want to visit because of me. It turns out he didn't want to visit because of May ... and Galen ... and a little bit because of me."

Lilac snickered, genuinely amused. "That sounds about right. Wesley is a complicated man. He's probably not ready to see May's ghost. He was absolutely crushed when she died. He went on a three-day bender ... and he did it in town. He's usually more for drinking at home."

For some reason, that made me unbelievably sad. "Well, he's a little irritated that I spent fifty bucks for a cab ride to his place this afternoon. I think that driver is probably hearing an earful about now. He says he's going to come up with a way to fix that, although I have no idea what that is."

"It sounds like you had a nice chat."

"We did. He gave me the lowdown on some of the history between Gus and Henry. It was eye-opening, to say the least."

"They're a colorful duo," Lilac agreed. "This situation will only make things worse. Ashley and Trish managed to overcome the feud for years, but they eventually succumbed – or that's how it seemed yesterday – so I think things will get worse before they get better."

"Yeah, well, I don't know what to make of it. I think Moonstone Bay is so small that everybody is up in each other's business, so it creates unnecessary tension."

"I don't think that's going to change."

"No. Definitely not." I sipped my tea. "Anyway, I actually had a reason for stopping by. I thought maybe you and I could take a walk around the festival when you finish your shift. I was hoping you could point out people who might be looking for employees."

"Oh, well, sure." Lilac didn't appear thrilled by the suggestion. "I don't see why I can't do that."

"Of course, I'm not sure I should really be taking on a full-time gig right now," I admitted. "Part of me wonders if I should be spending my days reading those magic books in May's library. I don't know anything about magic, even though I appear to be the beneficiary of a magical lineage. It's all so much to take in, and yet I feel as if I'm doing absolutely nothing."

Lilac furrowed her brow, her expression serious. "You really don't know anything about magic, do you?"

"Not even a little."

"Well, I think I can help you there." Her smile was unbelievably bright, which made me instantly suspicious. "In fact, I know I can. I agree you should be learning instead of wasting time every afternoon."

"And how can you help me with that?"

Lilac's smile turned sly. "There's someone I want to introduce you to."

"Who?"

"Let's just say she's an expert on certain witch subjects and leave it at that for now. I'll be done here in an hour. Swing back then and I'll take you to her."

I wanted more information but knew it was unfair to pressure Lilac when she had a business to run. "Okay. That sounds good."

"It's going to be great. Trust me."

PART OF ME THOUGHT I shouldn't have been surprised when Lilac led me to the fortune teller tent I'd caught a glimpse of the previous night. She was waiting when I returned to the bar and was unbelievably chipper as we walked along Main Street. She didn't reveal who we were going to see until it was too late for me to change my mind.

I read the sign hanging over the open tent flap. "Madame Selena, witch to the stars." That had to be a joke. "I'm not sure this is what I had in mind."

"And I'm not sure you have a choice in the matter." Lilac was firm. "I'm not a witch. I can't help you with witchy powers. You need someone who can teach you the ways of your people."

Now that she mentioned it, I wasn't all that sure what species Lilac belonged to. She didn't volunteer that information – and we'd only been hanging around together for two weeks, so it felt presumptuous to ask – but my curiosity was rampant. "What kinds of things could you teach me?"

Lilac merely shrugged. "To start out with, nothing. That's why I think you should talk to Madame Selena. She and May go back a long time."

That was slightly more interesting. "She and May were friends?"

"Well, I wouldn't use that word." Lilac's smile was sheepish. "It's more that they knew each other and crossed paths quite often. I don't think I'm the one who should explain their relationship. I'll let Madame Selena do that."

"I can't wait," I muttered, reluctantly following Lilac into the tent and pulling up short when the overpowering scent of lavender smacked into my olfactory senses. "What is that?"

"That is the power of our people," a woman replied, lifting her head as she swiveled to face me. She sat in a chair in the center of the room – it actually resembled a throne more than anything else – and she wore a turban so I couldn't see what color hair she boasted. "Lavender strengthens the mind, encourages love and boosts fertility."

Huh. I had no idea what to make of that. "The mind stuff sounds great," I said after a beat. "I'm not sure how I feel about being more fertile."

Madame Selena chuckled. "You might change your mind on that in the future. Come. Sit." She gestured toward a chair to her left. It was a simple folding chair, nothing like the throne she perched in, and I felt exposed as I shuffled across the tent. "You're Hadley Hunter."

"She is." Lilac bobbed her head, her enthusiasm on full display. "May was her grandmother."

"And Emma was your mother. I know." Madame Selena's eyes

never left my face. "You never set foot on Moonstone Bay until about two weeks ago."

"It's actually closer to three weeks now." My palms were sweaty, so I rubbed them against the knees of my cargo pants. "Are you really a witch?" I realized only after I opened my big mouth that the question might be construed as rude. "I mean ... are you?"

Instead of acting offended, Madame Selena merely smiled. "I am a witch. You are, too."

"So I've been told." I shifted on the chair. "Lilac thought maybe you could ... I don't know ... teach me a few things about being a witch. I was going to do research with May's books but I've always been better with a hands-on education.

"Like, for example, when I had science classes," I continued, recognizing I was blathering and unable to stop myself. "I was always more comfortable, earned better grades and everything, when we had labs than reading about the process in a book."

"I was that way, too." Madame Selena stretched out her rather short legs as she regarded me. "What have you been able to do so far?"

The question caught me off guard. "Oh, well, I'm not sure."

"She blew a guy who was trying to attack her with an ax out of a second-story window," Lilac offered helpfully.

I kind of wanted to strangle her for being so open with my secrets. "That was a fluke."

"Fluke?" Madame Selena arched a perfectly-manicured eyebrow. "I don't know that I would call it a fluke. I'm more apt to call it an interesting display for someone who had no idea at the time that she was a witch."

"That's putting it mildly," I drawled. "I'm still not sure how that happened."

"You protected yourself."

"But ... how?" I was frustrated. "How did I know to protect myself if I didn't even realize I had magic?" My fingers twitched as I continuously shifted positions on the uncomfortable chair. "I mean ... seriously. How could I protect myself that way when I didn't know it was possible?"

"Your brain didn't know it was possible," Madame Selena clarified. "Your instincts – your fight-or-flight response, so to speak – understood that you had power. I'm guessing that you displayed magical abilities long before you arrived on Moonstone Bay but you simply didn't realize that's what was happening."

I cocked my head, considering. "No. I don't think that's true. I would remember using magic."

"Unless you rationalized it as something else."

"Like what?" I didn't want to let my frustration out to play – I barely knew this woman, after all, and it wasn't her fault I'd grown up in the dark. "How could I have done magic and not realized it?"

Madame Selena shrugged. "I don't know. I obviously am not privy to your entire childhood. You're a witch, though, by birth. Given your lineage, you should be a strong witch. May was unbelievably powerful, and while I didn't know Emma as an adult, she was a very strong practitioner as a teenager."

"I wouldn't know. I never got to meet her."

Madame Selena's expression turned sympathetic. "That must have been hard for you. Still, I'm guessing you did things – probably as a teenager – that you didn't realize at the time. I don't want to distress you, but it might behoove you to think back on that time and look at your life from a different perspective."

I hated how pragmatic she sounded. "Even if I do that, what good could come of it? That won't help me control my powers."

"Are you struggling with out-of-control powers?"

That was an irritating question. "Well, no. I haven't really displayed any magic since ... um ... one night when Galen and I were taking a walk."

Madame Selena was intrigued. Her smile stretched the width of her face as she leaned forward. "And what were you and Galen doing at the time of the display?"

Letting our hormones run wild. Of course, she didn't need to know that. I cleared my throat. "He just wanted to show me that my magic could do more than throw a man out of a window. He walked me down to the water and kind of ... I don't know how to explain it ... he helped direct my magic and we kind of made a mermaid or something out of the water."

"Hmm." Madame Selena furrowed her brow. "That sounds like an elemental exercise. May was something of an air witch with earth witch tendencies. I didn't get to spend enough time with Emma to form a solid opinion, but I always thought she would lean toward being a fire witch. What you're describing seems to indicate you might be a water witch."

I had no idea what any of that meant. "I just want to be able to control it. I don't want to be so surprised when someone comes to visit one day that I accidentally throw him or her against a tree or something."

Madame Selena chuckled. "I don't think you have to worry about that, but I understand why you're struggling. I think I'll be able to help ...and I'm more than willing to. I believe you responded the way you did during the attack in your bedroom because something inside recognized you needed to fight – and fight hard – or die. That would hopefully be the exception rather than the rule."

I didn't want to appear overly hopeful, but I couldn't seem to stop myself. "So, you think you can give me lessons or something?"

"I think I can help. What you do with that help, well, that's entirely up to you."

That sounded more mysterious than anything else, but I was in a unique position. "Great. When do we start?"

9

NINE

"She basically said we could meet and she would show me a few things. Do you think that's a good idea or am I making a huge mistake?"

Galen found me at the festival not long after I'd finished with Madame Selena. I launched into the tale of my talk with her right away, not giving him a moment to speak until I wrapped up what turned into a rather rambunctious monologue.

"Um … I think that sounds okay." He absently smoothed my dark hair. "She's a bit of a nut, but she might be helpful."

"What do you mean? How is she a nut?"

"Everyone on this island has nutty tendencies. I'm including you in that statement, before you ask. Madame Selena is no different. But if you think you need help, she's a good place to start."

He wasn't nearly as excited at the prospect as I envisioned. "Oh, well, maybe I'll think about it a bit longer." I chewed my bottom lip. "Do you have examples of the nutty things she's done?"

Galen let loose a heavy sigh. "I can put together a list later if you think that will help."

It couldn't hurt. "That would be great."

"Good." He gave me a quick kiss, something I didn't allow before launching into my exciting news, and glanced around the festival. "Do you want to eat here or go someplace else?"

It was only now, after I'd had a few minutes to calm myself, that I realized he looked weary. In fact, he looked absolutely beaten down. He'd obviously had a long day and my diatribe didn't help. "Let's eat here," I suggested. "You can pick and I'll order and pay."

Galen snickered at the shift in my demeanor. "You don't have to pay."

"I want to. How about kebabs and rice?"

"That sounds fine." Galen trailed behind me as I headed toward the Middle Eastern-themed food truck, his eyes busy searching the crowd while I placed our orders. Once the food was ready, we picked a table that was isolated near the edge of the busy crowd and spent the next few minutes feeding our hunger.

Because I was me, though, I couldn't allow the silence to get a solid foothold. "Tell me about your day."

"My day was … interesting." He wiped the corners of his mouth with his napkin. "After you left, I spent several hours trying to talk down Gus and Henry. That didn't go well. They're both adamant that the other is evil and want me to do something about it."

"Are they evil?" It seemed the obvious question. "I kind of thought they were evil given how they were acting. I didn't get to see much before you kicked me out."

"I knew you would bring that up." Galen leaned back on the bench and gave me a long look. "I didn't kick you out to be mean. I needed to focus on them, and maintaining proper focus seems to be an issue for me whenever you're around. I much prefer focusing on you."

"Oh, that's cute." I made a face. "I'm not sure I believe it, but it's cute."

"It's true." Galen flicked the end of my nose. "I've had a long day. I'm sorry if you feel I kicked you out of my office to be mean."

The apology made me feel guilty. "I knew why you kicked me out. I'm not going to pretend I didn't pout about it for a bit – that's my way, after all – but I'm not angry. You had every right to kick me out.

You have a job to do, and right now that job includes investigating a murder. Did you get any more information on that, by the way?"

Galen shook his head. "Ashley is still our prime suspect. The prosecutor hasn't made a formal decision on charges yet, but it's coming."

I widened my eyes. "He's going to charge her with murder?"

"He is. He didn't say as much, but I've known him long enough to recognize the signs."

"Do you think she did it?"

"I don't know. I think there's more than enough evidence to suggest she's guilty."

I had no idea what to make of that. "Well, once the prosecutor decides, it's out of your hands, right? You can't dwell on it. It's not your fault."

"No, but something doesn't feel right about it." Galen dug his fork into his rice. "I don't want to spend our entire night talking about Trish's murder. Tell me about your day."

"I thought I already did."

"You didn't tell me about your visit to Wesley's place this afternoon."

Now it was my turn to sigh. "This island is thick with gossip. How did you even know that? The only person I told was Lilac. No one else knew."

"Wesley knew." Galen's expression lightened a bit. "I ran into him on the east side of town when he was trying to shake fifty bucks out of Aaron Travers because he claimed that Aaron ripped you off."

"Oh." I really should've seen that coming. "Yeah. Wesley wasn't happy about that."

"Don't worry. I stopped him before blood was shed. For the record, Aaron will probably give you ten free rides out to Wesley's house to make things square. If you're interested, I mean."

"I might be interested," I hedged. "I had a nice talk with Wesley this afternoon. He's an interesting guy. I was worried before that he didn't want to see me after the Ned Baxter thing, but it turns out I made up most of that in my head."

Galen smirked, the expression lighting up his handsome features.

"Well, at least you admit it. As for Wesley being a good guy, he mostly is. He's a bit nutty, too."

"I'm starting to think that everyone on this island is nutty, just like you said."

"I think people are nutty everywhere. Moonstone Bay is simply one of those places where everyone knows about everyone else's nutty behavior."

"Good point."

"I thought so."

GALEN WAS SO TIRED when he walked me home I couldn't help but worry about his draggy nature.

"Are you sure you should be walking home in this condition?"

Galen arched an eyebrow as he leaned against my front door and stared into my eyes. "I'm not drunk."

"No, but exhaustion is worse than being drunk. You need to sleep."

"That's the plan. I'm going home to sleep."

That seemed perfectly reasonable ... except for the fact that I wasn't keen on him leaving. "Or you could sleep here." The offer was out of my mouth before I gave it the appropriate amount of thought. I didn't want him to take it the wrong way. "I mean ... just to sleep. I wasn't inviting you to do anything else."

Galen's chuckle was warm and it sent a shot of energy straight to the nerves curling in my gut. "I knew what you meant." He didn't immediately respond to the offer, which made me uncomfortable.

"Anyway, it was just a thought." I shifted from one foot to the other. "Probably a really lame thought. I just didn't want you wandering around town when you're obviously so tired you can barely keep your eyes open."

"It's not a lame thought," Galen countered. "But it is a potentially dangerous one. Let me ask you a question: Are you going to make me sleep on the couch?"

I hadn't gotten that far in my planning. "I ... don't know. You said the couch was too short and uncomfortable for your frame."

"I stand by that."

"On the other hand, I only have one bed," I supplied. "If I let you share it with me, you might get ideas … and wandering hands … and a wandering tongue."

Galen's eyes momentarily filled with fire before he recovered enough to give me a considering look. "I think I can control myself if you're willing to take a chance. If you remember correctly, we've slept in the same bed a few times now … and I never let anything wander."

"No, but that was different."

"How?"

"We weren't dating then."

"Good point."

"If I invite you up now I'm afraid that our hormones will take over and clothes will end up shredded. It could be a mistake."

Galen barked out a raucous laugh as he shook his head. "I think you're the one worried about losing control of her hormones. I'm so tired all I can think about is putting my head on a pillow and passing out. If you don't think you can keep your hands to yourself, though, I understand. I'll leave you to your bed … alone."

Oh, now he was turning it into a dare. "I can control my hands."

"That's good. I can control my hands, too. I think we'll be fine."

"I can control my hands better than you," I muttered, digging in my purse for my keys. "Just you wait."

"It's not a competition."

"It is the way I play."

"Good to know."

I WOKE TO A WARM BODY nestled behind mine, Galen's breath warm on my ear as he slumbered. I barely remembered climbing the circular staircase to my bedroom – a fleeting worry that May would see us coming in together and disapprove wafting to the forefront of my brain. My heart pounded so hard as I brushed my teeth and hair in the bathroom that I thought it might leap from my chest. By the time I changed into simple knit shorts and a T-shirt and wandered back into the bedroom, Galen was already out and snoring.

I stared at him for what felt like forever and then sighed before killing the lights and crawling in next to him. His arm automatically came around me, even though he didn't stir otherwise, and I couldn't help but lament the fact that he wasn't more worked up about sharing a bed. Apparently I wasn't nearly as enticing as I thought.

Even though I was convinced his proximity would make it impossible to sleep, I dropped off quickly. There was something comfortable about his presence, the warm weight of his body against mine. I didn't wake once during the night, and now during the light of day I felt a bit iffy about how we should greet each other.

"Morning," Galen murmured as he kissed the ridge of my ear.

I jolted when I realized he was awake. "Morning. I ... how did you sleep?"

"Good." Galen kept his eyes shut as he hugged me tighter. "How did you sleep? Did you manage to keep your hands to yourself?"

I was insulted by the suggestion even though I knew he meant it as a joke. "Listen, buddy, if my hands decided to wander during the night you wouldn't have to ask."

"Good to know." Another light kiss to my ear. "You're warm in the morning. I like it. You're also quiet. That rarely happens."

"And you're full of yourself," I groused.

"I am," Galen agreed, finally wrenching his eyes open and meeting my steady gaze. "Thank you for letting me spend the night."

When he phrased it like that, I felt a little goofy. "You were tired. It was the neighborly thing to do."

"Neighborly, huh?" Galen tickled my ribs before wrestling me so I faced him, his strong arms clasped tightly around my back. "I'm not exactly feeling neighborly this morning."

"Oh, really?" I tried to ignore the way my heart pounded and my breath ran short. "Does that mean I win the wandering hands game?"

"If we were playing a game and my hands wandered we'd both win."

"You seem pretty sure about that."

"I am." Galen stared hard into my face for a long beat and then took me utterly by surprise when he gave me a quick kiss and released me. He rolled to his back and stared at the ceiling. "I don't know about you, but I'm starving. How about we move this party to the kitchen and I'll cook you breakfast?"

I was dumbfounded. "What?"

"I'll shower at home, but I have time to cook breakfast." Galen's smile was quick. "You're probably hungry, too. I'll meet you downstairs."

TWENTY MINUTES LATER I WAS still trying to soothe my bruised ego as I descended the stairs and found Galen standing in front of my stove, spatula in hand.

"You didn't have hash browns, but I did find a can of corned beef hash in the pantry," he announced. "I hope that's okay."

It should be criminal to look that good so early in the morning, I internally groused. His hair was messy, his face full of stubble, and his clothes were wrinkled and disheveled. He still looked ridiculously yummy.

I hated that.

"Corned beef hash is fine," I gritted out as I made my way to the coffee pot. "Whatever you want is … fine."

Galen lifted an eyebrow. "You seem tense."

"Do I? Huh. I have no idea why. I'm in a fantastic mood."

"You also seem sarcastic." Galen leaned his hip against the counter. "Do you want to tell me why your mood shifted so quickly?"

Not even a little. "I'm simply not a morning person."

"You were a morning person a half hour ago."

"Oh, you mean before you got me wound up and then turned your attention to breakfast?" I shouldn't have said that. The slow gleam of Galen's teeth as he smiled proved that. It was too late to take it back, and I was stuck with my absolutely ridiculous reaction. "Just … never mind." I turned my full attention to the coffee. "It doesn't matter."

"It obviously matters to you."

I didn't want to look at him because I knew he was having a good time at my expense. "It doesn't matter. You obviously have other things on your mind. What do you have planned for your day?"

Galen moved closer, his fingers skirting under my chin and forcing me to look at him. Instead of a smile, though, I found a frown. "I do have a lot going on. I didn't mean to upset you."

"You didn't upset me." That was a ridiculous lie. I was disappointed. I wanted to blame my out-of-control hormones … again … but it was easier to blame him. "I'm fine. I swear it."

"I don't happen to believe that." Galen released my chin. "If I was a little … um, abrupt … this morning, I didn't mean it as a slight to you. I just didn't want things to get out of control."

"Fine."

"And not for whatever stupid reason that's going through your head right now," Galen added. "If we're going to take that step – and it will be a glorious day when it happens – I don't want it to be when I have limited time and you have morning breath."

My mouth dropped open. "Excuse me?"

"That got a reaction out of you, eh?" Galen playfully swatted my rear end. "Listen, it's not that I didn't want to play a little longer. I simply knew that I wouldn't be able to control myself if I did and I don't want to rush things."

He made it sound so simple. "I don't want to rush things either. I mean … I didn't invite you over for that."

"I know. You invited me to stay because I was tired and you were worried about me. I saw it on your face. It was a nice moment."

"So … why are we fighting?"

"We're not. We're sparring."

"Is there a difference?"

Galen shrugged. "I don't want to ruin this by going too fast or doing something we can't take back. I want this to happen at a leisurely pace. I also want it to happen without hurt feelings."

He sounded so pragmatic I could do nothing but feel sheepish. "I'm not angry. I was … thrown."

"And I should've taken that into consideration. We're just getting started here. There's no reason to rush things."

"You're making me feel as if I'm the town harlot or something," I grumbled. "I wasn't trying to chase you and beg for sex or something. I just … you lost interest fast. It threw me."

"I didn't lose interest. In fact, it was the opposite. But I want it to be the right time for both of us. I have to be to work in an hour. This is not the right time."

"Fine." I threw up my hands. "Geez. I can't believe we're even having this discussion. I'm not upset." That was true. Mortified was a better description. "Can we please talk about something else?"

"Sure." Galen nodded. "So, I've been giving it a lot of thought and I've decided that I'm not sure Ashley is guilty. There's a lot of evidence piling up – circumstantial and otherwise – but it doesn't feel right."

The conversational shift was fast enough to cause me to gape. "I … well … I was thinking along those lines, too."

"I know. That's why I want to talk things through with you … but only if you can keep your hands to yourself and try not to tempt me over breakfast. You need to be a good girl instead of the town harlot."

I scowled. "I'm never going to live this down, am I?"

Galen shrugged. "I don't know. Let's find out. Set the table. I don't have much time and we have a lot to talk about."

10

TEN

"I have to get going."

Galen finished loading the breakfast dishes in the dishwasher – he cooked and cleaned, which made him practically perfect – and fixed me with a serious look.

"Do you want me to applaud?"

Galen's expression was rueful. "No. I was simply telling you because we're in a relationship and it's always wise to share things with your significant other if you want the lines of communication to remain open."

I made an exaggerated face. I knew exactly what he was doing … and I found it annoying rather than delightful. "You're feeling pretty good about yourself, aren't you?"

Galen adopted a breezy expression. "I have no idea what you mean."

"You're feeling good about yourself," I repeated. "You think I'm all hot for you and it's making your ego puff out."

"Oh, that's a horrible thing to say." Galen tapped my chin and grinned. "I'm merely worried that your residual disappointment about this morning's lack of hands-on experience will leave you sad and pouting all day."

Yup. He was definitely full of himself. "I wouldn't worry too much. It's not as if you're the only person on the island who is willing to show me how it's done. In fact, you kind of fell down on the job. I'm positive someone is willing to pick up your slack."

Galen's smile evaporated. "Do you think that's funny?"

I held my hands palms out and shrugged. "I have no idea what you're talking about. I was simply talking to hear myself talk … much like someone else I know."

The look Galen offered as he stared into my eyes was stern. "I know you're trying to pay me back for messing with you – trust me, I get it – but I don't like jokes about cheating."

"Fair enough." I could understand that. "We haven't talked about our relationship, so it can't really be considered cheating."

Galen folded his arms over his muscular chest. "How do you figure?"

"We have to define our relationship. So far, we've been on several dates. They've been nice dates, don't get me wrong, but we haven't talked about dating only each other or anything."

"I only date one woman at a time."

Oddly enough, even though he was agitated, I was glad to hear it. "I date only one man at a time. However, we didn't discuss that … or any of it. We're not at a point where either of us is whining, 'What do I mean to you' while looking for hints of unrest. How was I supposed to know you felt that way?"

Galen opened his mouth and then snapped it shut, narrowing his eyes as he stared hard. His intensity made me uncomfortable.

"I mean … you should just tell me you feel that way or something," I added lamely.

"I'm kind of sorry I started this game," Galen admitted, taking me by surprise. "It was funny when I could tease you about how hot you were for me. It took some of the pressure off me because I didn't want to react like an animal this morning.

"But now you're doing the typical girl thing," he continued. "You're turning what was supposed to be a light morning into something serious. I think it's going to result in me getting acid reflux."

I pressed my lips together, uncertain how to respond.

"Just for the record, we're only dating each other." Galen was firm. "I'm also sorry about messing with you this morning. I was embarrassed by that situation, too. I shouldn't have put it all on you. That's hardly fair."

"I wasn't fishing for you to pledge yourself to me or anything," I muttered, my cheeks burning under his intense scrutiny.

"I know that." Galen combed his fingers through my hair. "This is new for both of us. It's going to take time to iron out all the kinks. For once I want to take the time to do the ironing."

My stomach flipped, this time in pleasure. "Really?"

"Oh, now you're knowingly fishing." Galen surprised me when he gave me a long hug and a quick kiss. "We'll talk about this later if you want. I'm guessing we're both uncomfortable with the direction this conversation has taken and we'll likely pretend it didn't happen when we talk later."

I had a feeling he was right. "Will you call me if you get any new information on the case?"

Galen nodded. "Don't get your hopes up, though. Ashley has a lot of strikes against her right now."

"But you're going to continue searching for another suspect, right?"

"Yes." He gave me another kiss, his shoulders jolting at the sound of someone knocking on the front door. "Are you expecting someone?"

"Just the other guy I've been dating."

Galen scowled. "Really? After what I just said?"

I shrugged. "I have horrible comedic timing. I'm kind of a spaz. You should already know this. What do you want from me?"

Galen snorted as he moved toward the door. "Whoever it is, he or she has awful timing. I'll get rid of them."

I trailed behind, curious about who would bother visiting this early. If I'd learned one thing about Moonstone Bay, it was that island life didn't really mesh with early-morning activities. Those who had to get up early to work did so, but they weren't happy about it. Everyone else slept until at least nine.

"Whatever it is, we don't want any." Galen made the announcement before tugging open the door, pulling up short when he caught sight of Madame Selena. "Oh, it's you."

Even though it was early … and a weekday … Madame Selena was dressed to impress. She wore an ankle-length skirt and had her hair (which I had still yet to see) pulled back under an ornate turban. She wore sparkly shoes, had her overly long fingernails painted purple and had slathered on enough makeup that the Kardashians would've been jealous of her Sephora shopping basket.

"Good morning, Galen." Madame Selena looked grave as she surveyed his rough-and-tumble appearance. "I wasn't expecting you."

"Aren't you psychic?" Galen's tone wasn't exactly icy, but it wasn't welcoming either. "I thought you knew everything that happened on Moonstone Bay. Isn't that what the sign in your shop window says?"

"I believe the exact phrasing is that I know all and see all." If Madame Selena picked up on Galen's overt dislike she didn't show it. "As for being psychic, I try to keep my spirit helpers at bay unless I absolutely need them. I don't want to infringe on anyone's privacy."

"Yes, that's what I always think when your name pops up," Galen drawled.

Madame Selena waited on the other side of the screen for a long moment. Finally, she asked the obvious question. "Are you going to invite me in?"

"It's not my lighthouse." Galen walked away from the door, causing me to frown as I watched him meander toward the kitchen.

I scrambled to open the screen door and offer Madame Selena entry. "Did I know we were meeting today?"

"You should have." Madame Selena was blasé as she glanced around the lighthouse. "I thought you wanted to learn more about your powers."

"I do." That was true. "I just … didn't know we were meeting today."

"No time like the present." Madame Selena's smile was so bright it almost blinded me. It was also so fake it was almost painful and forced me to flick my eyes to the kitchen doorway, which Galen happened to be walking through. He'd put on his shoes and grabbed his badge and gun, telling me he was on his way out. "Oh, Galen, are you leaving?" Madame Selena made a tsking sound but didn't look altogether unhappy.

"I have work." Galen put his hand to the small of my back and prodded me toward the door. "Hadley, will you walk me out?"

"Um ... sure."

Galen didn't release the pressure until we were on the front porch and could talk without Madame Selena hearing. "Listen, I don't want to tell you your business ... ."

"But you're going to."

Galen exhaled heavily, as if tugging on his limited patience. "I just want you to be careful. Madame Selena is ... odd."

"This whole island is odd," I pointed out. "What is it about her that you don't like?"

"I didn't say I didn't like her."

"Your reaction to her showing up was fairly obvious."

"Ugh." Galen made a growling sound before briefly pressing his forehead to mine. "I want you to be careful. I don't think Madame Selena is dangerous, but I also don't think you need her. You're fully capable of figuring things out by yourself."

He had more faith in my newfound abilities than I did. "Three weeks ago I didn't believe magic was real."

"I know."

"I don't know how to move forward with this." I was at a loss. "I need help."

The look Galen shot me was almost pitying. "You really don't need help, but I understand why you believe otherwise. I swear you'll figure this out ... and I'll help where I can. If you feel you need Madame Selena, though, I won't stand in your way. She knows a lot about a great many things."

"And yet you don't seem to like her."

"She's nutty." Galen smirked as I rolled my eyes. "I'm sorry. She wears on me. Maybe she won't wear on you." He leaned forward and gave me a quick kiss. "I will be in touch if I have any information."

"Okay."

"I will also be in touch toward the end of my shift so we can make plans," he added.

"What if my other boyfriend wants to do something?"

Galen's expression darkened. "Why do you always have to take it too far?"

I shrugged. "I don't know. I think it's a gift."

"You might consider returning that particular gift for store credit." He gave me another kiss. "Have fun. I hope Madame Selena answers whatever questions you have. As for the rest … we'll talk tonight."

That sounded ominous. "Talk about what?"

"How hot you are for me and why you feel the need to cover for that with inappropriate jokes."

Now it was my turn to scowl. "You make me tired."

"Right back at you."

I WAS UNCOMFORTABLE WITH my new guest, but I remembered my manners long enough to offer tea and cookies. Madame Selena accepted both with grace and a bit of gluttony.

"These are very good cookies." She shoved a full one into her mouth and smiled, continuing to talk even as she chewed. "May never had cookies this good."

"Oh, well … ." It took everything I had not to stare as the crumbs clung to her lips. "I got them at the market."

"Not much of a baker, huh?" Madame Selena winked as she slurped her tea. "May wasn't a baker either. She always said she had better things to do."

I warmed to the conversation. "I don't know a lot about May. Were you close?"

"Um … I'm not sure I'd use that word." Madame Selena held up her empty teacup and I obediently got to my feet and filled it from the pot

I'd set on the small cart at the edge of the living room. "We were professional rivals of sorts. We respected one another. We realized there was enough room for both of us to operate without costing the other anything."

"That's good." I had no idea what else to say. "She hasn't been around much. May, I mean. She's here occasionally, but she disappears in the middle of a conversation ... kind of like she gets bored out of nowhere or something."

"I wouldn't take that personally." Madame Selena's smile was soothing as she accepted the fresh cup of tea I delivered. "May hasn't been back very long. It takes spirits a long time to learn about their new abilities."

I widened my eyes. "Is that true?"

"Yes."

"I guess that makes sense." I grabbed my own teacup and sipped. "Do you know how it works? The ghost thing, I mean. Why she came back as a ghost at all?"

"She made a choice."

"She chose to come back as a ghost?" I found the entire conversation illuminating. No matter what Galen thought, I believed that Madame Selena was going to expand my knowledge base exponentially. I basically knew nothing, so that wasn't saying much. "Why would she do that?"

Madame Selena shrugged, noncommittal. "Haven't you asked her that?"

That was a good question. "I guess not." I leaned back in my chair, conflicted. "When I first realized she was in the house I freaked out a bit. I didn't know ghosts were real until I found her in the kitchen. I didn't know witches and shifters were real either."

"On Moonstone Bay it's easy to forget that paranormal abilities and pagan traditions have been shunned in many places." Madame Selena sounded like a wise woman. That didn't stop me from worrying that Galen was right about her. Maybe she was nutty in a way that would be a hindrance instead of a help. "Here, the paranormal is ... well ... normal. Where you came from, the opposite is true. The 'normal' people on this island are the ones who stand out, if that makes sense."

It did. Er, well, at least in an odd sort of way. "That still doesn't explain why May would want to be a ghost," I pointed out. "Wouldn't it be better if she moved on and settled … on the other side?" Even as I said the words I found myself wondering if there was an other side. Every long-standing belief I'd ever held was suddenly up for grabs. "I mean … what about Heaven?"

Madame Selena pursed her lips as she regarded me. "I'm not one for getting into religious debates."

"That's not what I'm asking you to do." I meant it. "I'm simply wondering if … um … there's anything out there beyond this world. I mean, if May didn't come back as a ghost, what would've happened to her?"

"It depends on what she believes."

That was … interesting. "I'm not sure I follow."

"A person's belief system plays into their final resting place," she explained. "For example, if you believe in the Christian faith and you're a good person then you move on to Heaven. If you're a bad person, you get a one-way ticket to Hell."

That sounded frightening. "Wow. Um … wow."

"Yes. There are even grim reapers who show up to collect souls." Madame Selena sounded unbelievably knowledgeable. "That's why we aren't overloaded with ghosts. The reapers take care of it."

Huh. "If the reapers take care of it, why is May still here?"

"Sometimes the reapers fail and a soul chooses to stay behind. Obviously May decided to stay behind."

"But … why?"

"Perhaps she thought she had unfinished business."

"What would that business be?"

Madame Selena's eyes lit with mirth. "Have you ever considered, my dear, that her unfinished business is you?"

The question threw me for a loop. "No. I … no. Why would I be her unfinished business?"

"Because she lost her daughter and only had you left," Madame

Selena replied without hesitation. "True, she didn't know you. My understanding is that your father didn't allow that. You were still her flesh and blood. She left you the lighthouse. Part of her probably knew that you would come here. I'm guessing she wanted to stick around to meet you."

"I've asked her questions, though. I've pushed her on what happened with my mother. She doesn't want to answer. She conveniently disappears."

"That could be because she's weak."

"Or it could be because she doesn't want to answer my questions," I grumbled.

"That, too." Madame Selena beamed. "Only May can tell you what's going on. You need to be firm and ask her."

"Okay." I wasn't convinced. "What else are we going to do today?"

"I thought we would start with a long talk about the nature of being a witch."

That sounded unbelievably boring. "Sure." I feigned enthusiasm. "I love long talks about stuff like that."

"Good. You've got quite a few in your future."

I ignored the sinking feeling in the pit of my stomach and kept my smile in place. "I can't wait."

"Good. I have much to teach you. More importantly, you have a lot to learn."

"I guess we should get to it."

"Indeed. We'll start with the dawning of magic and the appearance of the first witch. That was before Jesus Christ, so we've got a lot to go through."

Crap. This was so not what I had in mind when I went looking for a mentor.

11

ELEVEN

Two hours with Madame Selena was about all I could take. I got Galen's "nutty" reference fifteen minutes in but managed to hold on … although just barely. It was almost lunchtime before I started cracking. At that point, I lied about having an appointment and managed to show Madame Selena the door after a bit of wrangling and a lot of lying. She was much more interested in going through May's magic books, but she finally left me to my non-existent appointment, offering up a wave and a promise to drop in again soon.

I wasn't looking forward to that.

Because I was a paranoid individual, I worried she would hide in the bushes and watch the lighthouse to see if I really did have somewhere to be. I didn't want to be caught lying so early in our relationship, so I changed my clothes, locked the lighthouse and headed to town. I searched the bushes for a hint of movement as I passed but came up empty. Instinctively I knew it was ridiculous to suspect Madame Selena of spying, but Galen said she was nutty, and I was starting to believe he was selling her condition – whatever it was – short.

Lilac's bar was quiet when I entered. She waved from behind the bar and I immediately headed in that direction, climbing onto a stool and accepting the iced tea she automatically offered with a smile.

"Thanks. I almost wish I could toss some whiskey in this to get the day started with a bang, but I'm guessing that's probably a bad idea, huh?"

Lilac arched an eyebrow. "It depends. What sorrows do you want to drink away? You didn't have a fight with Galen, did you?"

I thought back to our morning interlude. "I don't think 'fight' is the right word."

"What word would you use?"

"Banter. We bantered." And his huge ego somehow managed to double in size, I silently added. "It wasn't a big deal. You don't have to worry about it."

"Well, that's good. At least I think it's good." Lilac's gaze was probing. "You look … flustered."

I was fairly certain that wasn't a compliment. "I'm fine."

"You still look flustered."

"I had an early-morning visitor."

"Oh, are you talking about May?" Lilac offered me a sympathetic cluck that I didn't quite understand. "Did she see you and Galen doing the dirty?"

"No," I sputtered, wiping my mouth to clean up the sprayed iced tea. "Why would you even ask something like that?"

"Word spread before everything shut down last night that Galen was spending the night at your house. I figured May was the only one who would dare interrupt you guys."

Huh. That was so not the answer I was expecting. "First, Galen only spent the night because he was too tired to walk home."

"Galen's house is like a mile from the lighthouse."

"So?"

"So he could've walked a mile in fifteen minutes and been totally fine no matter how exhausted he was," Lilac replied. "I don't think I believe the 'he was exhausted' excuse you seem to want to spin. There's no reason to get all worked up. Everyone has a pool on when you guys are going to take things all the way. It's fine."

I pressed the tip of my tongue to the back of my teeth as I worked overtime to calm my frustration. "You have a pool?"

"Yes. That's normal. Don't worry about it."

Oh, why would I worry about that? Was she kidding? "I don't want you guys taking bets on that. It's ... gross."

"Trust me. There's nothing gross about it. We have to get our kicks somehow."

"Yes, well, nothing happened." I had no idea why I felt the need to explain myself to Lilac. It was a high school reaction, and I wasn't a fan of high school theatrics when I was in high school so I felt ridiculous for being mired in the conversation. "He slept. We woke up and had breakfast. That was it."

Lilac stared at me for a long moment. "Are you making that up?"

"No."

"Ugh." Lilac's pretty face twisted into a scowl. "What is wrong with you? That man is a prime piece of steak, honey. I would be rubbing myself all over him at the drop of a hat if I were in your position."

There was no way I would admit to what really happened. Even if I knew Lilac better, I'd never own up to that. "What's his deal?" I inclined my head in the direction of the man sitting at the end of the bar. I recognized him from the police station the previous day. He looked to be double-fisting shots of bourbon on the rocks this morning. "How long has he been here?"

"That's Gus Doyle."

"I know who he is." I tugged on my limited patience. "He got in a huge fight with Henry Conner at the police station yesterday. They were threatening each other with guns and chainsaws." That was a slight exaggeration, but that's how I pictured a fight going down between the two feisty and feuding men. "I kind of feel bad because of what happened with Trish."

"Oh, I wouldn't feel too bad for Gus." Lilac's eyes were thoughtful as she flicked them to the sad-looking man. "I'm sure he's feeling sorry enough for himself."

I was surprised by her reaction. "His daughter is dead."

"And this feud has been raging for decades." Lilac licked her lips.

"You said something about talking to Wesley yesterday. Didn't he tell you what's at the heart of this war?"

"Kind of, but not really." I searched my memory. "He just said that they were always fighting and hated each other."

"That's true. Their fathers started the feud long before the two of them were born. They carried it on, though, and they were happy to do it."

I wasn't sure what she meant by that. "Can you be more specific?"

"Sure." Lilac leaned closer. "Gus and Henry were both on the wrestling team in high school and they both insisted on being in the same weight class so they could wrestle only each other. We're on an island, so there's only one wrestling team, and the participants spend all their time going after the same people. When it came to Gus and Henry, the stories are legendary. Apparently there's even talk of genital punching."

Lilac was so earnest I could do nothing but nod. "Okay. That's ... quite the picture you've painted. That's not the stuff of lifelong feuds, though."

"I don't think you understand how seriously some people take wrestling ... or genital punching."

"There has to be more to it."

"Oh, there's more to it." Lilac risked a look at Gus and lowered her voice. "Gus also had an affair with Barbie Conner."

I furrowed my brow. "Barbie Conner?"

"Ashley's mother."

I ran the scenario through my head. "Wait ... so Barbie Conner is Henry's wife and she had an affair with Gus? That means she had an affair with her husband's mortal enemy. That can't be good."

"Oh, don't get your panties in a twist, Esmerelda," Lilac teased. "The only things more active than the feud over the years were the affairs. There are so many rumors about affairs between the Conners and Doyles that I have no idea which rumors are true."

Huh. I didn't see that coming. "So Gus slept with Ashley's mother. How did Henry take that?"

"Not well. He and Barbie divorced when Ashley was close to graduating high school. They split custody, although I remember seeing Ashley with Henry more than Barbie over the intervening years."

"Is Barbie still on the island?"

"Yeah. She lives on one of the side streets ... Magnolia, I think. She bought a place of her own shortly after the divorce. She doesn't participate in much town stuff. I think she fancies herself above it."

"You sound as if you don't like her."

"I don't like most of these people," Lilac admitted. "Barbie has always been full of herself. She's like a southern belle without the breeding or pedigree. It's hard to explain."

"It sounds like it." I rubbed my chin as I gazed at Gus. "Do you think it's possible that Henry killed Trish as payback for Gus having an affair with his wife?"

"I guess that's a possibility," Lilac hedged. "That was a long time ago. It wasn't as if Henry was even in love with Barbie. They didn't like each other at all. In fact, most people say that Henry was in love with Maureen but settled for Barbie when he couldn't have what he wanted."

"And who is Maureen?"

"Oh, sorry." Lilac's smile was sheepish. "I forget you're not up on all of this yet. Don't worry. You'll catch up."

That was a terrifying thought. "Who is Maureen?" I repeated.

"Maureen Doyle. Or, well, she used to be Maureen Doyle. She moved to the mainland when she split with Gus about five years ago. I hear she's remarried and only sees Trish, like, once a year."

Wow. It was like being trapped in a soap opera. I had no idea what to make of it. "So, you're saying Henry was in love with Gus's wife and Gus had an affair with Henry's wife."

"Pretty much."

"And now they're all divorced and unhappy."

"I would definitely agree with that."

"And Trish Doyle is dead," I added as an afterthought.

Lilac sobered. "Yeah. That's less funny."

There was no doubt about that.

I LEFT GUS TO HIS drinking for thirty minutes before I decided someone needed to curb his reckless habits. Lilac tried talking me out of approaching him – although her efforts were fairly feeble because she was mildly curious as to how things would turn out – but I was determined to talk to the man.

He barely lifted his eyes from the bottom of his glass when I took the open stool to his left.

"Hi." I hoped I didn't sound too chirpy. "I don't know if you remember, but I was at the police station yesterday."

Gus flicked his red-rimmed eyes to me. "I saw you."

"I'm Hadley Hunter."

"I know who you are. You're May and Wesley's granddaughter."

"Yes."

"You're also Galen Blackwood's girlfriend, which came as something of a surprise because he's never much showed an interest in having a full-time girlfriend before." Gus was clearly drunk. His pronunciation meandered a bit and his face was flushed with color. "How did you manage to bring down the esteemed sheriff, by the way? My Trish had a crush on him for years, but he barely showed her any attention."

Ugh. This was not the direction I wanted the conversation to go off the bat. "Oh, well … ." I didn't have an answer for him. From the moment Galen and I had met there had been a spark. It wasn't love at first sight or anything – I don't believe in that – but something chemical snapped off in both our brains. It was interesting … and a little daunting. "I don't know. We just seemed to click."

"I think that's how it is with people." Gus didn't seem especially bothered by my answer. "I've seen that happen with people before."

"Did it happen for you with Trish's mother?"

"With Maureen?" Gus's eyebrows flew up his forehead. "No. It most certainly didn't happen with Maureen. With her it was more of a Dumpster fire than anything else."

Oh, well, that was a lovely thought. "What about with Barbie?" Initially I wasn't going to push him too far on the issue. He was drunk enough that I figured he'd barely remember he didn't know me and proceed to babble. "Did you feel that way with her?"

Instead of immediately responding, Gus made a face. "Did I feel what way with her?"

My footing turned shaky. "I ... um ... well, I heard there might have been a thing between the two of you."

"Did you now?" Gus's unhappiness was obvious as he straightened on the stool. "And where did you hear that? Did Galen Blackwood tell you that? Did he tell you that I had an affair with Barbie and that somehow made it okay for my daughter to die? Is that what he told you?"

It was a mistake to confront him. I realized that now. But it was too late to turn back. "He didn't tell me that." I swallowed hard. "He never mentioned any of it. I heard other people on the island gossiping." That wasn't a total lie. Lilac was "other people" and she certainly liked to gossip. "Galen never said one thing about you and Barbie. Please don't think he did."

Gus scowled as he tipped back his glass and drained it. "I need another, Lilac," he barked, still glaring.

"I'm on it, Gus." Lilac's expression was sympathetic as she strode to the end of the bar and grabbed the empty glass. "Are you sure you want to keep doing this? You seem a little tipsy."

"I'm sure I want you to mind your own business and fill my glass," Gus shot back. "I didn't come here to be judged."

"No one is judging you." Lilac shot me a brief look. "As for the story about you and Barbie, don't take it out on Hadley. That story has been going around the island for years. You know that as well as anybody. Given everything that's happened ... well, people can't stop themselves from talking."

"That doesn't mean it's true." Gus was bitter as he watched Lilac fill a glass. "I never had an affair with Barbie. I know that story was going around, but it's not true."

"Then I believe you." Lilac was sympathetic as she handed Gus a fresh drink. "I'm sorry if the gossip upsets you. Moonstone Bay does gossip better than most places."

"Yeah. That's why I hate it here." Gus took a big gulp, the corners of his eyes leaking. "I never had an affair with Barbie. I mean ... does she even look like my type? Plus, even if I could get past the looks I could never get past her attitude. If you ask me, Henry started that story around the time of the divorce because he wanted to drum up island ill will and point it at me."

I couldn't help being surprised, and looked to Lilac for confirmation. "Is that possible?"

Lilac shrugged. "It wouldn't be the first time this island has gotten things wrong when it comes to the coconut phone gossip line."

"The worst part was when people started saying I was Ashley's father," Gus grumbled. "Ashley and Trish were already friends by then and it put a strain on their relationship. Henry didn't want them hanging out, but I was secretly relieved. Do you want to know why?"

"Because it meant they would end the feud and you wouldn't have to expend effort to do it yourself," I automatically answered, causing Gus's eyes to widen.

"That's exactly right." Gus bobbed his head. "I thought they would put an end to all of it. Instead, Ashley put an end to my baby."

My heart almost broke at the look on his face as he took another drink. He was a man mourning hard. I didn't understand that in practice but I did in theory. I didn't know my mother enough to miss her. She was simply gone from the start. I mourned her in my own way, though, because I recognized something was missing. I didn't know May to mourn her, yet I felt odd pangs of regret all the time when thinking about her.

For someone like Gus, someone who loved his daughter and hoped she'd be able to do the one thing he couldn't, the loss had to be crippling. I understood why he was drinking himself into oblivion in the middle of the afternoon. It was easier than carrying the emotional burden reality wanted to foist upon him.

"I'm sorry about Trish's death," I offered after a beat. "Are you sure that Ashley killed her, though? I'm not saying I doubt you or anything. I'm simply asking if you're sure."

Gus was morose instead of furious when he snagged my gaze. "The police are sure."

I knew better, but kept that knowledge to myself. "Well, I know things won't get better for you, but I hope you at least start to feel less lost." I awkwardly patted his hand. "I'm sure Trish wouldn't want you drinking your days away."

Gus snorted. "My daughter wasn't perfect. She was a good girl, but she would be happy to know that her death crushed me to the point where I couldn't function. That's simply who she was."

"It kind of is," Lilac agreed, a whiskey bottle in hand as she moved toward Gus's glass. "I called a cab, by the way. It'll be waiting on standby when you're done, Gus. Just let me know when you've hit your limit."

"Thanks, Lilac." Gus watched her pour him another drink. "I keep hoping I'll get so drunk that when I wake up this will all have been a dream."

I understood the inclination, but recognized he wanted a miracle that was never going to happen. "You should take some aspirin, too," I suggested. "You're going to feel terrible tomorrow."

"I'm going to feel terrible regardless. The alcohol has nothing to do with that."

I sighed. "Yeah. You're probably right."

12

TWELVE

I listened to Gus complain for a full two hours, waiting until he slurred so badly that I couldn't understand a single thing he said. Lilac waved me off when I offered to help her load him into a cab, saying it wasn't necessary and she had everything under control.

Then, for lack of something better to do, I found myself at the cemetery with nothing to watch but empty grounds that I wasn't allowed to visit. I stood at the spot Galen showed me more than a week before, the location boasting a picture window that allowed Moonstone Bay residents to watch their zombified loved ones shuffle about inside – without danger of attacking anyone, of course – after dark, and stared into nothing.

I didn't know what to make of Gus's story. He could've been lying. Maybe he did have an affair with Barbie Conner and he simply didn't want to own up to it. Maybe Henry Conner killed Trish Doyle as some form of payback. Or – and this was far more likely – perhaps Ashley decided to join the family feud and make her father proud by killing off his rival's daughter.

The notion made me sad and sick to my stomach.

I pressed my forehead against the glass, positioning myself as close as possible to the walled-off cemetery, and closed my eyes. Galen was worried when he showed me what was inside. He thought I might try to climb the wall to get to the mother I'd never known. I'd had no idea she was even buried on Moonstone Bay. My father kept an urn full of what he said were her ashes on our mantel when I was growing up. I'd yet to call him for a clarification. It seemed like a lot of work for an answer that wouldn't change anything.

Since then, I'd stayed away from the cemetery because ... well, because seeing my mother as a zombie didn't make me feel closer to her. It was the exact opposite, in fact. Meeting May's ghost and talking to her made me feel closer to my mother. Meeting Wesley and trying to build something with him made me feel closer to my mother. Looking at a zombie through a window made me feel ... nothing. I was left bereft and empty. I didn't know how to describe what I was feeling, so I decided to ignore it.

Why I came back now was a mystery to me.

The glass was cool on this side of the cemetery thanks to the overhanging foliage. The residents wanted the tourists to stay away, so they built the window in the back and were careful to patrol the area after dark so they could dissuade looky-loos from getting too close. During the day it was blissfully abandoned.

Galen explained that two workers entered the grounds regularly to mow and keep things neat. Other than that, the cemetery was off limits for everyone ... including him. Residents could look through the window but never touch. Not that anyone wanted to touch a zombie, of course.

Even though I had no idea why I chose to visit the cemetery now, I took advantage of the quiet and focused on Trish Doyle's murder. I didn't want to believe that Ashley Conner was capable of killing her friend, but if the evidence really was piling up against her maybe there was a reason behind it. Maybe she had snapped and killed Trish. Maybe she regretted it after the fact. That didn't change the outcome. Trish was dead and Ashley was in jail. That was unlikely to change in the near future.

The shuffling of what sounded like feet on foliage caused me to jerk my head to the right, narrowing my eyes as I searched the heavy underbrush for a sign of movement. I didn't see a person. Of course, the leaves were so thick anyone could hide in there without me knowing. If I was a better witch I figured I could reach out with my senses and somehow magically know if it was man or animal watching me. So far, though, I was a terrible witch.

I pursed my lips as I studied the spot, uncertain. "Hello?"

No one answered. I wasn't really expecting someone to pop out of the bushes and say, "I'm here!" Still, something inside wouldn't allow me to let it go. I squared my shoulders and spoke again. "Is anyone there?"

No voice answered, but something rustled in the underbrush, causing the hair on the back of my neck to stand on end.

I could have been brave and stormed to the spot where I was convinced someone watched me and confronted my rogue stalker. I could've been the heroine everybody cheers for because she's full of courage and sass. The idea didn't sit well with me, though. Sure, it could've been a small animal – maybe a cat or dog – screwing around in the bushes. My inner danger alarm didn't believe that. It was far more likely a killer in a hockey mask, and I was the sort of heroine who went to investigate a noise in the middle of a storm after her friends mysteriously started disappearing. Those types of heroines are never heard from again.

Instead of moving forward I took a step back. "I'll just be going now," I murmured. I stared for another beat and then turned on my heel and practically broke into a run as I made my escape. I was at the corner of the cemetery when I finally found the courage to look over my shoulder. I didn't see anyone, but the malevolence I thought I'd felt mere seconds before doubled as an involuntary shudder ran through my body. Someone was definitely there … watching me. And, if what I felt was even remotely true, someone wanted to hurt me.

I kept moving around the corner, desperate to put space between whatever was hiding in the bush and me, but I ran into something hard and solid, forcing me to swivel and prepare to fight.

"What the … ?"

Booker caught my hand before I could slap at him, making a face as he looked me up and down. He looked more frustrated with my reaction than worried I might do him physical damage. I couldn't blame him.

"What are you doing back here?"

I glanced over my shoulder again, exhaling heavily when the overpowering fear dissipated. I felt a bit sheepish given my ridiculous reaction. "Oh, um … ."

"They don't come out during the day." Booker gentled his voice as I met his gaze. "I know Galen showed you what's in there – that was smart of him, by the way, to be with you – but you can't see her during the day."

It took me a moment to realize he was talking about my mother. "I know that." I straightened. "I just … was doing something and ended up here. I'm not sure why."

Booker narrowed one eye. "You're not sure why you ended up here?"

"No. I was at Lilac's bar and ran into Gus Doyle. He made me sad. I ended up here."

"Uh-huh." Booker didn't look convinced. "What were you running from?"

I thought about telling him I believed someone was watching me from the bushes, but the more thought I gave that, the more I realized it was unlikely. It was probably my imagination running wild, which was a fairly normal occurrence in my world. "I was just heading back to town."

"Well … I'll walk with you." He didn't offer as much as demand I accept his services as bodyguard and reluctant tour guide, so I readily fell into step beside him. "What was Gus saying?"

I told him about our conversation, leaving nothing out. I wasn't sure I understood all of it because Gus was so very drunk, but when I was done Booker made a hissing sound as he shook his head.

"Getting drunk isn't going to help matters."

"I don't think he cares."

"I know, but … he's making things worse."

"For him, I'm not sure that's possible."

Booker heaved out a sigh. "You're feeling sorry for him, aren't you?"

"Don't you?" I didn't understand how anyone could look at a pathetic creature like Gus Doyle and not feel sympathy. "He lost his daughter. He's a wreck."

"I'm not saying it's not sad."

"Are you sad?" Curiosity got the better of me … again … and I blurted out the question. "I mean … are you sad because you were dating her and now she's dead? That would be normal. I know I'd feel sad if I were in your position."

"Ugh." Booker made a face as we hit the sidewalk in front of the cemetery. "I'm starting to regret offering to walk you back to town."

"You don't have to do it." Now that we were far away from the bushes of doom I felt brave and strong again. "If you have someplace else to be, I understand."

"Unfortunately for me, I have nowhere else to be. I finished work early. There's nothing more I can do this afternoon."

"So you have plenty of time to answer my question." I showed him my teeth as I adopted my best "you have to tell me what I want to hear because I'm adorable and sweet" smile. "There's no sense avoiding it."

"I'm not avoiding it." Booker was blasé. "I know you want me to feel guilty about dating two women at once, but I really don't feel that way."

I didn't doubt that. "Did you like either of them?"

"I liked both of them … for about an hour at a time. After that, they both got tedious."

I wrinkled my nose, appalled. "So you're saying that you liked having sex with them and that's it."

"Is there something wrong with that?"

I shrugged, unsure how to answer. "Did they want more from you?"

"Of course. That's a woman thing, though, and not an Ashley and Trish thing. In truth, they didn't want me because they really wanted me. They simply wanted me because everyone on the island wants me."

"Wow … and I thought Galen's ego was huge."

"It is. His ego is twice as big as mine."

"I'm sure he would say the same thing about you."

"But I'm right." Booker's grin was mischievous. "As for everyone on the island wanting me, it's true. Ask around. I'm like catnip and the women are the felines."

"I think I might throw up."

"You might not like it, but it's totally true." Booker refused to back down. "Women have always found me irresistible."

"And what about you? Have you ever found a woman irresistible?"

"Not really."

"I figured."

"I'm just not ready for a relationship." To my surprise, Booker turned serious. "A relationship takes work and I don't have the energy to work at one right now. I have other things going on. I know you don't want to hear it, but Trish and Ashley both understood that I was not in it for the long haul."

"You just said they wanted more."

"Yes, but they understood they weren't going to get more." Booker was firm. "I'm not going to make apologies for how I choose to live my life. I never lied to either of them. I never said I loved them. I never said I even wanted to entertain the idea of loving them. I was simply a guy who occasionally had needs and they were women who enjoyed meeting those needs. That's it."

"I guess that's fair," I grumbled, dragging a hand through my hair. "Why don't you want a relationship?"

Booker held his hands out and shrugged. "I don't know. I have a lot of other stuff going on right now. Not all of us are built to be the perfect boyfriend like Galen Blackwood."

His irritated tone caught me off guard. "What do you mean by that?"

"Nothing."

"Oh, no. You meant something."

"I didn't." Booker inclined his chin toward Main Street as we approached. "It's filling up early today. You should make an escape while you can."

"What is it with you guys hating festivals? I mean … I'm not always in the mood for a festival either, but it's hardly the end of the world."

"You might change your mind down the road. You're a newbie. The first festival is never bad. It's the hundredth festival that turns into a drag."

"Has anyone ever told you that you're a ray of freaking sunshine?"

Booker smirked. "It's been said a time or two. As for the festival, I don't want to dampen your enthusiasm. If you want to go to the festival I will walk you there to make sure you arrive safely."

That seemed like an odd way to phrase it but I decided to let it go. "Come on. They have these neat slush things that are amazing. They're blue and they make your tongue a weird teal color."

"I'm well aware of the Blue Slush Effect."

I was incredulous. "It has a name?"

Booker chuckled. "It does. As teens on this island, we had nothing better to do than go to the various festivals. It was expected. We've all enjoyed the Blue Slush Effect at one time or another."

"Good to know." I cast him a sidelong look as we walked. "What do you think about the whole Conner and Doyle family feud thing? Do you think that's why Trish is dead?"

"Wow. You just can't walk in silence, can you?"

"It was a simple question. If you don't want to answer, you don't have to answer."

"No, I'll answer." Booker's eyes flashed. "I would much rather answer that question than risk you going off on another tangent about why I don't have a girlfriend. As for the feud, like all feuds, it's ridiculous. I think it started out as something simple and turned into something dangerous."

"Does that mean you think Ashley killed Trish?"

Booker tilted his head to the side, slowing his pace as he considered the question. "I don't know. I've been giving it a lot of thought over the past two days, and I'm not sure I can see Ashley killing Trish no matter the situation."

"What if Ashley decided she wanted to make her father happy?" I pressed. "I mean, according to all the rumors going around, Henry thought Gus had an affair with his wife. Maybe Ashley got in a fight with Trish over you – she might not have believed you didn't want a girlfriend and wanted to stake her claim – and then she exacerbated the problem by listening to all her father's nonsense. Maybe she let anger lead her and did something she regrets."

"I guess that's possible." Booker stopped walking. "The thing is, I don't think Ashley has it in her to kill someone."

"Because she's a good person?"

"Because she's lazy." Booker grinned as I frowned. "I'm not casting aspersions, for the record. She's the first to admit she's lazy. I can't see her getting her hands dirty in that fashion. Also, well, she and Trish were friends. They had one fight. I don't think one fight is enough to cause a murder."

"Maybe she felt betrayed."

"Maybe she did," Booker conceded, "but I don't see it. That's not how she is. I've never seen anything that would indicate she was capable of snapping and killing her best friend."

I had no idea why I was pushing him when I tended to agree with him. "So who do you think did it if Ashley is innocent? Galen has her in custody. He says the prosecutor is going to decide on charges."

"If I knew who did it, you'd be the first I'd tell ... mostly because I figure it's the only way to shut you up and get you off my case," Booker replied, his eyes moving to the police station across the way. "As for the prosecutor, I think he's made up his mind about charges."

I followed his gaze, frowning when I caught sight of Galen and another man on the front walkway of the police station. They were across the road and I couldn't hear what they said, but I recognized the belligerent slant of Galen's shoulders as he openly argued with the other man.

"That's the prosecutor?"

Booker nodded. "Jack Winthrop. He's a real tool."

"Tell me how you really feel."

"He tries to throw his weight around and act like a big man on a small island," Booker supplied. "He should let Galen do the investigating and wait until he's done to get involved. He always fouls things up."

That was an interesting opinion. "Well ... why doesn't he do that?"

"You'll have to ask Jack."

The man wearing an overly expensive suit in 100-degree weather looked like the last person I wanted to have a conversation with. "I think I'll pass."

"That's probably a good plan."

Booker and I watched as Galen gestured wildly, yelling something we couldn't quite make out. The prosecutor returned the gesture – adding a rude one of his own – and then turned on his heel and stormed off. Galen's face was so red I worried he was about to blow a gasket.

I was considering crossing the street so I could offer him something – perhaps comfort or maybe a shot at enjoying the Blue Slush Effect – but his eyes slowly turned in our direction and the expression on his face didn't reflect delight. If anything, he looked absolutely furious.

"Uh-oh."

"Yeah, your prince charming is about to go rogue," Booker groused when Galen hit the street. "Batten down the hatches because this ride is about to get bumpy."

I had no idea what he meant, but I wasn't looking forward to the fallout.

13

THIRTEEN

I thought Galen was going to take his fury out on me – he was obviously carrying a mountain of it on his broad shoulders – but his focus was on Booker as he grew closer.

Galen didn't stop until he was standing in front of him, his chest heaving, hands clenched into fists at his side. The look he shot Booker was pure venom, but his voice was full of faux welcome. "Hey, man. Good to see you. What's up?"

Booker, always calm, wasn't the type to play games under most circumstances. For some reason he did the opposite. "Well, it's a lovely afternoon in Moonstone Bay," he drawled. "The sun is starting its inevitable descent into the horizon, the festival is about to crank up and I found your girlfriend hanging out by the cemetery, so I decided to walk her back to make sure she was safe. I think that just about covers everything."

Galen didn't mask his surprise as he deflated a bit and flicked his eyes to me. "Why were you by the cemetery? You can't see her during the day. If you need to see her again … well, I'll take you to her. We'll clear time and get it done."

"I wasn't there to see her." I felt stupid explaining myself a second time. "I was simply there to … think."

Galen merely blinked. "About what?"

"Life and stuff."

"Life and stuff?" Galen was incredulous. "That's a really pathetic answer. Think of a new answer and I'll come back to you in a second." He fixed his eyes on Booker and I could practically feel the electric sizzle of a brewing fight. "We need to talk."

"Oh, as lovely as that sounds, I've got other plans," Booker replied, folding his arms over his chest. "If you would like to call my secretary to make an appointment she might be able to fit you in next week. As for tonight, I'm booked up. Sorry."

Galen didn't crack a smile. "I'm not in the mood for whatever it is you're doing."

"And I'm not in the mood for any of this," Booker shot back. "I was trying to do a good thing and walk Hadley back to town. I didn't think you'd want her wandering around the cemetery on her own. I'm not in the mood to be smacked around because I did the right thing. You know that saying? No good deed goes unpunished, right? I'm starting to believe it's true."

Galen was unmoved by Booker's speech. "I guess it's good I'm not going to smack you around for that … even though you could've called me and I would've collected her."

I wasn't a fan of the way he phrased that. "Collect me?"

"Shh." Galen pressed a finger to his lips and pointed at me. "I will get to you in a second."

I rolled my eyes. "Lovely."

Galen planted his hands on his hips as he stared. "If it makes you feel better, I'm thankful that you made sure Hadley was safe. I will be forever in your debt for transporting her back to town and keeping her safe from the roving bunch of invisible hoodlums who often attack people as they walk between the cemetery and town, even though no one has ever reported such a crime. If that's not thanks enough, I would love to have a trophy created with your name on it so you can carry it around and get the accolades you so desperately need."

Booker snorted. "You're in a mood, man. I'm kind of used to you being in a snit because that's how you roll, but I'm too tired to put up with your crap right now. If you want to talk to me about something else – which we both know is crap for obvious reasons – you can make an appointment with my secretary."

"You don't have a secretary."

Booker smirked. "You're right. How did I overlook that?" He shifted his eyes to me. "You're looking for a job, right? That's what I heard in town earlier today. How would you like to be my secretary?"

"That's not even a little bit funny," Galen groused.

"I think it's hilarious."

After a moment of silence, I realized they were both focused on me. That was unnerving. "I'm going to say thanks but no thanks to the job offer." I sounded unnaturally chipper, but that couldn't be helped because my discomfort was threatening to take over. "I haven't actually decided if I'm going to get a job yet. Lilac thinks I should become a woman of leisure."

"Oh, if only." Galen briefly adopted a far-off expression before straightening. "As for you, Booker, I need information on your two girlfriends."

Booker remained blasé. "You'll have to be more specific. I have more than two girlfriends."

Galen scowled. "Why do you always have to make things so difficult?"

"I've often wondered the same thing about you."

"I need the lowdown on Trish and Ashley." Galen was firm. "You were dating both of them, right?"

"I was … hanging out … with both of them. Sporadically," Booker clarified. "I wasn't dating either of them. Dating involves dinner, dancing and holding hands on the beach. I believe you two are dating." His eyes briefly landed on me before continuing. "I was merely spending an hour here or there with Trish and Ashley. It wasn't a relationship."

"Oh, don't sell yourself short," Galen taunted. "What girl wouldn't jump at the chance to spend an hour with you every few weeks?"

Booker shrugged. "I have no idea. I think it's the perfect arrangement."

"What do you think, Hadley?" Galen focused on me. "Do you think that's a great deal for the female population of Moonstone Bay?"

I felt as if I were caught on two separate lines, with two fishermen from different boats fighting to see who was going to land me ... and then take me home before gutting and grilling me. "I don't think I want to be part of this conversation."

"I think it's too late for that." Galen's temper was on full display. "You were hanging out with him. He's your Booker. You must like what he has to offer, right?"

Now I was officially offended. "I ran into him by the cemetery." I took a step back because I was sick of the argument. I was also beyond tired of the attitude ... from both of them. Booker might have thought he was fooling me, but he wasn't. He knew exactly what buttons to push on Galen and he was masterful when it came time to push them. He was trying to drive Galen nutty, and doing a darned good job of it. "That's it. Nothing is going on."

Galen met my gaze, his expression shifting. "Where are you going?"

"Home." I was suddenly too tired to deal with either of them. All I wanted was a bottle of water and a nap. "I don't want to be here."

Galen obviously wasn't thrilled with the statement. "I thought we were going to dinner."

"And I thought you were a pleasant guy who didn't turn into a walking wall of testosterone at the drop of a hat," I shot back. "I know what you're doing here." I gestured between him and Booker. "I'm not some weapon that can be used when you want to win an argument with another guy. I'm not your property either. I don't deserve to be guilted for walking into town with Booker. We weren't doing anything."

"I didn't say you were," Galen protested. "When did I say you were doing something?" He looked to Booker for help. "This is your fault."

"I've been nothing but pleasant and helpful," Booker countered. "I think she's merely seeing you for what you really are."

"And what's that?"

"A tool."

I was at my limit. "Knock that off." I extended a finger in Booker's direction, causing his eyebrows to migrate north. "You're no better. You're trying to get Galen riled up because … well, because I think you like it. It's not funny. He's under a lot of pressure."

"So, wait … are you angry with him or me?" Galen wrinkled his forehead. "I vote for you being angry at him if I have a choice in the matter, by the way."

I shot him a withering look. "I'm angry with both of you. That's why I'm going home."

"What about our date?"

I shrugged. "Maybe we should take a night off." Even as I said the words, part of me regretted them. "I'm too tired to put up with this chest-thumping display."

"Hadley." Galen appeared contrite. "You don't have to do this. I'm sorry for how I acted. I … I'm tired, too."

I didn't doubt that. "So maybe you should get some rest." I kept my pinched smile in place as I took another step back. "I'll catch up with you tomorrow – maybe – and we'll compare notes or something."

"Hadley."

"No." I held up my hand. "You're not the only one who is tired. I had a long day, too. I'll talk to you tomorrow."

With those words, I left Booker and Galen to fight to the death and headed for home. The last thing I heard was Booker and Galen speaking at the same time.

"This is totally your fault!"

I CHANGED INTO KNIT shorts and a T-shirt when I got home, grabbing a banana and freshly-cut pineapple chunks to serve as dinner because I had nothing else worth eating in the lighthouse. I settled on the back patio to watch the sun set.

I was in a foul mood ... and then some. I had no idea what had gotten into Booker and Galen. Okay, I knew, but I didn't want to acknowledge it. They were both alpha males and they couldn't help themselves. In an ideal world they'd stow the testosterone and act like proper gentlemen. Sure, that was completely unlikely and unrealistic, but at the moment I craved it all the same.

I ate half the pineapple and ignored the banana as I watched the sun dip low against the horizon. It was a beautiful view, something I never thought I'd get to see on a regular basis when living on the mainland. I was thankful for it now ... even if I was surrounded by buttheads.

I was so lost in thought I didn't notice the figure moving along the patio until he was already on top of me. Galen, his arms laden with a bag of what looked to be food truck offerings, tendered a contrite smile as he moved to the table.

"Hey."

"Hello." I wasn't sure what to make out of his arrival. "I don't want to argue."

"We're not going to argue." Galen heaved out a sigh as he took the open chair to my left. "I'm sorry we fought earlier. That is not how I envisioned our evening going."

"You're kind of the reason it went that way."

"I know."

"I'm not going to apologize for walking with Booker."

"I know."

"I'm also not going to apologize for going to the cemetery," I added for good measure. "I don't even know how I ended up there. But I refuse to apologize for it."

"You shouldn't apologize for it." Galen smiled. "I am sorry. I really am. I shouldn't have reacted that way."

I knew it was unwise to forgive him so easily, but I was having trouble maintaining my fury. "Why did you react that way?"

"Because Booker drives me crazy."

"I figured that out on my own."

"He always has," Galen added. "We went to high school together.

Did you know that?"

I racked my brain. I couldn't be sure if I knew that, but it made sense because they looked roughly the same age. "No, but ... okay. Were you friends?"

"Not really." Galen answered without hesitation. "We weren't enemies, but we weren't friends. I hung around with the jock crowd and he hung around with the burnouts."

I bit the inside of my cheek to keep from laughing. "I see. Are you trying to warn me away from Booker because he's a pothead or something?"

Galen snorted. "No. I'm simply trying to explain that what happened today had very little to do with you and everything to do with us. I'm not always an easy man to get along with – I know that – but I try really hard not to be as difficult as I was this evening."

Because I'd seen that up close and personal on numerous occasions, I believed him. "What happened today?"

"The prosecutor is going forward with murder charges against Ashley. He won't even consider waiting. He's going for first-degree murder, and I can't help feeling that's the wrong course of action."

"Because you don't think the murder was pre-meditated?"

"I don't know." Galen threw up his hands in frustration. "That's half the problem right there. I simply don't know what happened or why. All I really have is Ashley and Trish fighting hours before one of them died, a longstanding family feud and a knife that looks a lot like a set I found in Ashley's home."

I didn't know about the last part, but it caused me to cringe. "That seems like strong evidence."

"It's certainly strong enough for the prosecutor's office." Galen dragged a restless hand through his hair. "I'm not saying Ashley didn't do it. I simply want more time to make sure she's the guilty party."

"And why do you think the prosecutor doesn't want that?"

"Because this is a tourist destination." Galen's answer was simple. "Things like this are not supposed to happen here. He wants to make it go away as soon as possible. Out of sight, out of mind. People will forget it even happened in a few weeks."

Oddly enough, I could see that. "If you don't believe Ashley is guilty, can't you just tell him?"

"He won't listen to me. He doesn't want to even consider anyone else might be guilty."

My heart went out to Galen and I awkwardly patted his hand. "I'm sorry. You've had a rough day. I should've taken that into account when you lost your marbles all over Main Street."

Galen snorted as he gripped my hand. "Yes, well, I guess I deserved that. I probably even deserved the 'marbles' comment, even though it's somewhat insulting. It's just … Booker knows exactly how to irritate me. We were kids together and he knew how to irritate me then. He's only gotten better with age."

"I noticed that." And, because I knew people like that in high school I allowed the remnants of anger pooling in the pit of my stomach to dissipate. "He only does it because he knows it bothers you."

"Do you think I don't know that?" Galen flashed a rueful smile. "I know it. I can't always help it. I was jealous when I saw you together, and something inside just snapped."

The admission caused me to squirm in my chair. "You were jealous? But … we weren't doing anything."

"I know. I'm not blaming you. I'm blaming Booker."

"Because he knows how to get under your skin?"

"Because he's always had a way with women that makes them go weak in the knees. I swear, if the women on this island were cartoon characters little hearts would pop out of their eyes whenever they see him. It's frustrating … and demoralizing at times."

I couldn't help but laugh at the cartoon heart visual. "Nice." I remembered the way the teenagers at the festival the other night looked at Galen. "I don't get the feeling you did all that bad in the dating department, and I'm referring to before we started going out. You don't have any reason to be jealous of Booker. You know that, right?"

"I'm not jealous because Booker gets around," Galen clarified. "I was jealous earlier because … you're the one person I'm interested in.

I mean … the only one. I don't see why he can't focus on the other five hundred women in town who would fall all over themselves to hang with him and leave you alone. And, yes, I know that sounds petty and proprietary. I can't help it."

Surprisingly, I understood where he was coming from. "You don't have to worry about Booker. We really did run into each other outside the cemetery. He was only walking me back."

"I know. I trust you. I just … it's Booker."

The face Galen made was adorable. "Well, he should clearly be flogged." I snickered when Galen's expression twisted to agitation. "What is in this bag?" I leaned forward, hoping to change the subject. "Whatever it is, it smells good."

"Fried green tomato sandwiches and elephant ears."

My eyebrows flew up. "Wow! I'm impressed. You went all out."

"I just wanted you to know that I was really sorry … because I am. I don't think of you as a possession or anything, however you phrased it in town. I am grateful to have you around, but I don't want to control you. What happened earlier was simply a timing issue."

"The prosecutor irritated you, Booker irritated you more, and I didn't help matters by taking off. I get it."

"You did the smart thing by taking off," Galen corrected. "That forced me to look at how I was acting and adjust my attitude."

"And Booker is still alive? You guys didn't start throwing punches after I left, did you?"

"No. He's fine. Unfortunately."

I snickered as I dug in the bag and came out with a container. "Well, it's fine now. Booker is off doing Booker things and we have a quiet night to ourselves. What could be better than that?"

Galen rested his hand on my knee and gave it a good squeeze. "Nothing could be better than that right now." He was earnest. "Absolutely nothing."

I found myself nodding in agreement, all my earlier anger disappearing. "Then let's eat, huh?"

"Definitely. I'm starving."

"That makes two of us."

14

FOURTEEN

We walked on the beach after dinner. Given our proximity to the downtown area, I could hear the revelry but was happy to be away from it … at least for tonight. Galen seemed content to leave his shoes close to the lighthouse and slosh around in the water, which never seemed to drop below a balmy seventy-five degrees from what I could tell. That was probably why Moonstone Bay was such a popular tourist destination.

"Did you always know you would stay here?" I asked as I slid into my flip-flops and watched Galen retrieve his shoes shortly before ten. "I mean … it's beautiful here. I don't know why you'd ever want to leave. It's a tropical paradise. Still, it's an island. It's a bit like being trapped at times."

Galen chuckled as he sat on the sand and tugged on a shoe. "I think everyone wonders what life would be like somewhere else. Of course I thought about fleeing to the mainland at some point, maybe setting up shop in Miami or St. Petersburg so I could remain close to the water, but when the time came to make that decision I realized I didn't want to leave."

"Do you ever regret that decision?"

Galen shook his head. "No. Are you regretting your decision to move here?"

"Absolutely not." I meant it. "This is the sort of place I dreamed about living when I was younger and suffering through brutal winters in Michigan. I understand that you've got a magical utopia here – in more ways than one – because I grew up somewhere else. I've already seen what the mainland has to offer and it's lacking. I like it here. I was simply asking if you have wanderlust."

Galen's grin was impish. "Since you got here, I'm afflicted with various forms of lust. Wander is not amongst them."

"Ha, ha." I flicked the ridge of his ear. "I guess I was just wondering because of what you said earlier. You grew up here and had occasion to fight with Booker quite often ... mostly about girls, apparently. Despite that, you volunteered him to help when I was attacked. It seems weird."

"Booker is a good handyman."

"And yet you still don't like him."

"I didn't say I didn't like him. I said he drove me crazy. That's true. He drives me crazy on a regular basis ... like eat my hair and try to bite my own nose crazy. That doesn't mean I don't like him. Er, well, at least occasionally."

I snickered as I extended a hand to help him to his feet. "I don't think I'll ever understand the way men interact with one another. It's nutty."

"Kind of like your buddy Madame Selena. How did things go with her, by the way?"

Oh, right. I should've expected that question. He was obviously eager to change the topic and Madame Selena was an easy option. "It was fine."

Galen waited for me to expand.

"She was a little manic," I conceded, rolling my eyes when Galen smirked. "Okay, she was totally obnoxious and seemed more interested in getting a look at May's books than anything else. She acted like that library was the holy grail of magic information. She didn't explain anything about being a witch or what I can do. She didn't offer to help me cast a spell or anything ... not that I want to as of yet. Essentially I'm exactly where I was twenty-four hours ago."

"That's not such a bad thing," Galen pointed out. "I know this is hard for you. I know it's not what you expected. But you're strong. You'll figure this out on your own."

"I hope you're right."

"I am right. I have faith in you. I wish you would have faith in yourself."

"It's not that easy when you have no idea where to start or what you're supposed to be doing."

"I guess that's fair."

We lapsed into amiable silence as we walked along the side of the lighthouse and headed toward the front door. I had every intention of kissing him goodnight and sending him on his way rather than inviting him to stay over. I was going to be strong tonight. I was determined. The open door at the front of the lighthouse threw me for a loop.

"Did you go inside first? I mean ... when you came looking for me. Did you come through the front door?"

Galen shook his head as he tilted his head back and scanned the imposing lighthouse façade. I had no idea what he was looking for, but I imagined it was lights or a hint of movement on the other side of the windows. "No. I knew you were around back."

"How?"

"I scented you."

That was a disturbing thought. I wondered what I smelled like. I imagined anise and cloves – two of my favorite scents – but figured it was far more likely I smelled like sweat and frustration. "That's a wolf thing, right?"

Galen nodded, all traces of mirth missing from his features. "That's definitely a wolf thing. I need you to stay here." He released my hand and reached for the door. "I'll be right back."

He had to be kidding. I gripped his arm so he couldn't race inside. "You're not leaving me out here, are you?"

"I ... you're safer out here."

"How do you know that?" I opted to be practical even though I wanted to shake him. "How do you know that someone didn't break into the lighthouse, realize we were outside, and hide in a bush so he or she can attack me later? If you leave me out here, whoever it is might take the opportunity and jump me while you're inside."

Galen made a face. "If you thought that you'd be hiding in my truck."

"Not really."

Galen growled. "Fine." He linked his fingers with mine and tugged me toward the open door. "You stay close and quiet. If I tell you to run, you run."

"You don't have to tell me twice. I'm keen to stay alive."

"Good to know."

Galen was intent as he quietly slipped through the open door. He kept me close, practically pinned to his side, and cocked his head as he surveyed the room. "Does anything look out of place?" he whispered.

I shook my head as I glanced around. The living room looked exactly as I'd left it, including the trashy magazine I'd flipped through earlier to take my mind off Booker and Galen's potential fight. "No. It looks the same."

"Okay. This way." Galen headed toward the stairs. "If someone is inside, it's obvious he or she is on the second or third floor. No one is down here. I'd be able to scent a third person on this floor."

"What are you going to do if you find someone?"

"Rip off a head."

I wanted to believe he was joking, but he looked so serious all I could do was swallow hard. "Okay. That sounds ... delightful."

Galen flashed a quick smile. "It will be okay. I ... ." Whatever he was about to say died on his lips as May flashed into existence in front of him, causing him to jolt back. "Hello!" He used his free hand to clutch at his chest. "You just about gave me a heart attack."

"Make a noise next time," I suggested, looking her up and down. She didn't appear flustered or upset, so I took that as a good sign. "Did the door blow open or something?"

May shook her head. "Someone was inside the lighthouse. I tried to get your attention on the beach but either you couldn't hear me or didn't want to be interrupted. Given the way you were looking at each other, I believe it was the latter. I didn't feel comfortable leaving the lighthouse, so I stuck close to make sure whoever it was didn't steal anything."

Galen slid his arm around my waist as he regarded my grandmother's ghostly countenance. "Well … who was it?"

May shrugged. "I have no idea. I couldn't see a face. He wore one of those hoodie things."

"Are you sure it was even a man?" I queried. "Women wear hoodies, too."

"Oh, well … ." May looked uncertain. "I didn't look that close. I didn't see breasts or anything. If it was a man, it wasn't a big man. If it was a woman, it was a decent-sized woman."

"Lovely," Galen muttered, shaking his head. "Let's go with the assumption that it was a man for now. Which rooms was he most interested in?"

"I have no idea. He barely made it inside before I knocked the broom over in the kitchen and frightened him to the point he rabbited. He ran so fast he left the door open. You two showed up a few minutes after that."

Galen flicked his eyes to the staircase. "You're sure no one is here, right? You're absolutely positive?"

May nodded, solemn. "Whoever it was ran as soon as I knocked over the broom. He obviously thought it was you two returning."

"What about a vehicle?" I asked. "Did he have a vehicle?"

"Not that I saw."

"We would've heard a vehicle," Galen reminded me. "Your driveway isn't that far from the patio. We would've heard if someone drove up."

"I didn't hear you drive up."

"Fine. I would've heard someone else drive up." Galen absently rubbed his hand over my back. "I don't understand why someone would try to break in when it was obvious we were here. I mean …

my truck is in the driveway. Anyone approaching would've heard us on the back porch."

"Unless we were already on the beach," I pointed out.

"Still ... we weren't quiet."

"Not everyone has your supersonic hearing."

"I guess." Galen exhaled heavily and searched the living room a second time. It looked completely normal. "I guess we can consider ourselves lucky. You need to lock your front door even when you're home. That's the safe thing to do and you should be practical."

Oh, that was rich. "Two nights ago you said I didn't have to lock my doors in Moonstone Bay."

"I said nothing of the sort."

I narrowed my eyes. "You did so. I remember because I pointed out that someone had already broken in and you said not to remind you."

"Yes, well ... ." Galen's lips twitched. "Fine. I was wrong. Is that what you want to hear?"

I grinned, triumphant. "Twice in one day. That has to be some sort of record."

"Whatever." Galen rolled his eyes. "I'm not comfortable with you spending the night here alone even though May clearly chased off whoever was trying to break in. That doesn't mean he or she won't return."

I knew where this was going. "You're going to suggest spending the night, aren't you?"

Galen snickered. "Only so I can be your bodyguard and make sure you're safe. That's what a good sheriff would do, and I am nothing if not diligent when it comes to my job."

Ugh. Whatever. "You're only suggesting this so you can make fun of me tomorrow morning. I don't want a repeat of that. I felt like an idiot."

"I know. I found it funny."

"Well, you won't find it funny tomorrow morning when you're the one in that position. I'm over that whole thing. You'll be the one whining."

"I have no doubt I will be whining." Galen strode to the door and shut it, engaging the locks before sliding the security chain into place. "I need to check the other door and all the windows before we head up to bed."

"I don't remember inviting you to stay."

"Oh, who are you kidding?" Galen puffed out his chest. "You'll cry if I leave and we both know it."

He was so full of himself it was almost painful. That didn't change the fact that I would sleep better knowing he was in the house. "I could make you sleep on the couch."

"You could, but you won't."

He was so smug. "You don't know that. I could change my mind."

"You won't." Galen moved toward the kitchen. "Don't make threats you can't keep."

"What makes you so sure I can't keep them?"

"I just told you. I'm exceedingly good at my job."

"We'll see."

"We certainly will."

IT TURNED OUT I COULDN'T maintain the threat. I barely put up a token fight. Also, once I told Galen about what happened at the cemetery – the part where I was convinced I was being watched but kind of forgot about it when I ran into Booker – he was practically glued to my side. He didn't seem to think I was imagining things. We were both thankful to share a bed … and wake next to one another in the morning.

"Good morning, Sunshine." Galen's smile was slow and lazy as he stretched next to me. "How did you sleep?"

That was a dangerous question. In truth, I had no business sleeping as hard as I did. I couldn't remember sleeping that well. It was a bitter pill to swallow. "I slept like crap because you snore."

Galen chuckled. "Oh, sweetheart, don't kid yourself. You're the one who snores."

"I do not!"

"You sound like a table saw hacking through rock," Galen countered. "Luckily, it only happens when you sleep on your back. I can quiet you if I shove you over to your side."

I was officially mortified. "No. That is … no."

"I'll record it for you next time."

"Don't even think about it."

Galen tickled me into submission as I tried to claw my way out of bed, laughing as he kissed my cheek and smoothed my flyaway hair. He seemed to be in a good mood despite everything that had happened the previous day. I couldn't fully understand his lazy attitude.

"What's the deal with you?" I asked after a beat, staring hard into a set of eyes that reminded me of a rolling surf. "I thought you'd be all business this morning."

"I thought so, too." Galen sobered, but only marginally. "It turns out all I needed was a good night's sleep to rebound. I feel better than I have since Trish Doyle turned up dead."

"That was three days ago."

"I still feel better."

"Well, good." I didn't know what else to say. "What's your plan moving forward?"

"Well, I've given it some thought." Galen rolled to his back and grabbed my hand so he could study my palm, his mind clearly busy. "I've decided that I don't care what the prosecutor's office has to say. Something doesn't feel right about this entire thing. I'm not done investigating even if they want me to be done."

I was impressed … and unbelievably relieved. "So, you're not letting it go. That's … good."

"I thought you would think so."

"I definitely think so." I licked my lips and gathered my thoughts. "Where will you start?"

"I'm not sure. I have a few ideas. Why do you care?"

"Because you care."

"Uh-huh. Are you sure that's the only reason?"

"Fine. I might be a little curious," I conceded. "It doesn't feel right to me either. I saw the look on Ashley's face at the festival. She was surprised … and a little bit devastated. If that was an act, it was the best act I've ever seen."

"I agree." Galen pressed a kiss to the palm of my hand. "We should get moving. You can shower first because you take longer to get ready. I'll run back to my house and shower and change. Then I'll pick you up and take you to town for breakfast so we can come up with a plan."

I was understandably confused. "We're coming up with a plan? As in you and me?" I wagged my finger back and forth for emphasis. "We're doing this together?"

Galen nodded. "We are."

"Is this because you're worried about leaving me alone in case someone breaks in? If so, let me remind you that I've taken care of myself on more than one occasion and I can do it again."

"I have no doubt that's true. You're still coming with me."

"And why is that?"

"Because there's no way you're going to stay out of this," Galen replied without hesitation. "You can't seem to help yourself from getting involved. I get it. I would like to break you of that inclination, but I know that won't happen.

"So, what does that mean?" he continued. "That means you're my new sidekick. Oh, before you even open your mouth to argue, that wasn't meant as a sexist statement. I am the sheriff. You're going to be my assistant on this one. That means you're essentially my sidekick, and I don't care if you hate the term."

"What … like the Robin to your Batman?"

Galen nodded. "If you like."

"More like the Gus to your Shawn," I muttered. "Even though everyone knows I should be Shawn."

"I have no idea what you're talking about."

"Only the best television show ever. *Psych*."

"I've never seen it. But if you love it that much we can binge it together." Galen gave me a soft shove with his hand. "Get in the shower. I want you to look pretty when you're Ethel to my Lucy."

He looked so pleased with himself for the reference that I couldn't hold onto my anger. “You think you’re funny, don’t you? It’s not going to be so funny when my sidekick overshadows your hero.”

“That’s not going to happen.”

“I wouldn’t be so sure.”

“Would you like to place a wager on it?”

“Absolutely.”

15

FIFTEEN

I had no idea how a sheriff's assistant was supposed to dress, so I opted for simple khaki cargo pants and a plain black shirt. Galen ran back to his house long enough to grab a change of clothes, and then we hit one of the diners for breakfast.

"I think you should've dressed in a cape," he said once our food was delivered. "If you're going to be a proper sidekick, you need a cape."

He was enjoying this far too much. "I've decided you're the sidekick. I'm going to solve this case and allow you to help."

He cocked a challenging eyebrow. "Oh, really?"

"Yup." I bobbed my head and mashed my over-easy eggs into my hash browns. "It makes the most sense. I have a keen mind for this sort of thing."

"Have you worked in the investigative field before?"

"No. That doesn't mean I won't be good at it."

"You're probably right." Galen leaned back in his seat and gave me a long once-over. "You still should consider a cape. I think you would look cute with it billowing behind you. Maybe a pair of those sexy

Wonder Woman boots and a nice bustier to go along with it. Wait … what were we talking about again?"

I decided to ignore the Wonder Woman comments. "Sherlock Holmes doesn't wear a cape."

"Ah. Does that make me Watson in this little scenario you've cooked up?"

"Pretty much."

"Good to know." He shoveled a forkful of pancakes into his mouth and thoughtfully chewed, swallowing before speaking again. "Okay, I'll play, Sherlock. You're in charge, so where do you think we should start?"

I actually expected the question and was ready. "The funeral home."

Galen furrowed his brow. "Why? We already know Trish is dead … and how she died. What good will stopping at the funeral home do us?"

"Because I called Lilac while you were at your house. By the way, I think I should probably see your house at some point, because I wasn't certain you didn't live in a box or something until someone mentioned you have a house. Lilac said that Maureen Doyle arrived on the first ferry this morning and was heading straight to the funeral home."

Galen's expression didn't change. "If you want to see my house you're more than welcome. I actually prefer visiting the lighthouse, because you're right on the water and have an outstanding view. My house is boring … and small. You live in a freaking lighthouse. There's nothing cooler than that."

I kind of agreed with him. "Are you talking about the ocean or me being outstanding to view?"

Galen cracked a smile. "That was cute."

"I do my best."

"If you're half as good at investigating as you are at flirting we might make some headway today. As for the funeral home, I still don't understand why you want to visit. How is Maureen going to help our investigation?"

"I want to know more about the feud, and she seems to be one of the few who got away."

"The feud?"

"You know … the feud. Wesley told me some about it. He said it started with Trish and Ashley's grandfathers, who then passed it on to their sons. He also said that Gus and Henry tried to pass the feud on to their daughters, but the girls were sick of it, so they basically ended it on their own terms."

"Unless maybe they didn't," Galen noted, his expression hard to read. "What do you think Maureen is going to tell you?"

I shrugged. "I don't know. Gus got really drunk at Lilac's bar yesterday – that's where I was before I headed to the cemetery – and he swore he didn't have an affair with Barbie Conner despite what the Moonstone Bay rumor mill claims."

"If Gus was drunk, how do you know he was telling the truth?"

I shrugged. That was a fair question. "I don't know. He seemed sincere. He was really upset."

"His daughter is dead."

"He didn't seem as if he was making up stories," I offered. "He never slipped up even though he was so drunk Lilac had to call someone to help pour him into a cab. If he was lying, don't you think he would have slipped up?"

"I guess." Galen ate some more, his mind clearly busy. "I guess we can go to the funeral home. It's actually not a bad idea."

I tried to refrain from being too smug. "Great."

"I don't want you to get your hopes up. Maureen might have nothing to give us."

"We won't know until we ask." I was prim and proper as I ate. "Besides that, I'm just getting started as Sherlock. This is only the beginning."

Galen snorted. "You make me laugh. No matter what, you always make me laugh. Perhaps you're the Jay to my Silent Bob."

I frowned. "I prefer Sherlock and Watson."

"Well, for now I'll give it to you. Finish up your breakfast and then we'll head to the funeral home. Even if we don't get anything from Maureen, I'm convinced you'll get a kick out of meeting Jareth."

"Who is Jareth?"

"Jareth Kern. He owns the funeral home. He's a little … different."

Since everyone on Moonstone Bay was different in my book, I wasn't particularly worried. "I'm looking forward to it."

"We'll see if you still believe that in an hour."

JARETH KERN WAS NOT what I expected. Sure, I hadn't spent much time in funeral homes – my mother was the only one close to me who died and I was an infant at the time so I didn't remember her service – but I had a pretty good idea what a funeral home director should be like.

I pictured him to be in his fifties, clad in a well-tailored suit, with slicked-back hair and a kindly expression. Instead I found a man who looked to be in his late thirties, was ghastly pale, and wore what I could only assume was a polyester-blend suit straight from the rack of some discount mall.

"Oh, you must be Hadley Hunter," Jareth enthused as we walked through the door of Eternal Twilight Funeral Home (seriously, that was the name, and I don't think it was meant to be ironic). He extended his hand and gripped mine before I had a chance to react to the gesture on my own terms. "I've heard so much about you. I'm so glad we could finally meet."

His hand was unbelievably cold, like, so cold I couldn't help but worry about his circulation. "Oh, well, I'm happy to meet you, too." I stared at his skin, marveling at the way the prominent veins spread like spider webs in certain spots. "I wish we could've met under happier circumstances."

"Oh, there's nothing happier than a death," Jareth said with a straight face. "Death is only the beginning, after all."

"Right." I tugged my hand back and instinctively moved closer to Galen in an effort to absorb some of his warmth. I was unbelievably cold after the brief skin contact. "I … um … this is a nice place."

Jareth beamed. "I like it."

Galen slid me a sidelong look, something unsaid lurking in the depths of his eyes. "Are you okay?"

How could I answer that? There was no polite way to say that Jareth gave me the creeps. Or that I was afraid to look too deeply into his eyes because I was sure monsters lived there. "I'm fine," I replied hurriedly. "I'm … fine."

Galen didn't look convinced. "You don't look fine." He flicked his eyes to Jareth. "Did you do something to her?"

Jareth squared his shoulders. "Of course not! What a thing to ask."

"She's off her game," Galen persisted. "You did something to her."

"What do you think he did to me?" I was confused. "He simply shook my hand."

"Did you look in his eyes?" Galen refused to back down. "Did you make eye contact with him?"

"I … don't … know." That was true. The more I tried to capture the memory, the more I couldn't remember looking into his eyes, even though it seemed that would be the normal thing to do. "Why does it matter?"

Galen pinned Jareth with a dark look. "I want you to knock it off. I'm serious. I mean … like, deathly serious. She's not used to all this. I know you like playing your games, but … stop it."

"Oh, fine." Jareth made a tsking sound with his tongue and pressed the back of his hand to his forehead. At that exact moment I felt as if the cloud that had invaded my mind – and wrapped around my heart – dissipated. "There's no reason to get worked up. I was merely testing her."

"Testing me?" I was baffled. "Why would you test me?"

"Because May worked up an immunity to my powers, and I wanted to see if you were capable of the same."

"Immunity. I … ." I looked to Galen for reassurance. "What's going on?"

"There's no reason to get upset." Galen's tone was conciliatory, soothing. "It's just, well, Jareth likes to sow his oats sometimes. That's what he was doing now. He won't do it again. I promise."

Galen turned a pointed stare to Jareth. "Tell her you won't do it again."

"Good grief." Jareth's easy smile had completely vanished. "Is that what you want to hear? I won't do it again. Stop being a killjoy."

Galen rubbed his hands up and down my arms. "Better?"

That was an interesting question. "I guess. What did he do?"

"It doesn't matter. He won't do it again."

"But ... what is he?" I asked the question even though I knew it would most likely come off as rude. Given whatever Jareth did to tick off Galen, I figured we were well past pretending to be polite. "I mean ... what are you?"

Jareth held his hands out and shrugged. "What are any of us?"

I didn't like his evasive answer and turned my full attention to Galen. "What is he?"

Galen pressed the heel of his hand to his forehead, frustration evident. "He's a vampire."

Son of a ... ! I didn't see that coming. "Are you serious? Vampires are real, too?"

Galen shrugged. "Did you think shifters and witches were the only storybook creatures that were real?"

"No. I thought mermaids existed, too."

Galen chuckled. "The world is bigger than you think, Hadley. There's a lot for you to see yet. That's the beauty of Moonstone Bay."

I cast a wary look at Jareth. He wasn't particularly beautiful. "I'm watching you." I extended a warning finger so he would be well aware of exactly how serious I was. "Now ... where is Maureen Doyle? We need to talk to her."

If Jareth was taken aback by the shift in my demeanor he didn't show it. "She's in the parlor." He crooked his arm in my direction. "Would you like me to lead you in?"

Not in this lifetime. "I think I'm good."

"I think she is, too." Galen put his hand to the small of my back and graced Jareth with a warning look. "Take us to Maureen. As for the rest, we'll talk about that later."

Jareth's smile slipped. "Why doesn't that surprise me?"

"Because you're not an idiot, despite the way you just acted."

"Maureen is this way. I'm sure she'll be happy to see a friendly face."

MAUREEN DOYLE WAS INDEED relieved to see a friendly face. She hopped to her feet when Galen swaggered into the room, paying me no mind as she threw her arms around his neck and began to sob against his chest.

"Please tell me you know who killed my daughter, Galen."

My heart clenched as the woman openly sobbed, Galen calmly rubbing her back as he attempted to soothe her. "I'm not happy about why you're here, Maureen, but I am glad to see you." Galen eased back so he could study the woman's face. "We have a few things to talk about."

"Of course." Maureen made room for Galen next to her on the couch, keeping her full attention on him and leaving me to sit on the matching sofa across the way. I tried not to cringe when Jareth sat next to me. "What do you know about Trish's death, Galen? I need to know who killed my daughter."

"Well, Ashley Conner is in custody and the prosecutor is charging her," Galen started.

"Ashley Conner?" Maureen's eyebrows flew up her forehead. "That can't be right. Those girls were friends for years … like, real friends. They weren't hanging out just to drive Gus and Henry crazy, no matter what those two idiots thought."

"They got in a fight the day Trish was killed."

"About?"

"My understanding is that it was about a man they were both seeing." Galen was obviously uncomfortable as he shifted on the couch. "I don't believe either relationship was serious."

Maureen pursed her lips. "I don't understand. Why were they dating the same guy?"

"I don't think 'dating' is the right word." Galen's discomfort clearly rose with each word. "It was Booker."

"Booker?" Maureen was astonished. "You can't be serious. Those girls threw away their friendship on Booker? The man is notorious for sleeping around. I mean … that's all he does."

"He looks good doing it, though," Jareth muttered, taking on a far-off expression, which only served to confuse me.

"The prosecutor is convinced that Ashley killed Trish, but I'm not sure that's true," Galen admitted. "The thing is, even though Trish and Ashley were angry with each other, Ashley looked genuinely shaken when she realized what had happened. She's also not the type to kill someone over one fight.

"Of course, I could be wrong," he continued. "I'm going to continue my investigation, even though that's not what the prosecutor's office wants."

"I agree with you about Ashley." Maureen was matter-of-fact. "The girl wasn't allowed in our home for obvious reasons, but she was always pleasant and fun to be around when I did have the occasion to spend time with her at a public event. Maybe it's just that I don't want to believe she's capable of killing Trish, but I would like you to continue looking."

"That's the plan." Galen lightly tapped her hand as he debated how to proceed. "I have some questions to ask you about the feud."

"Oh, geez." Maureen made a disgusted face. "I'm so sick of hearing about that feud. That feud ruined my marriage and stole my child from me. I don't want to talk about it."

I had no idea what she meant by that, but I was intrigued.

"We have to talk about it." Galen was firm. "Hadley talked to Gus at the bar yesterday. He got blitzed and was blathering on about a variety of things. He claims that he did not have an affair with Barbie Conner. While I don't like speculating about idle gossip, I always heard that was the reason your marriage broke up. Can you enlighten me?"

Maureen's face remained blank. "Who is Hadley?"

Galen gestured toward me. "She's helping me in a freelance

capacity. She's May Potter's granddaughter. I ... she was with me when Trish's body was discovered and wants to help me find out the truth."

"I see."

And, because she very clearly didn't see, I averted my eyes.

"I need to know the truth about why your marriage ended," Galen prodded. "It might be important."

"I understand. It's just that I promised Gus I'd never speak about it."

"I don't think you have a choice."

"Probably not." Maureen brushed her hair back. "Okay, here it is. Gus and Barbie weren't having the affair. I always thought Gus had a thing for Barbie – was even jealous a time or two when I thought she was throwing herself at him – but he swore up and down I was imagining things.

"I got so worked up at an Elks party one night that I ended up drinking with Henry," she continued. "He thought the same thing I did. We had a few too many drinks and one thing led to the next ... I'm sure you can figure out how things went."

I was officially horrified. "You slept with Henry?"

"It was one night that turned into a few months," Maureen conceded. "I don't know why I let it happen. I was lonely at the time. Gus and I were constantly arguing. I was weak and succumbed ... and it blew up my marriage.

"Trish took her father's side, of course," she continued. "She was furious and thought I'd betrayed her as much as Gus. I tried to talk to her, thought I could make things better, but she refused to even accept my calls."

"Is that why you left Moonstone Bay?" Galen asked.

Maureen nodded. "I thought a little space would do us good. I let Gus keep the bulk of the money in the divorce simply to get free and leave. After a few years, I met someone new. I invited Trish to the wedding, thought we could let bygones be bygones. She didn't even bother responding to the invitation."

My heart went out to the woman.

"Now she's dead," Maureen said, her voice thick with tears. "She's dead and we'll never be able to make up for lost time."

"Oh, that's just so sad." Jareth dabbed at his eye with a handkerchief and I couldn't help but notice that his tears were tinted red. "It's like a tragedy … and not a funny one like I prefer."

Everything about this day was turning into a tragedy.

16

SIXTEEN

"Are you going to explain the vampire?"

I waited until I was safely in Galen's truck before asking the obvious question upon exiting the funeral home.

"Jareth is … an acquired taste." Galen kept his gaze on the road. "I'm sorry he did whatever he did to you."

"Hmm." I made a noncommittal noise.

"What did he do to you?" Galen prodded.

"I have no idea." That was the truth. "I went cold all over and felt fuzzy. I'm not sure what happened."

"He probably tried to glamour you."

I ran the word through my busy brain. "So … that's true? I mean, vampires can really hypnotize people and make them think things?"

"I'm saying that vampires have many powers and that's one of them." Galen chose his words carefully. "Humans are susceptible to vampires. Shifters are to some degree. As for witches … that's more up in the air."

He seemed uncomfortable with the conversation so, naturally, I drilled down. "He said something about May being able to shut him out. Is that normal?"

"May was a very powerful witch."

That wasn't daunting or anything. "I'm not a powerful witch."

"You don't know that."

"I feel it."

Galen was calm as he turned off the main drag and onto a side street I didn't recognize. "Hadley, you don't strike me as the insecure sort so this ... mood ... confuses me. Why do you think you're not powerful?"

"I think that's obvious. I can't do any of the things May can do."

"You don't practice," Galen pointed out, parking in front of a nondescript bungalow with aquamarine trim. He left the engine running as he turned his full attention to me. "May practiced all the time. She researched. She loved living the life of a witch. You don't have to be her."

I swallowed hard. "You want me to be, though."

"I don't believe I ever said that."

"You did." I was firm. "You said you wanted me to touch Trish's body so I could see how she died. You only stopped yourself from pushing me to do it because you felt guilty."

"Wow. That's one messed up brain you've got there." Galen lightly rapped his knuckles on the side of my head. "That is not what happened. If you believe that, we need to have your vision and hearing checked."

I balked. "That is what happened."

"It's not." Galen kept his voice calm. "I shouldn't have brought that up. It wasn't fair to you. You're still getting used to living on Moonstone Bay. Bringing up the things May could do – things she worked six decades to perfect – wasn't fair to you. I'm to blame for thinking it was.

"You grew up believing you were normal," he continued. "You didn't know any different. Why would you? If you had contact with May while growing up things might have been different. You might be a skilled practitioner now, even more powerful than May. We can't go back in time and change things, though.

"So … are you at a disadvantage when it comes to magic now?" Galen queried. "I guess so. Some might think you're better off. You get to learn magic as an adult and not deal with all the immature stuff that adolescents deal with. I think you're getting the best of both worlds."

He was so earnest he caused my heart to flutter. "But it would be better for you if I could help."

"I want you to worry about what's best for you for right now," Galen stressed. "You can't learn everything overnight, and pushing yourself to be May is a bad idea. Do you want to know why?"

I wasn't sure. "Maybe."

Galen smirked. "Being May is a bad idea because you're Hadley. You need to learn this stuff at your own pace, embrace the life when you want and not when you think you should. Don't push yourself to be a superstar. Let it happen naturally."

"You seem convinced that I'm going to be a superstar. What if I'm not?"

"Then you'll still be Hadley." Galen tucked a strand of hair behind my ear and lowered his voice. "It's going to be okay. You're overwhelmed by all of this. I shouldn't have pushed you that night. It wasn't fair.

"I wish I could promise that people will stop comparing you to May – mostly because I think that's detrimental to your mental welfare – but I can't see it happening, so I'm afraid you'll have to get used to it," he continued. "May was beloved. I think you will be, too. But even if you're not, that's okay. Just be you."

I blew out a sigh. "I feel a little lost. When it comes to the stuff like you … and Lilac … and even Booker, I'm okay. I can figure it out. Sure, you're a pain in the butt when you want to be, but it's mostly in a charming way."

Galen chuckled. "That's good to know."

"It's just when I think about the other stuff … ." I trailed off, uncertain.

"Stuff like being a witch?"

"And Aurora being a mermaid … and you being a wolf … and that dude being a vampire ... and shark shifters being real. It all feels so overwhelming sometimes."

Galen offered a sympathetic cluck as he smoothed my hair. "That's normal. Anyone would feel overwhelmed in your position."

"I think you're just saying that to make me feel better."

"Is it working?"

I bit my bottom lip to keep from smiling. "Kind of."

"Well, that's good." Galen leaned forward and pressed a kiss to my cheek. "If you get overwhelmed, I'm here to talk. I don't know how much help I'll be, but I'm always here to listen. I don't want you internalizing this to the point that you explode. Let's talk about these things before they get out of hand, okay?"

"Yeah, well ... ." I sucked in a breath and purposely returned to the problem at hand. I needed time to think, and it wasn't going to happen if I had to explain my feelings in drawn-out fashion. "What's the deal with this place? Who lives here?"

"Henry Conner."

"Oh." Realization dawned. "Are you going to ask him about the affair?"

"Yes."

"Are you going to ask him if he killed Trish?"

"We'll see."

"Oh, are you going to ask him if he knows his wife never slept with Gus?"

"Ugh. You're the most annoying sidekick ever."

"I heard that."

"You were meant to."

HENRY CONNER, HIS EYES red-rimmed, didn't look happy when he opened his door and found us standing on his front porch. He stared for a long moment, blinked, and then made an unintelligible sound in the back of his throat.

Galen seemed to expect the reaction because he didn't appear upset by the greeting. "We need to talk."

"And what if I don't want to talk to you?" Henry challenged.

"I'm trying to make sure that the investigation into Trish Doyle's death is complete – and the prosecutor wants to close it and focus solely on Ashley – so I think you should reconsider."

"Ugh." Henry's frustration was palpable as he left the door open and disappeared into the drab hallway. Galen ushered me inside ahead of him before closing the door and prodding me toward what looked like a living room. "Ashley isn't a murderer, Galen. I'm not saying she's perfect or anything – you of all people know that – but she's no murderer. She wouldn't have killed Trish."

"I believe you, but I can't work on gut feelings alone." Galen settled on the couch, motioning for me to sit next to him, and focused on Henry. "There's a lot of evidence working against Ashley. You have to recognize that."

"What evidence?" Henry challenged. "As far as I can tell, you have no evidence."

"Well, for starters, she got into a fight with Trish at a bar earlier in the day. It happened in front of me, so I saw it, which isn't good for her."

"A fight is not a murder."

"I agree." Galen's tone was calm. "We have more than that, though. Ashley has no alibi. She was front and center at the beer tent – apparently dancing and drawing attention to herself – until she conveniently disappeared at the same time as the murder. She was gone for at least forty-five minutes that no one can account for. That's on top of the fact that the knife found lodged in Trish's throat matches a set Ashley had in her house."

Henry balked. "You mean kitchen knives that anyone could own? Last time I checked the grocery store only sold one set. Everyone on this island has the same knives."

Galen shook his head. "The handle was unique, like a fake mother-of-pearl material. It looked to be an old knife. Ashley had three knives in a drawer that matched it."

That was clearly news to Henry as he paled considerably. "But … that's still not proof."

"Henry, I'm doing my best here." Galen rubbed his hands over the knees of his trousers. "We have some questions to ask you and it's important you answer honestly. Do you understand?"

Henry didn't immediately answer, instead furrowing his brow and focusing on me.

"She's my assistant," Galen offered hurriedly. "She's helping me on this case. It's perfectly fine for her to be here."

"She's your girlfriend," Henry corrected. "Everyone in town knows you're courting her."

Ugh. What is it with that word? "I don't know that courting me is the correct way to put it," I hedged.

Galen cast me a sidelong look. "How would you put it?"

Whoops. That set him off. "Oh, well … courting is just such an odd word."

"Moonstone Bay is odd. Get over it." Galen focused on Henry. "She's with me and we're working together to find out the truth. She believes Ashley is innocent and refuses to take no for an answer, so you really want her on your side."

Henry scowled. "I never thought I'd see the day when our esteemed sheriff brought his girlfriend to work."

"Life is short." Galen was easygoing but firm. "Live a little. Now, as for our questions, I want to start with your relationship with Maureen Doyle. How would you describe it?"

Whatever Henry was expecting, that wasn't it. His mouth dropped open and incredulity practically rolled off him in waves. "Excuse me?"

Galen didn't back down. "You heard me. What was your relationship with Maureen Doyle?"

"I don't see where that's any of your business."

"It is if you want to continue helping Ashley."

I didn't believe for a second that Galen would abandon his investigation if Henry didn't cooperate. That wasn't fair to Ashley, after all. I had to give him credit for being a good bluffer. Henry was so uncomfortable with Galen's steady stare he could do nothing but move his lips – pursing and un-pursing them repeatedly – for a full minute. Finally, he found his voice.

"We had a thing," Henry barked, his eyes lit with fury. "It was a short thing, but it was a thing."

"My understanding is that it started at an Elks party, turned into a brief affair, and essentially ruined Maureen's marriage to Gus," Galen noted. "Is that how you see it?"

Henry was flabbergasted. "Who told you that?"

"It doesn't matter."

"It matters to me."

"Well, I'm not revealing my source." Galen leaned back on the couch and crossed his legs. He was in control of the interrogation even though Henry wanted to pretend otherwise, and he was sending a clear message of strength and determination with his stance. "Tell me about your relationship with Maureen. I'm especially interested in how it ended."

"It wasn't a big deal," Henry gritted out. "We got drunk at an Elks party. We were both annoyed with our spouses and one thing led to another. Before we even knew what was happening we were in a storage closet with our pants around our ankles."

I wrinkled my nose and muttered under my breath. "Lovely."

Henry scorched me with a look. "We were drunk. Things happen."

"Were you embarrassed after?" Galen asked, refusing to let Henry get off on a tangent. "I mean ... did you swear up and down it wouldn't happen again, or did you immediately start making plans for a second round?"

"Neither one of us said a thing. We just went back to the party and pretended it never happened."

"You had to meet up again," Galen pressed. "I know you had an ongoing affair for several months."

"It was closer to a year," Henry sneered. "After that first night we went several days without seeing one another. The guilt weighed on Maureen more than me. She called and wanted to meet to talk. We picked that little place out on the highway, the one close to the primary surf spot. We knew we wouldn't be discovered there.

"We talked, had lunch and agreed it should never happen again," he continued. “I walked her back to her car … and then we climbed in the back seat and did it again.”

“What?” My eyes goggled. “You did it in the car? How classy.”

“Hadley.” Galen sent me a warning look. “Let me handle this part of the questioning.”

If Henry was bothered by my reaction he didn’t show it. Instead, he merely shrugged. “You might think it was a forbidden love affair or something, that we actually longed to be together. That wasn’t the case.”

Maureen had said something similar before we’d left the funeral home.

“What was it then?” Galen asked, feigning ignorance. “What drew you together?”

“Loneliness.” Henry’s answer was simple. “We were both married to other people, but lonely. Gus was all about work and fighting with me. Barbie was all about spending the money I made and ignoring me. We didn’t seek each other out because of love. We did it because we were both lonely.”

I couldn’t help feeling sorry for him even as my dislike regarding his attitude grew. “What about Barbie and Gus?” I asked, refusing to risk glancing in Galen’s direction. He clearly wanted to handle the questioning, but I was curious. “Did you really believe they were having an affair or was it a convenient excuse to make yourself feel better because of what you were doing?”

“I believed it … for about thirty seconds,” Henry replied, dragging a hand through his thinning hair and staring at the ceiling. “Barbie announced it during a fight. I was halfway to Gus’s house to kill him before realizing she was full of crap. I knew she was just saying it to hurt me, but I wanted to strangle him all the same.”

“You obviously didn’t do that,” Galen noted.

“No. Instead I roused my lawyer out of bed – Ned Baxter – and had him put together divorce papers. It was a fairly quick and painless procedure because he had templates on file. He was always good that way.”

I grimaced at mention of Ned's name. "Ned Baxter was your attorney?"

Henry shrugged. "I had no idea he was a murderer. He was one of the best family lawyers on the island. He got me a divorce with minimal alimony, so I still kind of like him – even though he tried to kill you."

Galen quickly wrapped his hand around my wrist to quiet me before I could respond.

"So you basically let the island gossip train run in the wrong direction," Galen supplied. "You had the affair, but Gus and Barbie bore the brunt of the suspicion. That was a lucky break."

"It didn't feel lucky," Henry countered. "Everyone felt sorry for me because Gus stole my wife. That's how they saw it, anyway. You have no idea how annoying that is."

"Especially because you stole Gus's wife," I said.

Henry rolled his eyes. "I didn't steal her. We had sex for relief and that's it. When it came time to end the relationship it wasn't hard. I'm sure you're picturing some grand romantic thing, some tortured decision to go our separate ways for the benefit of our families. It wasn't like that."

Actually, I was picturing seedy hotels and areas in the middle of nowhere so the two could get in a quickie and then be on their way. "I'll take your word for it."

"You do that." Henry was obviously annoyed. "I don't see how my affair with Maureen matters. I didn't kill Trish. Ashley didn't either."

"I have to check out every avenue available," Galen replied pragmatically. "It's not a full investigation unless I look at all the angles."

"If I were you, I'd start with Booker."

I almost snorted in amusement but managed to hold it back … barely. Instead of joining in my mirth, Galen solemnly nodded.

"He's our next stop," Galen said, taking me by surprise. "I have quite a few questions to ask him. My understanding is that he was fine dating both Trish and Ashley. But the girls weren't fine with it. Booker has no motive."

"We both know he doesn't need a motive," Henry fired back. "He is who he is and that means he does things for no reason all the time."

What did that mean?

"I'm fully aware of Booker's nature," Galen said before I had a chance to push Henry on what he meant. "I'll take care of Booker. As I said, he's our next stop."

"Well, good. I hope you lock him up and throw away the key."

"We'll see where the day takes us," Galen said dryly. "As for you, we'll be in touch. We might have more questions."

"I might not be in the mood to answer them."

"I guess we'll have to wait to see."

17

SEVENTEEN

"You can't possibly think Booker is guilty."

We spent another twenty minutes at Henry's house – a span that felt as if it were dragging out forever – but I wisely kept my mouth shut until we were back in Galen's vehicle.

"I don't know what to think," Galen said as he started the truck. "If I'm absolutely forced to lodge an opinion, it would be that Booker is not involved. But I don't solve cases according to my opinion."

"But … ."

"He was dating both of the women," Galen reminded me. He seemed agitated, although I couldn't decide if it was the heat or Henry's bad attitude fueling him. Of course, my insistence on declaring Booker innocent might have something to do with it, too. "I have to talk to him."

"He says that women naturally fall at his feet and he can't do anything about it."

Galen rolled his eyes. "Of course he'd say that."

"He also says that both Trish and Ashley knew he wasn't in it for the long haul," I added.

"It seems you two have discussed this at length." Galen gripped the steering wheel so tightly his knuckles whitened. "It's nice you have faith in him."

"It's not that." I searched for the right words. "It's just ... he doesn't strike me as the murdering type."

"And can you describe the murdering type?"

I shrugged. "You know ... hinky."

"Hinky?"

"That's a word."

Galen snickered. "It is, but I don't believe it's a quantifiable word. I have no choice but to talk to Booker. I understand that makes you uncomfortable, maybe even a little angry. I can drop you at the lighthouse before I interview him, if that makes you feel better." What he didn't add is that it would clearly make him feel better to question Booker alone. He was terrified I'd get in the way.

I couldn't blame him for being worried, but that didn't mean I wanted to miss out on him questioning Booker. I honestly thought there was a chance I'd be able to offer some help. "You mean cut me out. You can't cut out your partner. That's not allowed."

"Sidekick. You're my sidekick."

"Partner sounds better."

"Oh, geez." Galen pointed his truck toward the beach. I knew exactly where he was going. "I don't want to cut you out. If you remember correctly, it was my idea to include you in the first place. I have to talk to Booker. I don't have a choice."

Actually, from his point of view, I understood. That didn't ease my nervousness. "Maybe I should talk to him for you."

"No."

"But ... after last night ... ." I didn't finish. I didn't have to. We both remembered what had happened the previous night.

"You think I'm going to beat the snot out of him because I'm jealous, don't you?"

"No." I would never imply anything of the sort. "I'm simply worried that you're already not in the best frame of mind where Booker is concerned."

"You don't need to worry about it." Galen pulled into the parking lot in front of the beach tourism center. Booker's aged van was two slots down. "Booker and I have been interacting for a very long time. It's not always pleasant and nice, but no one has ever died. We'll be fine."

I wasn't even remotely convinced. "Fine." I blew out a sigh. "If you guys start throwing punches, though, I'm out of here."

"I can guarantee we won't start throwing punches."

IT TURNS OUT THERE ARE different kinds of punches. There are the physical kind that men love throwing around in an effort to prove they're king of the hill. The other kind is more insidious. It's of a verbal nature, and it can cause people's skin to absolutely crawl with discomfort and worry.

Those were the kind of punches we were dealing with, and Booker landed the first jab in this bout. "Am I under arrest or are you here to deliver Hadley to me for safekeeping? I have to say, if it's the latter, I didn't think you were much of a sharer. I promise to bring her back to you in pristine condition."

Galen scowled as he took up position about six feet from Booker. It looked to be a safe distance, but I recognized right away that if they threw themselves at each other it wouldn't be safe at all. In fact, it would be rather dangerous.

"I've got Hadley's safety taken care of," Galen drawled, folding his arms across his chest. "We're here for official reasons."

"Really?" Booker flicked his gaze to me as his lips slowly curved. "I'd heard Hadley was looking for a job. I didn't realize she was going to be working for you. What are the benefits like in your office? Wait, don't tell me." He held up a hand. "You're paying her in kisses, aren't you?"

Galen remained calm on the outside, but I could feel the agitation building up inside of him. It would break loose soon if I didn't do something to head off this battle of wills … and testosterone. I'd never seen two men more keyed up while at the same time pretending all was normal. It was fascinating … and a little terrifying.

"I'm just helping out," I interjected quickly. "Galen isn't convinced Ashley is guilty – and I'm not either – and we want to work together to make sure that an innocent woman doesn't go to jail. I'd think you'd want to help with that."

Booker kept his gaze affixed to Galen for another moment before slowly turning to me. "We've had this discussion. I don't believe Ashley is the type to murder anyone. That doesn't mean I have information to offer."

"You were ... hanging out ... with both of them."

"Sleeping with," Galen corrected. "He was sleeping with both of them at the same time."

"Oh, it never happened at the same time." Booker's lips curved. "If it happened at the same time, I think all three of us would've been happier about the arrangement. I'm sure convincing them of that would've been difficult, but I've seen the outcome in my dreams and know things would've been fantastic if we all played well together at the same time."

"Oh, gross!" I wrinkled my nose. "You're not being cute or coy, by the way. You're being perverted and obnoxious. Besides, no woman really wants a threesome. That's simply the stuff of bad porn dreams."

Booker snorted. "I know a woman or two who would argue that point."

"I doubt it."

"More importantly, I think your boyfriend does, too."

I turned an incredulous look to Galen. "What?"

"Ignore him." Galen waved off my obvious interest in the new topic. "I need to ask you a few questions, Booker. It would be nice if, for once, you didn't make things difficult ... or try to deflect in a manner that gets Hadley worked up for no good reason."

"What would you have to look forward to if I made things easy?" Booker taunted.

Galen sucked in a breath and I could practically see his temper fraying. He promised no physical punches would be thrown, but I wasn't sure I believed that any longer. It might not be a matter of *if* that happened, but rather when.

"Just answer his questions," I prodded, moving between Galen and Booker. The last thing either of them wanted was to hurt me, and I knew they would fight the urge longer if that was a possibility. "You don't always have to make things so difficult."

Booker searched my face for a long beat. "Fine." He flicked his eyes to Galen. "What do you want to know?"

"Well, for starters, I'd like to know if Trish and Ashley were aware of each other," Galen started.

"They were friends. Of course they were aware of each other."

"I mean in your life," Galen clarified. "Were they aware you were dating both of them?"

"You'll have to ask them." Booker turned blasé as he picked up a paintbrush and focused on the window. "I wasn't keeping anything secret from either of them, but it's not as if we sat down and shared heart-to-heart conversations."

"How did it work?"

"Well, usually I called one of them and we agreed to meet at a bar," Booker replied. "We had drinks for an hour, listened to some music and then went back to her place for ... um ... the main event."

"What about the morning after?" I asked. "You must've talked about something then."

"You're assuming I spent the night. I never spent the night. That's the reason I wanted to stay at their homes. I didn't want to be the jerk to kick them out of mine after sex."

I felt sick to my stomach. "So you went with them long enough to have sex and then you took off? That is so ... sick."

Booker shrugged. "Like I told you before, not everyone is built for relationships." His gaze was back on Galen in a heartbeat. "We can't all be our esteemed sheriff here."

Whether he meant it to be a dig or not, it sounded like one. Galen reacted appropriately.

"You can slap at me all you want because I really don't care," Galen shot back. "I'm not ashamed to have one girlfriend. I know what you're doing, by the way, and I don't like it. You don't have to be so belligerent.

"I mean ... Trish is dead," he continued. "You didn't have to see a future with her to feel bad about her death. Any man – invested in the relationship or not – would feel something when he found out the woman he was spending time with was dead. Of course, you're not a normal man, are you?"

I widened my eyes when Booker took a step forward. "Maybe we should talk about something else."

They both ignored me. "I'm more of a man than you," Booker snapped. "Why else was I making sure your girlfriend was safe yesterday? You clearly didn't have time for her. Word on the street is that you kicked her out of your office. Nice, man." Booker shot him an enthusiastic thumbs-up.

"My girlfriend is none of your business," Galen fired back. "There's no reason for you to even look at her, as far as I'm concerned. She's my priority, not yours."

"Um, guys, let's not fight," I suggested.

It was as if I wasn't even sharing oxygen with them. They could no longer see or hear me.

"If she's your priority, why did she get taken advantage of by Aaron the other day?" Booker challenged. "If she's your priority, why does she always come to me when she needs help?"

"She's taking pity on you," Galen replied. "She's not going to you to ask for help, but to offer it. She can't help it. She has a big heart."

I tried one more time. "Guys, I'm serious. We should go back to talking about Trish."

"You're worried about that big heart, aren't you?" Booker supplied. "You're afraid she's going to open it to me and show you the door in the process. That's how things worked in high school. I'm still the same guy I was, and you're terrified you'll lose the same way you did back then. Heck, you're so worked up you look as if you're going to cry."

And ... I was done. I opened my mouth to tell them that, inform them of my plans to leave. They were too caught up in each other to even notice. I should've expected that, I thought as I walked away from the center and left them to posture and poke each other until someone lost an eye or a limb. Neither man was known for letting someone else take charge. Of course they would always lock horns. They fancied themselves the strongest men on the island, which meant taking a backseat to anyone was impossible.

"I hate men," I grumbled to myself as I headed toward town. I could still hear Galen and Booker shouting at each other as they took the fight up a notch. "I really just can't stand them."

Unfortunately for me, no one was around to hear.

"YOU LOOK LIKE roadkill run over twice."

Lilac immediately handed me an iced tea when I settled at her bar.

"Thanks." I downed half the glass before continuing. "I feel like I've been run over twice … and by two different men."

"Let me guess … Galen and Booker?"

I wasn't surprised she guessed Galen. Pegging Booker was another story. "How did you know?"

Lilac's grin was easy. "I heard there was a scene downtown last night, one that resulted in you storming off. I also heard Galen spent the night, which means he tracked you down to make up. I'm guessing he still wants to fight with Booker for form's sake today, huh?"

Last night. Of course. That altercation wasn't exactly private. That made sense. "They're puffing their chests out to see who's built better even as we speak." I drained the rest of the iced tea and handed over the glass for a refill. "I didn't even think they'd noticed I'd left."

"You have to understand, they have a … unique relationship," Lilac explained, lodging her elbows on the bar as she regarded me. "They've been in competition since … well, since before they could even speak."

I had no idea what to make of that. "Why?"

"You'll have to ask them."

Ugh. "I'm asking you."

"I honestly don't know." Lilac was sincere. "I only know they've always been going at each other. I was behind them in school, and the stories about the fights they got into were legendary. The stories about what they did together were legendary, too."

I remembered Booker's talk of threesomes. "You don't mean … ." Nope. No way. They were way too alpha for that. I couldn't even picture them doing anything of the sort. "Let's talk about something besides Galen and Booker and their honking huge egos," I suggested, shaking my head to dislodge the odd but somehow titillating image from my head. "What can you tell me about Henry Conner and Maureen Doyle?"

Lilac didn't appear surprised by the shift. "What do you want to know?"

"About their affair."

Lilac's lips curved down. "Their affair?" Her eyebrows migrated to her frizzy hairline. "I didn't know that they actually had an affair. There were whispers about it, but most everybody in town came down on the side of Gus and Barbie having an affair, not the other way around."

"Well, I think Moonstone Bay's gossip train broke down on that trip. I happen to know that Gus and Barbie weren't having an affair, but Henry and Maureen were." It was only after I shared the enticing tidbit that I realized Galen probably wouldn't be happy that I was talking out of turn. I was his sidekick, after all. Sidekicks weren't supposed to gossip.

Ah, well. I discarded my misgivings almost immediately. He was more worried about comparing egos – I wouldn't be at all surprised if the two of them found a measuring tape to settle their argument at some point – than paying attention to me and my big mouth. He'd get over it.

"So, Henry and Maureen were really having the affair, huh?" Lilac tapped her chin as she considered the new development. "There were whispers at one point but they went away. I'm kind of surprised, but not really, if that makes sense."

It made perfect sense. "My understanding is that it wasn't a great love affair. They didn't want to be together as much as they didn't want to be alone. Apparently their marriages were breaking up anyway."

"I don't know how true that is," Lilac said. "I mean … there were always rumors about the four squares of that triangle shifting in either direction. There were even rumors about Maureen and Barbie for a time."

Rumors no doubt started by a man. "So, you're saying that rumors of affairs date back even further than that?"

"Oh, to practically the beginning." Lilac nodded. "There were rumors when Maureen and Barbie ended up pregnant at the same time. Some people said they were swingers and it all happened at a key party."

I rubbed the tender spot between my eyebrows. "A key party? Wasn't that a thing in the seventies?"

"Yeah. Moonstone Bay has always been behind the times. We had eighties hair until 2010."

That figured. "You're saying that it's possible Gus might not be Trish's father and Henry might not be Ashley's. I mean … that's basically what you're saying, right?"

Lilac shrugged. "Anything is possible. Ashley does have Gus's coloring, and Trish did not inherit Maureen's hips. Of course, everything could be on the up-and-up, too. We'll probably never know."

That was true, yet I wasn't ready to let it go. "I don't suppose you know where Barbie Conner lives?"

Lilac's expression darkened. "Why? What do you have planned?"

Now it was my turn to play innocent. "I don't have anything planned. I'm simply asking out of curiosity."

Lilac didn't look convinced. "I don't know. If I send you over there and Galen finds out, he won't be happy."

"Galen is too worried about what Booker is doing right now to notice. Trust me."

"Okay, but you have to tell me what you find out."

That was something I could readily agree to. "You're on."

18

EIGHTEEN

Half the side streets in Moonstone Bay don't have signs – no joke – so I was forced to pick up a tourist map in one of the vestibules on Main Street before making my way to Magnolia Drive. Given the name, I expected big houses and lawns with ornate landscaping and decorative water elements. Instead, I found a block of ranch homes that looked exactly the same save for the color of the siding.

Barbie Conner lived in a gray house with white trim. It didn't stand out, but the woman who opened the door did. She had bottle-blond hair and super long lashes, the type you see on drag queens. She wore a pantsuit straight out of Hillary Clinton's presidential run wardrobe and an expression straight out of the punishing nuns' playbook.

I was understandably taken aback.

"I … um … hello."

Barbie barely registered a facial expression. At first I thought it was because she didn't know me. She was probably surprised to see a stranger on her doorstep. She disavowed me of that thought directly, though.

"Hadley Hunter, right? You're May Potter's granddaughter. I heard you were making the rounds with Galen Blackwood. I'm surprised it took you so long to find your way to me."

Apparently I was already famous in Moonstone Bay. That was something. Whether it was a good or bad something, though, I couldn't say.

"I was hoping we could have a little talk," I said, shifting from one foot to the other. "I have a few questions."

Instead of ordering me off her front porch, Barbie ushered me inside. "I was just about to make a pitcher of rum runners. Care to wet your whistle?"

Hmm. Perhaps that explained her lack of facial expressions. She was hammered and it wasn't even three yet. "I'm on the job," I lied. Sure, I was Galen's assistant in name only, but that didn't stop me from being serious. "Just a glass of water will be fine."

"Suit yourself." Barbie set about making drinks at a small corner bar, returning with a glass of water for me and a huge rum runner for herself before settling in the large wicker chair at the edge of the room. She sipped her drink, eyed me speculatively, and then flicked her fingers in my direction. "You said you had questions."

"Right." Her demeanor threw me. That was probably her intent. Still, I had a job to do and I was determined to get to the bottom of the affair rumor. "So, as you know, your daughter is being charged with Trish Doyle's murder and is incarcerated with no sign of getting out."

"You're just a sunny thing, aren't you?" Barbie sipped again, her forehead remaining dolphin smooth even though I was convinced there should be some form of facial movement. "No beating around the proverbial bush for you, huh?"

"I don't see how that will do anybody any good," I replied. "I'm not convinced Ashley killed Trish. In fact, I'm kind of leaning in the opposite direction and think she's innocent. Murder doesn't seem her style."

"Do you know my daughter?"

That was a tricky question. "Not really. I happened to be present when her friendship with Trish went south. They were angry but not stab-you-in-the-neck furious. I have trouble understanding why she would immediately turn to murder after a fight."

"If you're asking me to explain the inner-workings of my daughter's mind, you've come to the wrong person." Barbie crossed one leg over the other, giving me a nice glimpse of shoes that probably cost more than Booker's ancient van when it was new. "We aren't all that close."

"May I ask why?"

"Because she refuses to look at the bigger picture. I told her exactly how she should act, the people she should spend time with and the men she should pursue if she wants a safe financial future. She ignored every single thing I said to her."

"I think it's normal for daughters and mothers to battle on issues like that," I offered.

"Yes, but look at me." Barbie gestured toward her suit and shoes. "I'm clearly a good role model. I managed to squeeze a decent settlement out of Henry even though he lied about me having an affair. Everyone said it was impossible at the time, but I made it happen. If I didn't, would I be able to get Botox every week and look this young?"

That explained her lack of facial expressions. I should've figured that out on my own. "Do you think Henry purposely spread the story about you and Gus having an affair simply to make sure you'd get less in the divorce?"

"Henry has always been a tool … with a little tool." Barbie laughed at her own joke, the sound utterly humorless. "He saw he had an opening and took it. I knew he was really the one having the affair and I tried to tell the judge that. I couldn't prove it, though. He and Maureen stopped seeing each other around that time, and my private investigator couldn't get the photos I needed.

"It's too bad, really," she continued. "I would've gotten twice the settlement I did if I could've proved infidelity. Henry was far too smart to allow that, though. I did get more than he wanted because I outsmarted him, but it was nowhere near as much as I wanted. I had to settle … and I hate settling."

That was interesting. A new wrinkle of sorts, although clearly not on Barbie's face. "The judge didn't believe you?"

"The judge said he didn't care about infidelity by either party. He said he was only interested in a fair monetary distribution. That's a laugh, right? I should've gotten more."

"How much money did you bring into the relationship?"

Barbie screwed up her face into a close approximation of a scowl. "I don't work. Why would I possibly want to work?"

I definitely should've taken a few moments to read this situation better. "Still, you were aware of the feud between your husband and Gus. How did you feel about it?"

"I thought it was juvenile and petty."

"Did you tell your husband that?"

"Of course not," Barbie scoffed. "That feud kept him busy so he wasn't constantly bugging me for things … like dinner on the table and my credit card receipts. As long as he was focused on Gus I could do whatever I wanted. That's the way I liked things."

She was completely unlikable. I could see why Henry wanted to divorce her … and why he was looking for an escape. Maureen was ten times more genuine than Barbie even pretended to be. "So you just ignored the feud because it benefitted you."

"Pretty much." Barbie studied her nailbeds. "Why are you interested in this? I know you're not friends with Ashley. She wouldn't be able to tolerate you because of her crush on Galen."

"Well … I happened to be with Galen when he discovered Trish's body. It made me sad. I was also there when Ashley saw the body, and I'm convinced she's innocent. I want to make sure the guilty party doesn't go free. As for the other, I'm not so sure Ashley has a crush on Galen. She was involved with Booker … at least until a few days ago. I think it's far more likely she has a crush on him."

"Honey, half the women on this island have been involved with Booker at one time or another," Barbie drawled. "He's not known for his relationship skills as much as for his 'if the van is rocking, don't come knocking' skills."

I was mortified on behalf of her daughter. "You probably shouldn't say things like that. I mean ... Ashley was clearly interested in Booker no matter what his motivations were in the relationship."

Barbie snorted. "Um, no. Ashley and I didn't spend a lot of time together, but the girl wasn't an idiot. She didn't always make the right choices when it came to men and makeup – definitely when it came to makeup because a pair of false eyelashes would've done wonders for that rather plain face – but she knew there was no future with Booker. She still had hope that she'd snag Galen if she waited him out."

I had no idea what to make of that. "Oh, well ... ."

Barbie barreled forward as if I hadn't started speaking. "Ashley has loved Galen from afar for years. He's the island's most coveted bachelor. Do you want to know why? I'll tell you why. It's because he isn't against settling down eventually. Booker will never settle down. Galen wants to do the whole family thing.

"Now, even though he's an attractive man I never thought he was a proper object of affection for Ashley," she continued. "He doesn't make enough money. The one thing my daughter inherited from me is expensive taste. She needs a man who makes a lot of money to pay for the things she wants. Neither Galen nor Booker fit that bill."

"The heart doesn't always care about things like that," I argued. "Sometimes the heart simply wants what it wants."

"And luckily the brain is around to fix that." Barbie finished off her drink. "Ashley didn't kill Trish. I'm certain of that because there's no money in murder, especially on this island. I mean ... just ask Ned Baxter. That didn't go well for him, did it?"

I shifted in my chair. "I think we're getting off topic."

"Trish was a worthless girl who was never going anywhere in life," Barbie supplied. "I never liked her. I never understood why Ashley hung out with her. Quite frankly, I'm happy they're no longer friends."

"They're no longer friends because Trish is dead."

"And it worked out wonderfully to Ashley's advantage," Barbie noted. "She needs to stop focusing on friendships that gain her nothing. She needs to find a man. Her father won't fund her lifestyle forever."

"Does he fund it now?"

"Mostly."

Hmm. That was a bit of news I hadn't been privy to before. "Does he want to fund her lifestyle?"

"Who knows what Henry wants?" Barbie turned imperious. "If I knew what that man really wanted out of life we'd still be married and I'd have my hands on his money. As it stands, Ashley is getting older. Her prospects are running out. Fighting over Booker – killing over him – makes no sense. Ashley is a sensible girl."

I considered asking about Ashley's paternity, just going for it, but I knew it was a waste of time. Barbie Conner was in her own world and it wasn't one I wanted to visit for an extended stay. "Well, thanks for answering my questions. I can show myself out."

I FELT AS IF I needed a shower after leaving Barbie's house. The feeling only grew when I touched the door jamb upon exiting the house and found myself overwhelmed by a flash of something I shouldn't have seen. I couldn't explain it. In five seconds time I saw an entire five-minute conversation from the past … and it wasn't pretty.

I didn't want Barbie to know what I saw. She was in her own little world, so it wasn't hard to cover. I did a decent job of putting on a bright smile and escaped. I wanted to lie down badly, but that wasn't an option given the fact that I wasn't home. Instead, I headed downtown, my mind racing, and pulled up short when I caught sight of Booker leaning against a light post in front of the fruit stand on the corner.

"What are you doing here?"

Booker slid me a sidelong look as he shined an apple against his shirt. "Are you asking if I killed your boyfriend and am on the lam?"

"No. Wait … you guys didn't fight, did you?"

"You saw us. We always fight."

"I mean with your fists." I held up mine for emphasis, causing Booker to frown.

"Don't hold your wrist at an angle like that if you're going to hit someone." He straightened my arm. "You'll break something if you do. Don't put your thumb like that either." He studied my new fist. "Much better. You could do real damage to someone with that."

I rolled my eyes as I dropped my arms. "Ha, ha. You're so funny."

"I was a comedian in another life."

"I have no doubt." I rolled my neck until it cracked. "Galen is alive, right? He's not hurt or anything, is he?"

"Galen is perfectly fine."

"You didn't lock him in the tourist center and throw away the key?"

"He left under his own power." Booker bit into the apple and thoughtfully chewed, swallowing before speaking again. "He wasn't happy when he realized you took off, by the way. I haven't heard him curse that much since the time we were on opposing volleyball teams and the island trophy was on the line."

"How long did it take you guys to even notice I was gone?"

"I noticed right away. That's because I'm observant and in tune with your emotions."

"You're full of crap."

Booker's smile was sheepish. "I have no idea. You were gone from the beach when we realized. We couldn't even see you walking down the sidewalk. Galen was upset … but mostly at himself. If you play your cards right, he'll grovel when it comes time to make up."

"Why would he grovel?"

"Because he feels he let you down. I'm sure he feels guilty about ignoring you to the point you wandered off. Where did you go, by the way?"

"To see Lilac."

"Yeah, I stopped in at Lilac's place about an hour ago. You weren't there."

"Then I went to Barbie Conner's house," I admitted. "I wanted to ask her a few questions."

"And how is she?"

"Soused."

"Sounds about right."

"Her face doesn't move either," I added. "This island needs a recovery group for those who overindulge in Botox. She could be a founding member."

Booker snorted. "She's looked exactly the same for years. I don't even notice now."

"Yeah, well, I think the only thing she notices is herself," I lamented, momentarily wondering if I should mention the flash to Booker and then immediately deciding against it. "She doesn't even seem to care that Ashley is in jail. She did say that she doesn't think Ashley would murder someone over you. Apparently you don't make enough money to concern Barbie."

"Ah, I dodged a bullet." Booker's eyes gleamed. "You look offended on my behalf because of that. Don't get yourself worked up. That's simply how Barbie is. I don't think she means anything by it."

"It's offensive."

"I'm not offended."

"She made digs about Galen, too."

"Ah, now we're getting to the root of it." Booker took another bite of his apple. "I know you're upset because you think I was using those women – perhaps even playing one against the other – but that's not what was going down."

"I don't think that's what was going down for you," I countered. "I think those girls were head-over-heels for you whether they wanted to admit it or not."

"Then that was their mistake."

"Because you're not the relationship sort?"

"Basically." Booker bobbed his head. "I am my own person and I'm content with my life right now. That doesn't mean I don't want human companionship from time to time. I try to be forthright about my needs when that happens. If someone happens to get hurt in the process … well, that is not my intent."

I could only sigh. "You just don't understand. I wish you did, but I'm starting to think you're incapable."

"Oh, I understand. But I choose to live my life a different way."

"Well, what's done is done." I squared my shoulders. "Barbie wasn't much help. She let a few things slip. I'm going to have to own up to interviewing her without Galen. It seemed like a good idea at the time, but now I'm not so sure."

"You'll be fine."

"How do you know that?"

"Because Galen is so busy beating himself up over you disappearing without anyone noticing that he'll probably forgive just about anything you did," Booker replied. "I mean … now might be a good time to rob a bank. He feels so guilty you'd get away with it. He's quite smitten with you."

Smitten? "I don't think he would like you using that word."

"Why do you think I picked it?" Booker turned mischievous. "I've never seen him this worked up over a woman. I kind of want to torture him over it because … well, that's what we do. But I won't, because that would hurt you and I'm genuinely fond of you."

"Even though I thought you were a murderer?"

Booker sobered. "We've already talked about that. You were in a bad position. I don't blame you for what happened."

"You could have been killed."

"Not likely."

"But Ned was a murderer," I persisted. "You got lucky that he was in such a hurry to get to me that he didn't try to finish you off."

"You don't have to worry about that." Booker was so sincere it caused me to be suspicious.

"Why don't I have to worry about that? I mean … you can die, right?" I had no idea what he was, but I was becoming more certain that he wasn't a normal human being. "You're not like … immortal, are you?"

"You mean like the guys on *Highlander*?" Booker's smile was back. "You don't have to worry about that. I'm not immortal and I don't run around chopping off heads with swords. As for the rest … it's really not important."

I thought about pushing him, but now didn't seem the time. "I should probably get going. I need to find Galen."

"Don't worry. I'm sure he'll find you."

I was almost positive that was true.

19

NINETEEN

I needed time to think.

I was happy to leave Booker and his bad attitude behind. Instead of seeking out Galen – which I knew would be the mature thing to do – I decided to slink away and let him find me. I had things to ponder, and I couldn't do that with an audience.

I don't know what possessed me to return to the cemetery. I felt like an idiot for doing it and yet that didn't deter me. It was as if I were Harry Potter in the first book when he found the mirror that let him see his heart's desire. It just so happened that his heart's desire was to know the parents who died when he was an infant. It wasn't quite the same for me, but it wasn't all that different either.

I sat on the ground near the window and put my back to a broad tree. I cast a quick look to my right, to the foliage that made me nervous the previous day, but unlike before, I was fairly certain I was alone. That was for the best.

I closed my eyes and exhaled heavily, resting my hands on my knees. I wanted to breathe myself into a flow state, allow my mind to float on a cloud and essentially re-enter the vision I thought I'd had at Barbie Conner's house. It was a technique I remembered reading about when one of my friends in Michigan insisted I start yoga. I found the stretching and contorting in a hot room unbearable. I liked the idea of a flow state very much, though, and I was determined to get a better look at the earlier flashes. Somehow I knew they were important.

At first my mind was too busy to allow me to summon the vision a second time. I kept wondering about Booker and what he was … and Galen and how he would react when I saw him … and May and why she wouldn't answer questions. My brain was a mess.

I was determined to make it happen, though, so I focused. Galen believed I could figure out everything that was happening on my own. I was hopeful he was right because otherwise … well, otherwise I had no idea what to do.

I concentrated on my breathing to the exclusion of everything else, shutting out the noises that surrounded me and focused on inhaling and exhaling.

In.

Out.

In.

Out.

Before I even realized what was happening I slipped into the vision and allowed it to take over. It was loud, ugly and emotionally brutal … and yet I sat through it all the same. I heard the voices as they swirled, saw the faces, but I was a passive participant rather than an active member of the family.

"You're late," Barbie spat, leaning against the counter as she looked Ashley up and down. It wasn't the same Ashley I'd met a few days before, but rather a younger model. Given the length of her skirt, I figured she had to be in high school … and probably very popular with the boys. "How many times have I told you not to be late when I have things scheduled with the girls?"

Ashley rolled her eyes. "I don't see why you care what I do … whether you're hanging with your drunken friends or not. I don't need you here when I get home. Just … go." Ashley made impatient shooing motions with her hands. "Seriously, go away."

Barbie grabbed a glass of wine from the counter. "Maybe I simply enjoy spending time with you. Did you ever consider that?"

"No."

"That's good because I never enjoy spending time with you," Barbie spat, causing me to inadvertently cringe. I couldn't imagine a more hateful woman. She had no redeeming qualities as far as I could tell. "Why are you so late?" she demanded, clearly opting to change the subject rather than continue the fight. "Did you have detention again?"

Ashley shot her mother a withering look. "I haven't had detention since eighth grade and you know it. That was years ago and one freaking time."

"Then where were you?"

"I was at the coffee shop on Main Street." Ashley averted her eyes and focused on the leather backpack she carried. It was much trendier than anything I owned at the same age. That was probably her mother's doing. Barbie would want Ashley to dress a certain way even if she was a terrible mother because Barbie obviously believed Ashley's appearance reflected on her.

"What were you doing at the coffee shop?"

"Um ... drinking coffee."

Barbie narrowed her green eyes. She wasn't nearly as Botoxed then as she was now. She looked far more natural ... and evil ... in the past. It made me shudder.

"And who were you drinking coffee with?" Barbie challenged. "Was it a boy? Wait ... do you have a crush on a boy?"

"Oh, I hate it when you pretend to care about my life," Ashley complained, adopting a whining tone that set my teeth on edge. "Why can't you crawl in your bottle like you usually do and ignore me?"

"Because that's what you want and I don't care to make you happy," Barbie drawled. "Now ... talk. Who were you with at the coffee shop? Don't tell me it was that Carpenter boy. He's not going to amount to anything and his family has no money to leave him. He's not a suitable match."

"I wasn't with him." Ashley was mortified. "Why would you think that?"

"Because you're being evasive."

"I am not."

"You are so."

"I am not."

"Then who were you with?" Barbie clearly scented blood in the water and started circling. "If you were really minding your own business and not doing anything to be ashamed about you would've already told me to shut me up. Now I know you're lying."

"I'm not lying!" Ashley's nostrils flared. "I wasn't with a boy. You don't need to get all worked up for nothing because whatever you're thinking ... well, didn't happen."

"Fine." Barbie held up her hands, the one gripping the wine glass splashing a little on the floor.. "Tell me who you were with and I'll leave it alone. I'm due to head off anyway."

Ashley blinked several times before answering. "It doesn't matter."

"It matters to me."

"But ... ." Ashley heaved out a sigh. "Fine. I was with Trish Doyle, if you must know."

Barbie's expression twisted into something hateful. "Oh, geez! Please tell me you're not entertaining the idea of becoming a lesbian. That is not going to happen on my watch, so you shove that thought out of your head right now."

"I'm not a lesbian," Ashley fired back. "Why do you always go there? It's so ... stupid. It's possible to be friends with a woman and not be a lesbian."

"I know that. I have friends and I'm not even close to being a lesbian."

"You have horrible women you like to gossip and drink with," Ashley corrected. "You don't have friends."

"And Trish Doyle is not your friend," Barbie fired back. "You only started hanging around with her to irritate your father – something I happily supported at the time – but now it's getting ridiculous. She's low class and beneath you."

Ashley glowered at her mother. "She's funny and I like her. I don't care what you say. We're friends."

"You're not friends."

"We are!" Ashley slapped her hands on the counter. "We're friends and I like her. I don't, however, like you."

"Oh, well, that feeling is mutual," Barbie drawled. "There are a lot of things I wish I could take back in this life, but having you is the biggest."

Ashley snorted and turned on her heel. "Have another drink, mother. I don't think you're sloshed enough and it's almost five. You're behind schedule."

She breezed through the kitchen door, barely acknowledging her father as he walked into the room. Henry Conner merely raised an eyebrow when he saw his only child storming out of the room. He loosened his tie and regarded his wife with a cynical look.

"You look more sober than usual."

"Oh, your wit astounds me, Henry," Barbie supplied, rolling her eyes. "I think you missed your calling. You should've been a comedian."

"And give up all this?" Henry made a face as he shuffled to the small bar cart and searched through the contents until he came up with a bottle of whiskey. "I thought you had plans tonight."

"I'm leaving in a few minutes." Barbie sobered. "We have to talk about Ashley before I go."

"Why? She seemed perfectly normal to me. She's clearly angry with you and will spend the night pouting in her room. What's different about that?"

"She's spending too much time with the Doyle girl." Barbie lowered her voice. "You know that's not a good idea."

Henry poured two fingers of whiskey into a tumbler. "I know it's not a good idea, but there's no talking her out of it. What do you want me to do?"

"Forbid her from hanging out with Trish Doyle."

"And when that has the opposite effect and she only spends more time with Trish, what do you want me to do then?" Henry challenged. "She's a teenager, Barbie. She's going to do whatever it is that she thinks will irritate us most. That's how teenagers are wired."

"Then you've got to give her something to make her not want to spend time with Trish," Barbie shot back. "Raise her allowance ... or buy her a new car. Bribe her until she doesn't want to spend time with that girl."

"I'm not going to bribe our daughter." Henry took a long swig of his whiskey. "She can't be bought. She's not you."

"Everyone can be bought," Barbie sneered. "Ashley is no different. She can't keep hanging around that girl. It's too dangerous. The truth might come out and then what? Where will we be if that happens?"

Henry didn't immediately answer, instead shrugging as he finished off the whiskey. When he finally did speak, he sounded defeated. "Who knows? Maybe we'd all be better off if the truth came out."

"You know that isn't true."

"I don't know that." Henry placed the empty glass in the sink. "I don't know anything anymore."

"And that's why you're a complete waste of space," Barbie sneered. "Fine. If you won't handle it, I will."

Henry balked. "What are you going to do?"

"Don't you worry about it. I've got everything under control."

"HADLEY?"

A worried voice from the real world jolted me out of the vision. I was fairly certain that was all there was to see, but I wouldn't have minded hanging around for another minute or two … if only to see if I might be able to smack Barbie Conner around a bit for being such a horrible person. Ah, well, it was too late now.

I shielded my eyes from the blinding sun as I focused on the figure moving closer. I wasn't surprised when I realized it was Galen. I knew he'd find me. He always did.

"What are you doing here?"

"Looking for you," Galen replied, worry flitting across his handsome features as he dropped down to sit next to me. "Are you okay?"

"I'm fine." It was the truth. Kind of. "How did you know where I'd be?"

"Booker mentioned seeing you downtown. He said you looked … upset. I thought maybe you'd end up here so I gave it a shot."

"Oh, well … ."

Galen gripped my hand, cutting off whatever I was about to say. "I'm sorry I didn't notice you take off earlier. I didn't mean to get so wrapped up with Booker that I ignored you. That seriously is the last thing I wanted."

He was so earnest my heart went out to him even though I remained mildly agitated. "I know. What's your deal with him? Why do you guys hate each other so much?"

"We don't hate each other. Did you not hear the part of the story about how Booker sought me out to tell me he ran into you?"

"I figured he did that to mess with you."

"He did. He was also worried. He said you were pale and upset. Then he told me you talked to Barbie Conner, and I figured that was probably normal for anyone who spends time with that hateful woman."

"Ha, ha." I rubbed the back of my neck. "She's not very nice."

"If you'd waited for me I could've told you that."

"I was mad at you at the time."

"I figured." He picked up my hand and flipped it over so he could trace his fingers over my palm. "You still should've waited for me. It's hard to conduct an official interview when you don't have authorization."

"I thought you were my sidekick."

Galen snorted. "Yes, well, you still should've waited for me. Barbie is a lush, so I'm not too worried about it. She probably won't even remember you were there. Did she tell you anything?"

"Not much, but … ." I broke off and bit my bottom lip, unsure.

"What?" Galen was gentle as he prodded. "What happened?"

I told him about the vision, including the small exercise I conducted to explore further when I arrived at the cemetery. When I finished, he was impressed, which wasn't the reaction I expected. "I thought you would be angry."

"Why? Because you're learning to control your powers?"

"Well, no," I hedged. "More because I questioned Barbie without you being present. You haven't yelled about that at all. Are you feeling okay?"

Galen barked out a laugh. "I'm feeling fine. I already said there's no reason to be angry. Barbie won't remember you were there. I doubt she has information to share anyway. She hasn't even bothered to visit Ashley in jail."

The news didn't surprise me. "Ashley turned out a lot better than she should have given the lack of parental interest she was dealing with. Still, what do you make about the last part of the vision? The part about the secret?"

Galen shrugged. "I don't know. There have been so many rumors about the Conners and Doyles over the years that it's hard to fathom which rumor it could be. You said Ashley looked like a teenager in the vision, right?"

I nodded, searching my memory. "She said she was coming from having coffee with Trish. Barbie thought she had detention. She looked about sixteen or so."

Galen thoughtfully rubbed his chin. "I don't know. I need to give it some thought. Maybe I'll put together a list of all the rumors I've heard about the two families and let you look it over."

"That sounds like a good idea ... and I'm not just saying that because I'm a busybody."

Galen chuckled, smoothing my hair as he leaned forward and gave me a soft kiss. "Are we okay? I really am sorry about earlier. I won't let it happen again."

"We're okay." I meant it. "I wasn't furious or anything. I was a little hurt. I was mostly worried that you and Booker would kill each other. You were getting a little intense."

"We've always been that way. You don't have to worry about it. We've only come to blows a handful of times. The last we were in our early twenties. We have maturity calming us now."

I wasn't so sure about that. "And you're not going to tell me his big secret?"

"No." Galen shook his head. "If Booker wants to tell you, it's his secret to share. I can't do that to him."

"Even though you hate him?"

"I don't hate him. I simply don't like him a lot of the time. The thing is, with the big stuff, I trust him. Why do you think I called him the night you were attacked? I needed to know the job would get done ... and done correctly. He was the first person on my list that night.

"Booker is more than one thing," he continued. "Everyone on this island is more than one thing, and that includes you. If he wants you to know what he is, he'll tell you."

I couldn't help being disappointed. "Fine. I guess I can live with that."

"Good."

"But I'm not happy about living with it," I warned.

"I figured." Galen slowly stood and extended his hand to help me to my feet. "I was thinking we would keep things quiet tonight. How does takeout sound? We can take it back to the lighthouse, eat, and then take a walk."

"Does that mean you're spending the night again?"

Galen shrugged. "Do you have a problem with that?"

"No." I meant it. "You have to watch your wandering hands, though. They're starting to get a mind of their own."

Galen snickered as he linked our fingers. "You're making that up because you want me to be embarrassed. It won't work."

"We'll see."

"We will."

I was quiet for a moment and then I opened my mouth, which is never a good sign. "My other boyfriend isn't ashamed of his wandering hands."

"Ugh. Why can't you just let that 'other boyfriend' stuff go? It's not funny."

"When I find a bad joke to latch on to I always keep it way too long," I explained. "It's unattractive and annoying. You'll get used to it."

Galen chuckled. "Thanks for the warning."

"Don't mention it."

"How does pizza sound?"

"Worse than Chinese."

"At least you're not afraid to form an opinion."

"You never have to worry about that."

"Good to know."

20

TWENTY

Galen was still holding firm regarding Booker's secret as we shared cereal and coffee on the back patio the next morning.

"I'm not telling you."

"Just give me a hint," I pressed. "I'm sure I will be able to figure it out if you give me a hint."

"No." Galen shook his head. "Ask Booker."

"I already asked him." I kicked back in my chair and folded my arms over my chest. "He won't answer."

"Did you really ask him or did you merely hint around and expect him to fill in the blanks out of the goodness of his heart?"

"Um … hmm."

"That's what I thought." Galen finished his coffee and stood. "I need to run to my house and take a shower and change. I would suggest, if this is really bothering you, that tracking down Booker should be your first order of business."

I arched an eyebrow, amused. "I thought you didn't want me spending time with Booker."

"I never said that."

"You sort of implied it."

"Only in your head. I have no problem with you hanging out with Booker as long as you don't engage in any funny business."

"Right. So, no dressing up as clowns? No tooting horns and putting on ridiculously large shoes. I think we can manage that."

Galen scowled. "Your sense of humor is the oddest thing."

"Wesley says I get it from him."

"Now that is a frightening thought." Galen leaned over and gave me a quick kiss. "I will call you later if I come across any tasks you can help me with. It will probably be after lunch."

"I'll be waiting." I watched him move toward the side of the house, something occurring to me. "By the way, um, if you want to keep some clothes here – a razor and other stuff, too – you can do that."

Galen's face reflected amusement when he glanced back at me. "That's progress, huh?"

"It's just ... there's no need for you to have to run across town all the time when I have room in my bathroom."

"Good to know." Galen ran a hand over his stubbled chin. "While we're talking about domestic things, if you wanted to run to the grocery store and stock up on things to eat – especially breakfast items – it wouldn't be the worst thing in the world."

I pursed my lips. "Are you attacking my culinary skills?"

"I happen to love cereal."

"Good."

"That was the last of it, though. You're also out of eggs, fresh fruit, yogurt and anything else that could be considered a breakfast food. I don't want to tell you how to eat or anything, but breakfast is the most important meal of the day."

He wasn't wrong. "I'll run to the store."

"Good girl." He mock saluted. "I will call you as soon as I can. If I have something you can help with, I'm more than willing to spend another day with you as my sidekick. I have to go to the prosecutor's office straightaway, though, and I doubt very much he'd find you as charming as I do."

"You're probably right." I sipped my coffee. "I'll be around when you get a new lead."

"What if I don't get a new lead?"

"You will."

"How can you be so sure?"

I shrugged. "You're you. I'm pretty sure you don't quit until you're satisfied with the outcome."

Galen shot me a hot and flirty look. "You have no idea how right you are about that."

I swallowed hard. "So … um … I'll talk to you later, okay?" It was an effort to get out the words without fanning my face, which felt as if it was on fire thanks to Galen's innuendo.

"You definitely will."

THE FIRST ORDER OF business was tracking down Booker. He was exactly where I'd expected him to be, finishing up work on the beach tourism center. He barely acknowledged my appearance when I turned up in the open doorway.

"You're almost done, huh?"

Booker nodded. "I will be glad to get out of here. I don't ever remember getting so many visitors to a gig before."

If he expected me to feel guilty he was going to be bitterly disappointed. "I came to ask you a question."

As if sensing I was about to turn things serious, Booker opted to take control of the conversation. "Did Galen find you yesterday?"

"He did."

"Did you guys make up?"

"We were never really fighting."

"That's not how it felt to me."

"Well … we're fine." I shifted from one foot to the other, uncomfortable. "I'm going to ask you a question. You don't have to answer it, although I think you already know that. It's just … I can't stop thinking about it. People keep saying weird things about you and I have to know."

Booker kept his eyes on the lettering he was finishing up, his fingers steady and his gaze even. "I've been expecting this for a bit. Lay it on me."

"Okay, well … ." I licked my lips and squared my shoulders. "What are you?"

"I'm a Pisces. Some people say that means I'm moody, think the world is out to get me, and occasionally dramatic, but I don't put much stock in astrology."

I knew exactly what he was trying to do. "You know what I mean." I refused to back down. "Everyone on this island has a secret. Galen told me that and then he proved it when he turned into a big freaking wolf on the highway one night to save me from a stalker who turned out to be hired by Ned."

"So, because Galen can turn into a wolf you're wondering if I can do something similar," Booker mused. "To satisfy your curiosity, the answer is no. I'm not a shifter. I don't get hairy under the full moon … or any other day of the week, for that matter. In truth, I struggle growing a full beard. I'm often jealous of Galen's hair-sprouting skills."

Somehow I'd already deduced he wasn't a shifter, although I had no idea how. "I know. You're not a vampire either. I met that weird dude who runs the funeral home yesterday, by the way. He did something to fuzz my brain and upset Galen. He promised not to do it again, but I'm not so sure. I didn't ask Galen specifics about vampires because it didn't seem like the time, but that's totally coming."

"He's a bloodsucker," Booker supplied. "He can't go out in direct sunlight, but he can work during the day … as you saw. He survives on animal blood, which he gets from the area farms. He's been strictly forbidden to snack on tourists, so if you see him doing anything of the sort you should definitely report him to Galen. Other than that, he's a normal guy."

"He's creepy."

"He's definitely creepy," Booker agreed. "A lot of people are creepy, though."

I waited for him to expand, to volunteer information, but he focused all his attention on the letters he'd so painstakingly applied to the window the previous day. Apparently he only had touch-ups left and then he was done.

"Booker … ."

"I know you want me to tell you what I am, but it's not something I normally do," Booker supplied. "I try to keep my private business private."

"But Galen knows."

"And he obviously didn't tell you, which is driving you insane." Booker's lips quirked. "The thing is, this island is full of paranormal beings, but it works because we basically stay out of each other's business. We all know about each other, but we never mention it. It's like an unspoken rule or something."

"Except everyone has something to say about your romantic habits and I didn't grow up on this island," I countered. "I have no idea what's real or mythology. I didn't know I was a witch until a few weeks ago and I'm still trying to deal with that.

"For example, did you know I had some sort of psychic flash while I was at Barbie Conner's house yesterday?" I continued. "I mean … it was an actual flash. I saw a fight between her and Ashley and then I listened as Henry and Barbie talked about having a secret."

"I'm guessing this was before they divorced," Booker noted. "My understanding is that they rarely talk since the divorce, and there were all sorts of weird accusations in the divorce paperwork."

"Is that really important considering the conversation we're having?"

"I'm just pointing it out."

"This is all new to me," I pressed. "I get that you don't want to talk about it and I'll respect your decision not to tell me." I paused a beat. "Okay, I won't respect it, but I'll figure out a way to deal. I know it's none of my business. I just … wanted to know."

Booker didn't immediately say anything, instead focusing on his task. When it became apparent he wasn't going to start spilling his guts I heaved out a sigh.

"I should get going." I turned to leave. "I promised Galen I'd pick up some groceries. Apparently I'm not very domestic. I need to learn to get better at that."

Still nothing from Booker.

"So, um, I guess I'll see you around." The moment my feet hit the front walk he finally spoke.

"Wait," he barked, his temper on full display as he cursed under his breath and stomped his foot. "Wait a minute."

I tried to tamp down my excitement, instead pasting a puzzled expression on my face as I swiveled. "What?"

"Oh, don't play innocent with me." Booker screwed up his face into a frustrated expression. "You're about to get your way and you know it."

I was so excited I could barely contain myself. "You don't have to. I understand your need for privacy."

Booker extended a warning finger. "You are the world's worst actress," he groused. "I mean ... seriously. You're not fooling anyone."

I didn't care about fooling anyone if he was about to share his deep, dark secret. "I'm sorry if I'm making this difficult for you."

"Knock it off." Booker's eyes flashed as he licked his lips and returned the paintbrush he held to a small palette on the ground. "Okay, I'm going to tell you. The only reason I'm going to do it is because I know someone else eventually will. My money is on Lilac – she can't keep her mouth shut – but I know it will happen. I figure it's better you hear it from me."

The way he phrased it had me worried. Perhaps he was something bad and our relationship would be forever changed by the revelation. The possibility gave me pause. "Um ... ."

Booker ignored my indecision. "Here it is ... and if you laugh I won't talk to you ever again."

Laugh? That didn't sound so bad. "If you're a shark shifter I'm totally going to throw you a party."

"I already told you I'm not a shifter."

"Oh, right." Crap. He did tell me that. "So ... what are you?"

Booker sucked in a breath. "I'm a cupid. Now, reach into my bag over there and grab the flask in the pocket. I need a drink."

A cupid? That was so not what I was expecting. I did as he instructed, though, taking advantage of the momentary distraction to run the notion through my head. When I straightened and handed him the metal flask he was watching me closely. I figured it was for signs of laughter, but I was more confused than anything else.

"I don't understand," I said after a beat. "Cupids are supposed to wear diapers and fly around so they can shoot people with love arrows. You look nothing like a cupid."

Booker made an exaggerated face as he downed a shot of whatever was in the flask. "You're letting pop culture fuel your knowledge base. That's not what a cupid is."

"So ... what is a cupid? Are you saying you don't help people fall in love?" Saying the words triggered something in my brain. "Wait ... everyone and their brother says that people are magically attracted to you. Is that a cupid thing?"

Despite my excitement, Booker remained morose as he nodded. "Yeah. That's a cupid thing. Women are naturally attracted to me. That's why I go through them so quickly."

"I don't understand. Wouldn't you be infatuated with the idea of love if you were a cupid?"

"I *am* a cupid and I am not infatuated with the idea of love," Booker shot back. "It's not like that."

"How is it?"

"Well ... women are drawn to me." He was no-nonsense. "They can't stop themselves from wanting me."

"Which is how you ended up dating two women at once."

"Which is how I ended up having sex with two women at once," Booker corrected. "I don't date. Do you want to know why?"

Actually, I did. "Yes."

"Because the things these women feel for me – or at least think they feel for me – aren't real," he replied. "They're attracted to me because of what I am and not who I am. It's chemical. Pheromones and all that other jazz. It's not funny, so don't laugh."

The last thing I wanted to do was laugh now that I knew a little more about his predicament. "I'm sorry." I held up my hands in capitulation. "I truly am sorry. I didn't even think about how hard this is on you. It must be difficult constantly wondering if what people feel is real."

"It's not real."

"You don't know that," I countered. "Just because the first jolt of lust might not be real, that doesn't mean that true love can't spring from it."

"Yes, but I will never know if what people claim to feel is real or a byproduct of what I am. That's why I'm destined to be alone."

That made me inexplicably sad. "I don't believe that. I'm sure there's a way around your little problem."

"Oh, honey, it's not a *little* problem."

I frowned. "That's such a man thing to say."

"It's true."

"Whatever." My mind was already working. "I'll conduct some research. I'll figure it out."

"And I thought my day couldn't get any worse." Booker slapped his hand to his forehead. "I'm going to regret telling you. I just know it."

"You won't. It's going to work out. In fact … wait a second." Something occurred to me. "You said that women throw themselves at you. Is that all women?"

"Basically."

"But I've never felt inexplicably drawn to you," I pointed out. "I was never warm for your form and rubbing myself against you whenever you visited. To me you were just a normal guy."

Booker chuckled, although the sound was hollow and humorless. "That is the rub, isn't it? You're apparently immune to my charms. May was, too."

"So maybe all witches are immune to your powers," I suggested. "We just need to find you a witch."

Booker snagged my gaze for a long moment and I felt something heavy pass between us. Luckily for us both, he didn't bring it up. "I've been around other witches. They come to the island all the time and they throw themselves at me like everybody else."

"That could just be because they're on vacation," I argued. "Sometimes you want to hook up when you're on vacation. It doesn't necessarily mean anything. You're pretty. You would make an appealing hook-up option."

"Oh, I think that's the nicest thing anyone has ever said to me," Booker mocked, pressing his hand to the spot above his heart. "I'm going to write about that in my journal later. Thank you so very much."

I rolled my eyes. "I was just saying that maybe witches are an option for you. We can test the idea. There's no reason to be all morose about things. You might be able to find a woman who is immune to you."

"That would be nice." Booker offered a half-smile that didn't make it all the way to his eyes. "That was one of the reasons I liked hanging around May so much. You have no idea how frustrating it is to have someone constantly propositioning you in a sexual manner."

"You might be surprised. Women have that happen all the time."

"Yeah, well, it's a pain," Booker muttered. "That's why I never get serious with anyone. That's why I don't date. I'm doomed to this life and I'm fine with it."

He didn't sound fine with it. "Wait … weren't your mother and father cupids? I mean … that's how you're a cupid, right?"

"My father was," Booker replied. "My mother was something else."

"A witch?"

"Just … something." Booker vehemently shook his head. "We're not getting into that, so don't even try. I already spilled my guts once today. It's not going to happen a second time."

"That's fine. The cupid thing is more than enough to work with for the time being."

He looked hopeful. "You're going to stay out of it?"

That seemed unlikely. "We'll figure something out. Maybe there's a spell or something we can try."

Booker scowled. "You don't even know how to be a proper witch. I'm not letting you cast a spell."

"Oh, don't be a spoilsport." I was lost in my own head. "Where would I find books on cupids? Wait, never mind. You're not going to tell me. I'll figure it out on my own."

"Yup, I'm definitely going to regret telling you," Booker groused, making a disgusted sound in the back of his throat. "This is going to come back and bite me in the behind."

"I think you're exaggerating."

"And I think I'm done talking to you for the day." Booker made a shooing motion with his hands. "Go away."

"Oh, I'm not even close to being done."

"That's exactly what I was afraid of."

21

TWENTY-ONE

I considered stopping by the station to see Galen once I'd finished talking to Booker. Okay, to be fair, Booker simply got tired of talking to me, so he sent me on my way. I had plenty of questions to ask him, but he wasn't in the mood to answer. It was a small island and there was no place to hide, so I left Booker to his work and headed to the grocery store.

I stocked up to the point I figured Galen would be wowed when next he looked inside my refrigerator – even grabbing an extra toothbrush and razor in case he forgot to bring one to the lighthouse – and then headed home.

I took an extra-long time putting things away in the hope that May would appear so I could ask her about Booker's cupid lineage. Other than once or twice on other floors, she almost always showed up for visits when I was in the kitchen. She didn't appear today, which was disheartening.

In fact, it had been days since I'd seen her. I ran the realization through my head as I climbed the spiral staircase to the library on the third floor, frowning as I did the math. She was there the night we thought someone might have broken in, but she disappeared as quickly as she appeared. That was almost forty-eight hours ago and I hadn't heard a peep from her since. That was unusual, to say the least. Even though she wasn't forthright and eager to spend time with me – especially when I had questions that needed answers – she almost always popped up every day, even if she stayed for only a few minutes.

Worry about May took a backseat when I hit the library – which was more of an office-laboratory combined – and a blast of cold air hit me in the face. I shuddered as I glanced around, confusion washing over me. There was something off about the room … although I had no idea what.

My first instinct was to flee. Yeah, I'm not the bravest soul when it comes to situations that horror movies have warned me about. One of my biggest fears was becoming a cautionary tale. Like, for example, I didn't want to turn into an idiotic babysitter who forgets her charges and gets put in a bed with a tombstone like the chick from the original *Halloween*. I also didn't want to visit a summer camp because good things could never happen there.

Now, standing in a room in my own home that felt decidedly inhospitable, I certainly wanted to run. I steeled myself, though, and instead focused on the contents of the room and refused to let myself bolt back down the stairs.

On second glance, everything seemed to be in its place … if slightly off. I headed to the bench at the far wall, the one that held an assortment of beakers and test tubes, and looked over the box of ingredients I found there not long after moving in. At the time, I didn't know what to make of the equipment. Now I knew May used it to mix potions and other things – although my witch knowledge was so lacking I had no idea what those other things were – but the box looked as if someone had been rummaging inside.

Everything was there – hemlock, nightshade, rosemary, lavender, bittersweet, caraway – I recognized the labels on the bags from my first search. Something about the way they were organized felt off. I was almost certain the lavender and bittersweet weren't next to each other before.

I was careful when touching the bag of lavender – I still had the warning about it increasing fertility in my head, thanks to Madame Selena – and moved it to the front of the box as I turned to stare at the rest of the room.

It was the same, yet different. I didn't like the feeling washing over me, as if someone had invaded my space and ruined something that was supposed to feel safe.

I turned to the bookshelves next. I hadn't conducted a proper inventory upon discovering the contents and mentally kicked myself for that now. I should have a list of everything in the room. How else would I know if something went missing?

"May?" I called out to my grandmother, hopeful she'd visit even if she wasn't in the mood. I needed her more experienced eyes to look around and detect if something was missing. "May, I need you."

Nothing. Not so much as a whisper. She didn't appear at my elbow and cause me to jump, or call out to warn me she was coming. There was no sign of her. That made me uncomfortable.

On a hunch, I moved to the ornate bookstand in the center of the room. That's where May's Book of Shadows was prominently displayed. I'd flipped through the book a time or two – mostly out of curiosity – but I hadn't taken the time to study it. That was also on my to-do list, although I often found things to distract me from the task because I wasn't much of a reader unless it involved snarky heroines and sarcastic sidekicks.

The book looked to be intact as I flipped through it. Everything was in its place and where it was supposed to be. The room still felt off. Of course, I could be imagining it. That's what I told myself, anyway. I rarely visited the third floor. That's probably why I felt like a stranger in my own house.

I gave the Book of Shadows another lingering look before closing it and turning my full attention to the bookshelf by the door. I wouldn't find the information I was looking for in a spell book. A history book was more my speed today.

I found what I was looking for quickly. "*Mystical Creatures of Moonstone Bay.*" I read the title aloud. "By Monique Maven." Hmm. I'd never heard the name. Still, if she was local, that probably meant she was an expert.

I sat cross-legged on the floor and opened the book, flipping through the pages until I found the section I was looking for. "Cupids in human form," I read, tapping my bottom lip. "He might not want to tell me how it is for him, but I'm certainly going to find out one way or another. I hope he's ready for a new list of questions because when I'm done here I'm going to make a list and track him down again."

I tried to force my worry about someone being in the lighthouse from my head. There was nothing to steal here, after all. Everything in the upstairs room appeared to be present and accounted for, which meant I had nothing to worry about.

Even though I was trying to be practical I couldn't shake my feelings of unease. I kept reading. I read about cupids being able to control feelings – whether good or bad – and I read about one particular cupid going rogue hundreds of years ago and becoming the Devil of Fornication. No joke. That's a real thing. I can't decide if I want to meet him or not. I mean, as far as devils go, he didn't sound half bad.

I read about how cupids supposedly have an affinity for dolphins, which could explain why Booker's father opted to settle here. I especially enjoyed the part of the story where even the dolphins fell in love with the cupid water enthusiasts ... and then tried to do really lewd things to them. I read about another cupid who apparently contracted syphilis and didn't get treated. He went crazy and started shooting people in the head with arrows, which I found fantastical and mildly frightening.

I got so caught up in the book I managed to forget my discomfort. I couldn't entirely shake the feeling of dread settling over the room, though. I feared that wasn't going anywhere.

I SPENT HOURS ON the third floor reading about cupids. There was so much information I was more confused than when I started. I headed to the kitchen, grabbed a banana and bottle of water, and moved toward the back patio. I needed a break from reading – it was dense stuff – and I was eager to take that break outside.

I didn't even get a chance to sit before I noticed a figure walking the beach. At first I assumed it was Aurora – I hadn't seen her in days, now that I thought about it – but a simple glance told me that wasn't the case. The person walking was a fully-clothed man, not a naked female.

My heart did a slow roll when I realized who it was.

I left the banana on the small bistro table and headed toward the beach, clutching the bottle of water as I crossed the sand. The man didn't look in my direction, instead stopping long enough to stare at the bright blue ocean and keeping his back to me. He remained locked in that position until I joined him.

"Gus." I shielded my eyes from the sun, internally lambasting myself for not thinking ahead and grabbing a pair of sunglasses from the counter. "What are you doing out here?"

Gus merely shrugged. "Taking a walk. That's not against the rules."

"I know." I wasn't sure how to address him. We'd become rather chummy at the bar, but he probably didn't remember much of that. "Do you know who I am?"

Gus nodded. "Hadley Hunter. May and Wesley's granddaughter. Emma's daughter."

"Right."

"We talked at Lilac's place the other day," he added. "You drank with me."

Technically that wasn't true. I didn't do any drinking because he did enough for ten people. I didn't think pointing that out was a good idea, so I nodded. "I did. We had a long talk."

"Oh, I'm sure." Gus ran his hand over his head. I could feel the frustration wafting off him in waves. "I got really drunk."

"I was there."

"I probably said some stupid things."

My heart went out to him most in this stupid mess, although I wasn't sure why. Maureen was certainly a victim, too – and Trish – but Gus was struggling the most. I wasn't even sure he realized how much he was struggling. “It’s okay. I say stupid things all the time. It doesn’t matter if I’m drunk or sober. You’re allowed to say stupid things.”

“I can’t even remember the stupid things I said.”

“We just talked a bit. It was nothing big,” I supplied, lowering myself to the sand and patting it so Gus would feel comfortable enough to sit. His face was ruddy from the sun and I wanted him to take a break. “We talked about Trish … and the feud. You made sure I understood that you’d never had an affair with Barbie Conner even though that was the rumor.”

Gus snorted as he got comfortable on the ground, accepting the bottle of water I handed him with a nod of thanks. “Have you met Barbie?”

“I have.”

“You probably understand why it’s important for me to clear up that rumor.” He twisted the cap off the bottle and took a long swig. “She’s a horrible woman, although she wasn’t as bad when we were younger. She’s gotten progressively worse through the years.”

“She’s definitely a horrible woman,” I agreed. “She’s so horrible I don’t think she realizes how she comes off to people.”

“Oh, don’t kid yourself.” Gus sneered and shook his head. “She understands how people see her. She encourages it. Have you met the group of women she hangs out with?”

“I can’t say I have.”

“They’re awful. They think they’re somehow better than everyone else on the island.” Gus took another drink. “Barbie is their ringleader. She encourages them to be awful to everyone else while stabbing each other in the back whenever the mood arises.”

I didn’t know Barbie’s friends, but I had known women like that. “That doesn’t sound like anyone I’d want to spend time with.”

“No.”

“Barbie is a stupid name anyway.”

Gus snickered. “Her real name is Barbara. She chose to go by Barbie instead of Barb. Can you believe that?”

“No.” I really couldn’t. “How are you feeling otherwise?”

Gus's mouth twisted into a frown. "How am I supposed to feel? My daughter is dead. She's gone. She's at the funeral home right now. We're planning a service for her – but her mother insists on doing all the work and I keep dodging her calls – and then she's going to be cremated."

"Well … ."

"Burned!" Gus barked, making me jolt. "They're going to burn my baby's body."

I didn't know how to react. "Well, I'm sure if you go to the funeral director and convey your concerns he'll come up with a different solution. You could pick out a nice coffin and cemetery plot."

The look Gus shot me was incredulous. "Has no one explained to you about the cemetery?"

"Oh." I felt stupid as realization dawned. "Right. The zombies. I hadn't even considered that." I felt like a moron. "How does that work on Moonstone Bay?"

"Everyone is cremated, whether they like it or not," Gus replied, focusing on the rolling ocean waves. They looked somehow more shimmery than usual. I didn't blame him for being entranced. "No one new can go into the cemetery. No one old can come out."

"And it's because of a curse gone wonky, right?"

Gus shrugged. "Galen could better answer that question. I just know my baby can't be buried there. We have to burn her."

My heart went out to him. "I know this is hard for you … ."

"Do you?" Gus's eyes were accusatory when they latched onto mine. "Do you know this is hard for me? Who have you lost? I lost my daughter. A father isn't supposed to outlive his child."

"He's not," I agreed, my eyes pricking with unshed tears. "As for losing someone, I have. I lost my mother. The thing is, I lost her before I ever had a chance to know her. At least you got to know your daughter. She knew you loved her."

Gus looked miserable as he buried his face in his arms. "I don't remember the last time I told her I loved her."

"She knew."

"The last time I saw her she said she was meeting Ashley for drinks downtown." Gus was inconsolable as he sobbed. "I gave her grief about it. I told her they shouldn't be friends. I told her Ashley wasn't worth her time."

I felt helpless. "I'm sure Trish understands that you didn't mean what you said."

Gus's eyes were filled with loathing when he raised them this time. "Oh, I meant it. That monster killed my baby. How could I not mean it?"

I was taken aback. "I'm not sure Ashley did kill Trish."

"She did!"

I shrank back in the face of his fury. "Okay. She did." I held up my hands in capitulation, but only because I was worried Gus would lose whatever shred of sanity he had left and attack me. "It was my mistake. I won't make it again."

As if sensing my distress, Gus deflated a bit. "I didn't mean to frighten you."

"I wasn't frightened." That was a lie. "In fact … ." Whatever I was about to say died on my lips as the shimmering from the ocean water grew in size. It was like a cloud of … something … as it rolled forward. It didn't keep pace with the waves, moving slower, but it was definitely coming. "What is that?"

Gus's face was blank as he turned to stare at the water. "Are you talking about the boat? That's Edgar Fletcher's boat. At least I think it is. It's too far out to be certain. I'm sure he's just fishing."

"Not the boat." How could he even see the boat through the shimmering? "I'm talking about the glare. I … it's like a big cloud."

"What are you talking about?" Gus wrinkled his nose. "I don't see any shimmering."

That couldn't be right. "But … ." Something started clicking in my ear. I didn't recognize the sound at first, thinking perhaps Gus was clacking his teeth or making some sort of sound with his tongue. By the time I recognized what it was – a ticking clock counting down – it was almost too late.

"Oh, my … !" I grabbed Gus's arm and gave him a tug, trying to pull him from where he sat and toward the underbrush near the line of trees closer to the house. "Run, Gus!"

His expression reflected confusion as he watched me scramble to my feet. "Why are we running?"

"Because something bad is about to happen."

"What?"

I never got a chance to answer. The roar of the gun was so deafening it forced me to cover my ears, and the cloud of shimmering light hit me full on. I wanted to scream, warn him to flee for his life, but my voice was drowned out by the shimmering.

For a time all I saw was light. I couldn't stand it, so I screamed and lashed out with everything inside of me. Whatever I managed to tap into – and I had a feeling it was magic – lumbered away from my chest and smacked into the shimmer, causing it to explode into shards.

I gasped for breath as the light returned to normal and the buzzing in my ears dissipated. I took stock of myself, relieved that I couldn't find a bullet wound. "I need to call Galen," I gritted out. "I need … Galen needs to know."

When Gus didn't respond I turned to him. It only took a second to realize why he hadn't said anything. He would never say anything again. His eyes were wide and sightless … and fixated on the sun … and there was an ugly wound spreading fresh blood across his chest.

He was dead.

Something very bad had just happened.

Very, very bad.

22

TWENTY-TWO

I sat on the beach a long time, perhaps in shock. No, definitely in shock. I remained a few feet from Gus, doing my best not to stare into his lifeless eyes. I knew I should call someone, but I was too far gone to find my phone or remember a number.

Someone else must have called, because people started swarming the beach a few minutes later. Two were emergency paramedics who breezed by me and went straight to Gus. I could hear their words, understand them even, but they barely registered.

"Shot in the chest."

"Looks like he died instantly."

"I wonder where he was shot from."

"Probably lucky whoever it was didn't go for both of them."

I wanted to say something – at least tell them to shut up – but I couldn't find my voice.

Galen was the third to arrive. Instead of going to Gus, he walked straight toward me. "Hadley?"

I shifted my head in his direction, although I didn't make eye contact. "Gus is dead."

"I know." Galen hunkered down in front of me, giving me no

choice but to look at him. "Honey, were you hit?" He turned his eyes to the paramedics. "Have you looked her over?"

"She's got a little blood on her shoulder there from the splatter," one of the paramedics replied. "As far as we can tell, Gus was the only one hit. We didn't want to approach her in case she freaked. She's been shaking her head and kind of staring into nothing."

"She looks fine," the other paramedic said.

"Oh, well, thank you for your astute medical opinion," Galen drawled, moving his hand to my hair. His voice turned soft and sweet. "Hadley, I need my men to go over the beach and the paramedics have to take Gus away. Would you please come inside with me?"

"Sure." I felt detached and wobbly as I got to unsteady feet. "We were just talking when it happened."

"Okay." Galen placed his hand to the small of my back.

"I think he was trying to work out some things, maybe even hurt himself. He looked so sad, but ... someone else did it for him."

"Yes, well, we'll figure that out. Don't worry."

"I'm not worried. You'll find who did it." I believed that. Faith didn't stop me from getting wretchedly sick, though. Suddenly, I dropped to my knees on the sand and vomited, my stomach turning itself inside out as I struggled to maintain control of ... well, something.

"Oh, honey ... ." Galen sounded upset as he knelt behind me and rubbed my back. "Get it out."

"I don't even know why I'm sick." I used the back of my hand to wipe my mouth. "It's weird. I shouldn't be sick."

"You can be whatever you need to be." Galen kept rubbing. "Tell me when you feel good enough to walk again. I really do want to get you back inside."

"Okay."

"In fact, if you're done throwing up, how about I carry you?" His eyes brightened. "That way you won't have to walk."

Something about the way he said it – the look of excitement on his face – snapped me back to reality. "You can't carry me in public!" I was incensed. "I can walk on my own two feet."

Instead of being insulted, Galen chuckled. "Well, at least you're sounding a little more like your regular self. I'm glad. As much as I'd like to play the hero and carry you, I'm much more excited to hear you yell at me."

I wiped my mouth one more time and slowly got to my feet. "Me, too."

"Finally something we agree on, huh?"

I DISAPPEARED UPSTAIRS to brush my teeth and change my clothes, leaving Galen to question his deputies in my kitchen. When I returned, I found a bottle of water on the counter and Lilac and Booker standing close to the table, their heads bent toward Galen as they whispered.

"None of that," I ordered, my temper flaring. "I don't want you guys talking behind my back."

Booker, a master at covering his emotions, merely stared back. "What makes you think we were talking about you?"

Lilac, who always blurted out whatever came to her mind, couldn't resist. "We're so sorry." Her eyes filled with tears. "We're all so worried about you. Galen said you were acting like a zombie when he showed up … and then you puked. Both of those things sound terrible."

"Ugh." Galen slid Lilac an annoyed look as he slipped around her and walked toward me. "Don't listen to Lilac. That's not how I phrased it."

"No?" Now that I had settled a bit, I was in the mood to fight. "What word did you use?"

"I said you were quiet, and that concerned me."

"You said 'zombie-like,'" Lilac argued. "I remember exactly what you said. You said 'Hadley was acting zombie-like and I thought she might have lost her marbles all over the beach so I need you guys to get over here.' I was very worried."

I didn't want to laugh – it seemed inappropriate given what had happened on the beach thirty minutes ago – but I couldn't stop myself. "Well, at least people care enough to worry I'm losing my marbles." I rubbed my forehead, a rare tension headache brewing. "I need to sit down."

I grabbed the bottle of water from the counter and slid into one of the chairs at the table, my temper threatening to come out and play when I saw the worried looks Galen and Booker exchanged when they thought I wasn't looking.

"Stop that," I hissed finally, extending a warning finger. "I won't fall apart. And, contrary to popular opinion, my marbles won't spill out all over the beach."

"Of course they won't." Lilac made a sympathetic clucking sound as she sat next to me. "We're in the kitchen now. If your marbles spill, it won't be out there."

"I don't think that's helping, Lilac," Galen complained, moving to the open chair to my left and drawing my attention to him. "How are you feeling?"

"Annoyed."

"That's good. I like it when you're annoyed. It makes my blood run hot."

"Well, as long as you're happy." I offered a tight smile as I twisted the cap off the bottle of water. "Do you have any idea who did this?"

"No." Galen shook his head. "We're still working on it. We believe the shot came from a spot down the beach, close to that stand of trees near where we took off our shoes before wading the other night. Do you know the one I'm talking about?"

I dully nodded. "Yeah."

"Did you see anyone hanging around those trees before it happened?"

"If I had, don't you think I would've said something?"

"I think you were in shock when I first got here." Galen was calm as he rested his hand over mine. "I'm not sure you remembered anything at the time."

"I remember everything." That was mostly true. "You don't have to treat me as if I'm breakable. I'm not going to break."

"It's okay if you do," Lilac offered, her eyes shining with sincerity.

"What you saw out there ... anyone would break because of that. It's okay."

"Well, I won't." I was firm. "I'm fine."

Galen squeezed my hand. "Okay. Tell me what you remember."

"Starting when?"

"Um ... how about when we separated after breakfast?"

"I tracked down Booker at the tourism center and bugged him until he gave in and told me what he was," I replied dully. "He wasn't happy, but he did it. Then I went to the grocery store. I bought steaks for dinner tonight – mushrooms, onions, potatoes ... you know the whole yummy pile of things we'd need because I thought we could grill. I got stuff for breakfast ... and I even bought you a razor and toothbrush in case you forgot what I'd said this morning."

Galen tucked a strand of hair behind my ear. "I didn't forget. Thanks for that. It might come in handy tonight. Then what happened?"

"I came home and put the groceries away," I answered. "I called for May because I had questions about cupids, but she didn't answer."

"Oh, can we not talk about that?" Booker made a face. "There's a dead body outside. Let's focus on that."

"Leave her alone," Galen chided, his expression darkening. "I told her to tell me everything. That's what she's doing."

"Oh, you just want her to say something goofy about what I told her," Booker grumbled. "I know how you are."

"Yes, I want to turn Gus's death into open season for jokes about you being the island's resident sex maniac," Galen drawled. "That's exactly how I roll."

"Knock it off," I ordered, annoyed. "We're talking about me right now, not you guys and your complicated relationship."

Galen sobered. "I'm sorry. Continue."

"I decided to go to the third floor because I needed a book," I volunteered. "I remember the room felt off, like someone had been there and changed things while I was gone."

Galen straightened his shoulders. "Wait ... what?"

I nodded. "I thought for sure someone had been in the room. Things seemed off."

"Why didn't you call me?"

"Because nothing was missing. I thought some of the herbs were out of place and that maybe someone had opened the Book of Shadows. But nothing was missing. It was a feeling I had no proof to back up. I mean … I'm not even sure of everything that's in that room. I haven't conducted an inventory or anything."

Galen opened his mouth to say something and then apparently changed his mind. "Okay. We'll talk about that later. Tell me what happened next."

"I went downstairs to grab a banana and bottle of water." I searched my memory for the proper chain of events. "I went out to the patio because I was going to take a break from researching."

"What were you researching?"

"Cupids. I can't wait to see you ride a dolphin, by the way, Booker."

Booker scowled. "I knew telling you was a mistake. I just … knew it."

Galen snickered. "I'm happy you told her. I was getting sick of fending off questions."

"You should've told her. It would've saved time."

"That's what I said," I interjected. "He said it wasn't his secret to tell."

"And I stand by that." Galen moved his hand to the back of my neck and rubbed at the tension there. "So, you were upstairs researching and decided to come downstairs on a break. What happened then?"

I shrugged. "Not much. I saw Gus walking the beach and went out to talk to him. He was distraught, talking about Trish and how his life was essentially ruined. I think he was going to kill himself. Er, well, I think that was the plan … although I'm not sure how I know that. I think I might've picked up a stray thought from his brain or something. Either way, he didn't do it. Maybe he was trying to gear himself up for it or something."

"He had a gun in his pocket," Galen noted.

The information took me by surprise. “He did?”

Galen nodded. “A small handgun. It was loaded. If you think he was considering killing himself, it’s a fairly good bet that he was.”

“Someone beat him to it, then,” Booker mused, taking the remaining seat at the end of the table and rubbing his chin as he ran the scenario through his head. “Someone had to be watching what was going down on the beach and decided to act at a certain time.”

“Do you remember what was happening right before the shot was fired?” Galen asked gently.

“I … .” I broke off, my memory clicking firmly into place. “I remember thinking that something bad was going to happen. I remember trying to get Gus to run … but he wouldn’t.”

Galen’s eyebrows flew up. “You knew something bad was going to happen?”

“It was as if I had an inner danger alarm in my head and it was screaming at me to get out,” I replied. “At first it wasn’t easy because of the shimmering.”

“Shimmering?”

“What? Oh, the water was shimmering.” I shook my head to dislodge myself from the reverie. “I don’t know how else to explain it. The water was shimmering, like there was a floating cloud and it was heading my way. I felt kind of dreamy while it was shimmering, but it was as if I knew somehow – like really deep down – that it shouldn’t be shimmering and I managed to break through. I’m not explaining it very well.”

“You’re doing fine.” Galen patted my hand and flicked his eyes to Booker. “What do you make of that?”

“It sounds as if someone tried to put her under a spell,” Booker replied without hesitation. “If I had to guess, I think whoever did the shooting wanted Hadley out of the picture for the deed, perhaps so she wouldn’t fight what was about to happen.”

“Or maybe it was something else,” Lilac suggested. “Maybe someone tried to put Hadley under a spell because he or she wanted to frame her for Gus’s death. I mean … Hadley somehow slipped through the cracks. That's amazing, by the way, for a novice." She beamed at me.

Unfortunately, I couldn't return the smile. "Wait a second ... are you saying that you think someone hid in the bushes, tried to put a spell on me, shot Gus with the intention of framing me for murder and then managed to escape without anyone seeing him or her?"

"I think that's it in a nutshell," Galen replied. "You were out of it when I arrived. At first I thought it was simply because of Gus's death. That would be enough to drive anyone around the bend. Now I think it was more than that."

"It was the remnants of the spell," Lilac said, nodding. "I'm sure you're right. When whoever it was realized Hadley was free of the spell they had to run because it was either that or get caught. Finishing the frame job wasn't an option because Hadley was conscious ... and possibly a real threat."

I balked. "I'm not a threat."

"Oh, really?" Booker challenged. "That story about you throwing an ax-wielding assailant out of a second-story window has made the rounds on the island. I've been asked about it at least three times. Whether you like it or not, you are a threat ... and people know it."

"I've been questioned about it too," Galen admitted ruefully. "People are curious about Hadley. That first show of power could've been a fluke, though, and our culprit might've thought she couldn't pull it off a second time."

"The shimmering she described, that sounds like a powerful spell," Lilac argued. "I think there are only two or three people on the island capable of casting a spell like that. I mean ... she might be one of them eventually, but that's a large bit of magic."

They were talking around me as if I wasn't present, and it was driving me insane. "You guys know I can hear you, right?"

"You have a very strong presence that's hard to forget," Galen drawled. "Of course we know you're here." He patted my hand and gave my fingers a squeeze. "It's just ... you shouldn't have been able to break that spell. You've barely tapped into your magic. My guess is you did it instinctively – because that seems to be how you do everything – but what you managed to accomplish today is fairly amazing."

"Yes, she's a true goddess amongst men," Booker drawled, annoyance dancing across his handsome features. "We need to focus on the individuals who could pull this off. One of them clearly has a grudge against Hadley … although, for the life of me I can't figure out why. What benefit would anyone find in framing her for murder?"

"Maybe someone wants to buy the lighthouse," Lilac suggested. "It is a prime piece of land."

"So soon after Ned failed at the endeavor?" Galen didn't look convinced as he shook his head. "No, this is about something else. Who could weave the bit of magic Hadley described?"

"I'm not a hundred percent sure, but those witches out on the north shore might be able to," Lilac replied.

"The ones from that hippie commune who refuse to shower and shave their pits?" Booker made a face. "Why would they possibly leave La-La Land and come to town to kill Hadley? They haven't even met her."

"They're feminists," Lilac argued. "Feminists don't shave their pits."

I didn't point out that was stereotypical … and often altogether wrong. It didn't seem like the time.

"Who else could cast the spell?" Galen persisted. "I mean … who here has enough magic to do what was done today?"

"Off the top of my head the only one I can absolutely say without hesitation is capable of doing what Hadley described is Madame Selena," Lilac replied. "I have no idea why she'd want to attack in this manner. I mean … it's not like her."

"No, it's not." Galen's eyes were thoughtful as they snagged mine. "But she is a nut."

"Oh, she's the nuttiest of the nutty," Booker agreed. "That doesn't explain why she'd go after Hadley. What's her motive?"

"She and May were never really tight," Galen pointed out. "I never got the feeling May liked her all that well."

"Madame Selena essentially said that to me," I said. "She said they weren't friends, but they respected one another."

"I don't think May respected her all that much," Booker argued. "May thought she had evil tendencies."

"How do you know that?" Galen asked.

"She told me. We hung around a lot because she was immune to my charms. You know that."

"I know." Galen's expression softened. "You did a lot of odd jobs around the lighthouse for her, and for free most of the time. You were good to her."

"She was good to me." Booker furrowed his brow. "Other than Madame Selena, can you think of anyone strong enough to cast a spell on Hadley?"

Lilac and Galen shook their heads in unison.

"No," Lilac said finally. "Maybe the north shore witches, but like you said, they have no motive. They haven't even met Hadley, and they never come to town."

"So, Madame Selena is our prime suspect." Galen rolled his neck and stared at the ceiling. "She'd better hope I don't get my hands on her if she's guilty."

"I think that goes for all of us," Lilac said.

"So how do we find her?" I asked.

"That shouldn't be hard," Galen replied. "She usually hangs out at her house, storefront or festival tent. There's not a lot of variation in her schedule. I'll make a call. If we can track her down for questioning, I want to do it tonight."

23

TWENTY-THREE

Galen's deputies searched the entire island – at least the areas they could get easy access to – for signs of Madame Selena, but came up empty. Lilac and Booker left after dinner. We all enjoyed the fresh steaks, Booker grilling them as he ignored the evidence and medical teams toiling on the beach. Lilac added corn and potato salad to the mix and we had a virtual feast.

Once Galen realized I was flagging, he suggested Lilac and Booker call it a night. Lilac obviously wasn't thrilled with the idea, but Booker was smart enough to trick her into leaving.

"Come on." He slid his arm over her shoulders. "I'll take you to the festival and visit the beer tent with you. If I remember correctly, that's one of your favorite activities. I'm sure you'll forget Hadley's woes relatively quickly."

Lilac made a face. "Exactly what sort of friend are you accusing me of being?"

"The best kind."

"Oh, well, I guess that's okay." Lilac's cheeks turned pink as Booker winked. "Let's go to the beer tent. You've won me over."

I grabbed Booker's arm before he could disappear into the night, lowering my voice so Lilac didn't overhear. "Don't do your Booker thing," I warned. "She's not another notch for your bedpost."

Booker chuckled. "What makes you think she's not already a notch?"

I was taken aback. "I … is she?"

Booker shrugged. "I don't kiss and tell." He took a step away from me and fixed Galen with a serious look. "I'll keep my ear to the ground. If I hear anything about Selena I'll call you."

"I don't care what time it is," Galen stressed, standing so close to me that I could feel his warmth against my back. He ran hotter than anyone I'd ever met. I figured that had to be a wolf thing. "She can't have gotten off this island. That means she's here."

"And if she were innocent, she'd be at her tent," Booker surmised. "I get what you're thinking. She realized right away that she screwed things up and is on the run. Where do you think she'd go?"

"I have no idea." Galen rubbed his hand up and down my back, the action soothing as I battled to stay awake. "All she has is that golf cart thing, the purple one with the storage bins for all her stuff. That won't go unnoticed."

"I'll keep my ear to the ground," Booker repeated. "Some of her pals might be at the beer tent."

I knit my eyebrows, suspicious. "Is that why you suggested going to the beer tent? Lilac thinks you did it to cheer her up. Don't disappoint her."

Booker flicked the end of my nose. "You can't have it both ways. I can either take her to bed or disappoint her."

"That is not funny."

Booker chuckled. "Everything you say is funny. Don't worry about Lilac. We've been friends for years. She's in good hands. I won't let anything happen to her."

"It's true," Galen offered. "Booker and Lilac are friends … and not the sort of friends that will make your head implode. You have nothing to worry about."

Weariness forced me to believe them. "Fine. I'm too tired to get worked up anyway. Call if you find Madame Selena. I'll be able to sleep better if I know where she is."

"I'm on it."

Galen locked the door, double-checking that it was securely fastened before sliding the security chain in place. Then he did the same with the back door before hitting the lights and pointing me toward the staircase.

"You're practically living here now," I noted as I climbed. "You've been here every night for … well, days."

"It's not for fun," Galen argued. "I'd be happier if I were practically living here because you couldn't keep your hands off me."

I snorted, genuinely amused. "One day I'm sure it will happen."

"Not tonight." Galen didn't sound particularly sad about the realization. "Tonight you're getting some sleep. Then, tomorrow, we'll find Madame Selena and figure all this out. Once that happens, we can focus on the fun stuff again."

"Yeah." I didn't bother going into the bathroom to change my clothes, instead stripping out of my shorts and climbing into bed wearing nothing but a T-shirt. I was too tired to go through my normal nightly routine, the one I spazzed over whenever Galen decided to sleep over. There was no frantic brushing of the hair or strategic makeup removal. There was no diligent cleaning of the teeth. For tonight, I simply wanted sleep. "Do you think Madame Selena had something to do with Trish's murder?"

I couldn't see Galen's reaction because he'd hit the lights just as I finished asking the question. I heard him at the end of the bed for a moment, probably stripping down to his own form of pajamas. When he slid into bed next to me, he was shirtless and warm.

"I don't know," Galen replied finally, sliding his arm under my waist and positioning me so my head was on his shoulder. "Under normal circumstances she would jump to the head of the suspect line. I've been thinking about it a bit, and I can't come up with a motive for her."

I was exhausted and yet my mind remained busy as I snuggled closer to Galen. He rubbed soothing circles on my back. I knew it was an attempt to lull me to sleep. I was fine with it, although I remained focused on the case. "Maybe she was having an affair with Henry or something. He is divorced, after all, and they're roughly the same age."

"I guess that's a possibility." Galen's lips brushed my forehead. "Go to sleep. We'll talk about this tomorrow."

"Okay." I stifled a yawn. "Or maybe Madame Selena was having an affair with Gus and he left her everything in his will ... but only if Trish predeceased him. That would explain why she killed both of them."

Galen chuckled. "Your mind is a fascinating place. "Get some sleep and we'll revisit it in the morning."

"Okay." I was already drifting. "I'm sorry in advance if I snore."

"Don't worry about it. I kind of like it."

I was still wondering if that was true when I slipped under.

I WOKE IN THE EXACT same position, my head on Galen's shoulder and my hand on his bare chest. I thought he was still asleep because the morning sun was barely filtering through the window, but he shook me of that belief when he placed his hand on top of mine and kissed my forehead.

"How are you feeling?"

I tilted my chin so I could look into his eyes. "Okay. I thought you were still asleep."

"I've only been up a few minutes."

"Doing what?"

"Watching you sleep." Galen's grin was quick and easy. "You make little sighing noises when you're out. It's kind of cute."

I pursed my lips. "I'll have to take your word for it."

"You definitely will." He smoothed my hair. "Are you ready to greet the day or do you want to fondle me some more?"

I was aghast. "I haven't fondled you!"

"You have so. You rub your hand all over my chest and make purring noises in your sleep. Frankly, I think I'm a majestic gentleman for not taking advantage of you given those noises. Sometimes they're sighs, but other times they're kitty growling noises."

Oh, now he was just making things up. "Do you think I'm going to fall for that?"

Galen shrugged. "I don't know. I was mildly hopeful."

"Well, I'm not." I propped myself on an elbow and stared down at him. It should be criminal to look that good first thing in the morning. Like … a felony or something. Even as I wanted to engage in lustful thoughts, the reality of the previous day came crashing back. "Do we have any news on Madame Selena yet?"

Galen shook his head, sobering. "Not so far. It's barely light out. Trust me, finding that purple golf cart won't be hard now that we have the sun to give us a hand."

"Okay." I chewed my bottom lip. "What are we going to do until then?"

Galen's grin was wolfish. "Well, if you're open to suggestions … ." His fingers danced over my midriff, causing me to slap his hand away.

"No way. You said you wanted time for that particular event and we both know we could be interrupted at any moment." Plus, I rationalized, I had morning breath and bedhead. Neither were flattering when it came to looking back on a special memory.

"Fair enough." Galen dropped his hand. "I guess we could start with breakfast."

"That sounds like a fine idea." I moved to climb out of bed, but Galen grabbed me and snuggled close before I could escape. "This does not look like breakfast preparations to me."

He barked out a laugh. "You're cute."

I didn't feel cute. I was really starting to regret not brushing my teeth before passing out. "I'm also hungry … and have to go to the bathroom."

"Just one minute." Galen stared hard into my eyes. That let me know the conversation was about to turn serious. "I know you're trying to figure out this witch thing – you think it has to change you when it really doesn't – but I want to remind you that you took care of yourself yesterday. That's the second time you saved yourself, and you did it on instinct.

"I would like to be the hero in this story and say I was the one who raced in at the last second and saved the day, but I can't lay claim to that title," he continued. "You're the hero. You did it ... and you didn't need Madame Selena to figure it out."

"I don't think I'm going to need Madame Selena to figure anything out," I clarified. "She's very clearly evil and I don't want her around. I'm allergic to evil."

"Definitely cute." Galen briefly rubbed his nose against mine, refusing to let me squirm free. My bladder situation was becoming dire. "Just think about what I said." He was earnest. "You did it all on your own. You're strong ... and capable ... and you don't need a mentor. You don't need to be afraid of being who you are because you've always been this person."

His words bolstered me. "That's nice."

"Good."

"I really have to go to the bathroom, though."

Galen gave me a quick kiss before releasing me. "Go. I'll head down to the kitchen and start breakfast. If we're lucky, we should have news relatively quickly."

"I don't generally believe in luck, but I'm crossing my fingers today."

"That makes two of us."

"IS THIS HER CART?"

We'd barely finished breakfast when news came in from one of Galen's deputies that something that looked suspiciously like Madame Selena's golf cart was tipped on its side and partially obscured in the underbrush on the highway that led out of town.

We loaded the dishes in the dishwasher and then immediately hopped into Galen's truck so we could look ourselves. By the time we arrived, Booker was on scene and waiting. Instead of reacting with anger at his appearance, Galen was all business.

"What do we know?"

"We know that this cart was not here as of midnight," Deputy Richard Lynn replied, his uniform pressed and starched. "We were up and down this highway three times after your call. We would've seen it."

"Can you be sure?" Booker asked, crouching near the front wheel of the garish purple cart. "Unless you were looking directly at this spot, you might not have seen it."

"I don't believe that's true, sir," Lynn replied, his shoulders squared as if he were about ready to begin a report. "The reason it was so easy to find this morning is because some of the contents of the jars on the back of the cart were glowing."

I cocked an eyebrow, intrigued despite myself. "Glowing?"

Lynn nodded. "It's since dissipated – mostly – but we believe the crash happened around 3 a.m. or so because the glowing contents would've ignited around the time of impact. It's fairy dust – the laughing kind – and it's only good for a few hours."

Galen nodded as if what his deputy had just related to him wasn't utter nonsense. "I guess that makes sense. Except ... what was Madame Selena doing on the road at that hour?"

"And where did she think she was going?" Booker added, making a face as he leaned closer to stare at the vinyl seat. "Hey, Galen, can you come over here a minute?"

I expected Galen to ignore the request, but he readily acquiesced. Their relationship was something I probably would never be able to wrap my head around. One minute they were growling and posturing like total macho jerkwads and the next they were working together for a common goal. It made absolutely no sense.

"What do you have?" Galen asked, crouching next to Booker. His nostrils flared before the other man could answer. "That's blood."

"I figured as much." Booker flicked me a glance. "There's a decent amount on the steering wheel and pooling on the ground here. It's not enough to suggest a death, but it is enough to make me wonder if someone was seriously hurt in this little mishap."

Curious, I scurried to the other side of the cart. I saw the blood smeared on the steering wheel, but it was less apparent in the green grass close to where the two men crouched. "Do you think she hurt herself in the crash or was injured before that?"

Galen shrugged. "I don't know that we have evidence either way. Just out of curiosity, why would you think that she was hurt before the crash?"

"I don't necessarily believe that," I hedged. "It's just … look around." I gestured toward the trees, which were unnaturally tight at this particular point. "There's no curve and lots of cover. I can't help wondering why Madame Selena would wreck here. The road is a lot curvier back toward town."

"I hear you, but I'm not sure I understand," Galen prodded. "How does that equate with her already being hurt?"

"I don't know." I held my hands up and shrugged. "These trees provide natural cover. What if someone was in them and knew when Madame Selena would pass by? What if someone hid in there to shoot at her as she passed?"

Galen glanced to Booker. "Do you get what she's suggesting?"

Booker nodded. "I think I do. She's basically saying Madame Selena wasn't working alone. That perhaps she had a partner and now that we're on to her the partner realized Madame Selena was dead weight."

Galen thoughtfully rubbed his chin. "Like maybe Madame Selena might have a tendency to talk to clear herself and throw someone else to the wolves, so to speak, in an effort to get away with whatever she's been plotting. I guess that makes sense. Hadley brought it up last night, but I've been struggling to find a motive for Madame Selena to kill Trish."

Booker widened his eyes. "You think this has something to do with Trish's murder? But … how?"

"How could it not?" Galen challenged. "It's not as if the crime rate on this island is sky high. We've had two murders within a week here – a father and daughter. They have to be related."

"I thought we agreed last night that framing Hadley was the

intent," Booker argued. "Someone wanted to take her out of the equation."

"But why? I doubt it's because she's dating me or hanging with you. I doubt it's because she frequents Lilac's bar. She doesn't have a job, but she has been asking questions about Trish's murder ... and she's been with me a few times when it happened."

Things clicked into place. "You think someone wanted to frame me for Gus's murder because whoever it is thinks I might help you get close to uncovering the truth."

"It's just a hypothesis right now," Galen stressed. "But if you were a murder suspect I sure as heck wouldn't be spending all my time trying to clear Ashley. Whoever did this wants us to believe Ashley is guilty and let it go. When Hadley and I started asking questions not long after news went public that Ashley was being charged, it became obvious quickly that we weren't going to let it go."

"Then how does Madame Selena play into this?" Booker queried. "She had no motive to kill Trish."

"I agree," Galen said. "That's what was stymieing me. Motive is a problem. Then I remembered Madame Selena will do practically anything for money. What if someone hired her to help frame Hadley, and when it backfired that person realized Madame Selena could tear down everything our suspect worked so hard to build?"

"That kind of makes sense," Booker admitted. "But if you look at the victims, that doesn't give us many options for a suspect."

"Basically Henry and Barbie," I suggested.

"And Maureen," Galen added. "We can't forget Maureen. She didn't get much from her divorce because of the affair. All those documents were sealed, but I opened them after I saw Maureen at the funeral home the other day. She barely got anything in that divorce."

What Galen was suggesting made me uncomfortable. "But ... she said she regretted the affair because Trish wouldn't talk to her. Why would she kill her own daughter if she was upset about the girl not paying attention to her?"

"Maybe Maureen realized Trish was never going to let her back in," Galen suggested. "Maybe she decided she was upset about her divorce settlement and wanted more. If she killed Gus, then Trish would inherit and she'd get nothing. If she killed them both …how much do you want to bet Maureen is now the sole beneficiary of Gus's will because Trish is dead?"

I rubbed the back of my neck as my stomach flipped. "That's really cold-hearted. I'm not sure I buy that from Maureen. She was one of the only people in that group I even liked."

"Yeah, well, we need to look at all of them." Galen was firm. "One of them did this. We need to figure out which one."

He was forgetting one thing. "What about Madame Selena?" I asked. "Do you think she's dead?"

Galen turned his eyes back to the drying blood. "I don't know. If she's not, I'm going to guess she wishes she was right about now. I don't know where to look for her. We need to focus on what we have and go from there. If we're lucky, we'll find Madame Selena. If we're not, well, she was involved in this. We're simply not sure how deeply she was mired in the muck."

"I guess."

"Come on." Galen extended his hand as he stood. "You can be my sidekick again and we'll figure this out. We're finally getting close. I feel it."

24

TWENTY-FOUR

We went to the funeral home to talk to Maureen. Visitation was scheduled to start at noon, everything was set up … including an open casket (the cremation was scheduled for later, according to Jareth). Maureen was surprised to find us in the parlor waiting for her when she arrived.

"What's going on?"

Galen was in no mood to take things slow. "I'm sure you heard about Gus. We need to talk about a few things."

"I haven't heard a word from Gus." Maureen made a face. "He hasn't returned any of my calls. He's not even helping plan the services. If he called and complained that I'm cutting him out … well … he should try returning a phone call."

I was baffled. "He can't return your calls. He's dead."

Galen slid me a sidelong look that was full of warning. The damage was already done, and I couldn't take the statement back.

"What?" Maureen was horrified, her hand flying to her mouth. "What do you mean that Gus is dead?"

"There was an incident yesterday," Galen replied, calmly grabbing

Maureen's arm and directing her toward the parlor sofa. "I would've thought someone had told you."

"I spent the night in my hotel room." Maureen's eyes brimmed with tears. She was either a really good actress or telling the truth. I couldn't decide which. "I put out the 'do not disturb' sign. I don't understand. What happened to Gus?"

Galen kept his gaze on Maureen and sucked in a breath. There was no easy way to deliver the news. "Gus was on the beach by the lighthouse yesterday. He was despondent and talking about Trish."

"She was his daughter. Of course he's despondent."

"He had a gun in his pocket."

"But ... are you saying Gus killed himself?" Maureen immediately started shaking her head. "He wouldn't do that. He's not wired that way."

"Whether he really would've gone through with it is up for debate. It ultimately doesn't matter, though, because someone else did the deed for him."

"But ... who?"

"We don't know." Galen projected a cool confidence as he eased Maureen into reality. "Someone – and we have no idea who at this point – but someone fired a gun from a stand of trees near the lighthouse.

"Hadley happened to be with Gus on the beach when it happened," he continued. "There was some sort of spell that we believe was meant to confuse her. She recognized what was happening and tried to get Gus to run, but it was too late. He died on the beach."

Maureen pressed her lips together as she worried her hands in her lap. She didn't immediately speak.

"He died quickly," Galen offered. "He didn't suffer."

"Oh, he suffered." Maureen found her voice, but it was weak. "He suffered a lot throughout the years, and I caused part of it. Trish's death must have wrecked him. He would never consider doing ... what you're suggesting ... otherwise." She turned her gaze to me and there was something accusatory about the shine of her eyes. "What did he say to you?"

I shrugged, uncertain if I should answer. I risked a glance at Galen and he simply nodded. "He was mostly babbling about how upset he was about Trish's death. He didn't make a lot of sense sometimes. He was fighting off tears.

"His face was red, like from too much sun," I continued. "That's how I knew he'd been out there for a long time. I think he was just wandering, trying to fill the void he was feeling with … something. It wasn't working."

"And he was on your property?"

"Well, it wasn't technically my property," I hedged. "The beach belongs to the city, right?" I looked to Galen for confirmation. "It was close to the lighthouse. I could easily make out who he was from my patio."

"But you got away," Maureen pointed out. "How were you so lucky?"

Galen cleared his throat to get her attention, directing her ire to him. "This is just a working theory right now, but we believe whoever shot Gus used a spell to distract Hadley. It was meant to confound her, muck up her brain so she didn't have any idea what was happening. In that scenario, our suspect could've set her up for Gus's murder and turned attention to her."

"But … why?"

"We're not sure," Galen admitted. "Hadley managed to break from the spell even though she didn't realize what it was. When that happened, whoever shot Gus made a break for it. Hadley didn't see who it was because she was distracted by other things."

"What other things?"

"Gus." Galen was matter of fact. "He was dead, and only a few feet from her. She was still shocky when I got to the beach only a few minutes later."

"I see." Maureen rubbed her forehead. "So, basically you're saying that Gus died because of her."

"That's not what I'm saying at all." Galen's voice took on an edge of warning. "Don't blame Hadley for this. It's not her fault."

"Who else should I blame?"

"The person who did this," Galen replied honestly. "We believe that Gus's shooting and Trish's death are tied together. What we're trying to figure out is how. We need your help to do that."

"And how can I help?" Maureen turned bitter. "I wasn't even a part of their lives for the past few years. I don't know what they were involved in … or who they were hanging out with … or even what they were thinking. I wasn't a part of their lives."

"I understand that." Galen refused to break under the weight of her words. "Here's the thing, Maureen: Ashley has been in jail since the night of Trish's death. She couldn't have been on the beach yesterday. That means she had nothing to do with Gus's death."

The reality of what he was saying finally hit home for Maureen. "So you think she's innocent."

Galen nodded once. "I do."

"So do I. Who do you think is guilty?"

"Well, to be honest, we're considering you as a possible suspect."

I openly gaped at Galen's statement. "Wow!"

Galen ignored my reaction. "You didn't get much in the divorce, Maureen. I unsealed the documents after I talked to you the other day. You left the marriage with twenty grand in assets. That's it."

"And that somehow makes me a murderer?" Maureen widened her eyes to saucer-like proportions. "What dreamland are you living in, Galen? Even if I would've had the guts to kill Gus – which I didn't – I never would've killed my own daughter. I was on the mainland when she was killed, for crying out loud."

"And I plan to confirm your alibi." Galen didn't back down. "That's next on my list of things to do. I can't rule you out, Maureen. You said it yourself the other day, Trish wanted nothing to do with you. When you combine that with the fact that Gus screwed you in the divorce, you had motive to kill both of them."

Maureen was dumbfounded. "And what is that motive?"

"Money. Gus had no one to leave his fortune to but you."

Instead of acting guilty or insulted, Maureen snorted out a laugh. "Have you actually checked Gus's will?"

Galen looked around the room. "No."

"So you don't even know if the theory you're floating is sound."

"No, but ... I'll find out by the end of the day."

"I'll wait here while you do that." Maureen turned smug, folding her arms over her chest. "I'll wait right here for your apology when you check Gus's will and find out I'm in line to get nothing. There's no way I killed Gus and Trish for money!" She practically screamed the words. "Now, until you're ready to apologize, get out of my face."

Galen shifted his eyes to me. I could read the conflict there. Had we made a big mistake? I was starting to think so.

WE REMAINED AT THE funeral home while Galen dealt with Gus's lawyer on the phone. He insisted the man immediately fax a copy of the will to him, but he was running into a brick wall in the form of a belligerent attorney.

With nothing better to do – there was no way I was going to shoot the breeze with a bereft Maureen – I made my way into the front parlor and looked around at the items on display. This was the funeral home's sales wing and it made me uncomfortable.

"Hello again!"

Jareth entered the room on silent feet and was practically on top of me before he spoke. I didn't as much as sense him until he was directly behind me, and then I had to swallow a squeal so he wouldn't realize he'd practically scared the life out of me.

"Hello," I gritted out, forcing a smile as I turned. Jareth was only a foot away and that distance was nowhere near comfortable. "How are you?" I took an exaggerated step away from him, causing the amused man to bark out a laugh.

"I'm fine ... and you're frightened of me."

"I am not."

"You are."

I was firm. "You just happen to make my skin crawl now that I know you did something to my brain. If you expect me to apologize for that ... well ... forget it."

"I like that you're bold and say what comes to your mind."

"And I like it when you keep your distance." I waved my hand for effect. "Don't come close enough to touch me."

For the first time since the conversation started, Jareth looked legitimately concerned. "You think I'm going to do something to you. I don't understand why."

"Really?" I cocked an eyebrow. "You don't understand why I'm uncomfortable around you even though Galen swears up and down you did something to invade my mind the day we were introduced? I can't imagine why I'd be upset about that. Really, it's not you, it's me."

Jareth was back to smiling. "Ah, that."

"Yes, that."

"I was not trying to invade your mind. I was merely trying to see if I could ... influence would be the correct word ... your feelings. Vampires are known for that. May managed to build up an immunity of sorts to my powers. I was always fascinated by her ability, and we often tested one another as a game of sorts."

"I'm not May."

"You're certainly not," Jareth agreed. "You're a unique person all your own. I have a feeling, given all that I'm hearing, that you'll find a way to keep me out sooner or later."

It would probably be later because I had no intention of spending time with him to test his theory. "Sure. Whatever." I glanced over my shoulder to where Galen continued arguing on the phone with the attorney. "I wonder how long this is going to take."

"Probably not much longer. Galen always gets what he wants."

The remark seemed a little pointed. "And what's that supposed to mean?"

"Simply that I find it cute how you two have found your way to one another so quickly given your short time on the island," Jareth replied. "Before you, Galen was not much for dating ... at least for more than one night."

"So I've heard."

"He was more interested in competing with Booker to see who could snag more women on weekends."

That was something I hadn't heard, although it didn't exactly surprise me. "Well, you'll have to ask Galen why he decided to give up his extracurricular activities. I'm not privy to the inner workings of his mind."

"Don't sell yourself short. I think you're privy to more than you realize."

"And how do you figure that?"

"You're powerful," Jareth answered simply. "You manage to show strength without even realizing you're doing it. I find you ... fascinating."

"And I find you freaky."

"I really wish you would loosen up and like me," Jareth lamented. "I think we could have great fun together."

"And I think that would've been much more likely before you invaded my mind."

"Pshaw. You're stuck on that, and it's annoying." Jareth twisted his lips. "All right, how about we change things up? I'll apologize – again – for looking inside of your head. I'll also promise never to do it again. In exchange, I would like you to give me a second chance."

I balked. "A second chance for what?"

"Exploration."

That sounded unlikely ... and oddly intriguing. "I'll think about it." I leaned against the display shelf on the wall and crossed my arms as I regarded him. "I don't know much about vampires."

"There's not much to know. I don't feed off humans and I'm a good boy with the tourists. I'm utterly boring."

"I don't believe that."

"Well, it's true." When Jareth beamed he showed off a row of teeth that looked suspiciously normal.

"Why don't you have fangs?" The question was out of my mouth before I realized how obnoxious it sounded. "I mean ... how do you drink blood if you don't have fangs? You can't bite anyone's neck with those teeth. They're not sharp enough."

Jareth chuckled, genuinely amused. "You are witty and delightful. I can see why you caught Galen's fancy. Of course, I'm despondent over that. I thought eventually Galen would turn his attention in my direction and we'd live happily ever after."

I wrinkled my forehead. "He's not gay."

"He could be."

"You probably shouldn't mention that idea to him," I suggested. Despite my misgivings, I was starting to like Jareth. That made me uncomfortable on an entirely different level. "Can I ask you something?" I didn't wait for an answer before barreling forward. "I need information on magic and I think the only way to get it is to talk to May."

"I was under the impression that May's spirit is still hanging around," Jareth noted, frowning. "Why not just ask her when she pops in for a visit?"

"Her visits are few and far between. She won't answer questions when I pose them."

"Okay, what's your question?"

"Is there anyone else on the island who can answer my questions? And, before you say 'Madame Selena,' you should know she could very well be dead or wishing she was dead. She's also the person I think cast the spell yesterday, so I don't trust her."

Jareth's shoulders shook as he bent at the waist and laughed. "Oh, I really like you. I promise never to look inside your head again if we can hang out. I suggest a night at the bar to really get to know one another."

"I'll consider it if you answer me," I said. "I need someone to help me with the magic. You've been around a long time … and you're a vampire. You must know someone."

Jareth slowly sobered. "I still think May is your best bet. Why not simply ask her to hang around and help you? She's your grandmother. She used to talk about you all the time. I would think she wants to help you more than anything."

"Except she's barely around."

"Then force her to stick around and answer your questions."

I was understandably confused. "And how do I do that?"

"By holding a séance, of course." Jareth made a face. "You're a witch, dear. You should be adept at séances even if you're new to the game."

I was intrigued. "And how do I conduct a séance?"

"I'm not familiar with all the intricacies, but I'm certain May has a book. Perhaps in that charming third-floor library?"

I narrowed my eyes. "How do you know about the library?"

"Because we made potions together at times. She was trying to come up with something to cure my bloodlust."

"Oh." That sounded nice. "Did she succeed?"

"Nope. She did, however, make me want to try steak once."

"How did that go?"

"I threw up. My body is not equipped for human food."

"Fair enough." I licked my lips. "If I wanted to conduct a séance and force her to answer my questions, what would I need?"

"The people closest to her in life."

"So … Wesley?" My heart sank. "He's not ready to visit the lighthouse yet, and as far as I can tell that's the only place she can visit."

"He's your grandfather," Jareth pointed out. "If you ask it of him, he'll come."

Surprisingly, I knew Jareth was right. "Okay, well … I'll consider it."

"You do that."

I flicked my eyes to Galen when I heard his footsteps. He didn't look happy as he approached.

"So I got the attorney to go through the will with me," he announced with little preamble. "Maureen is right. She inherits nothing. Even if Gus had died first and Trish had inherited before dying, Maureen would still get nothing. Gus and Trish have their wills set up so all the money goes to charity."

"Huh." I was impressed at their revenge diligence and confused as to where to look next. "Maureen has no motive."

"None," Galen confirmed. "Also, I'm pretty sure her alibi for Trish's murder will hold up. She was on the mainland."

"So where do we go next? Henry or Barbie?"

"I'm not sure. I need to think."

"Great. While you do that, I need to hold a séance."

Galen didn't seem surprised by my announcement. "Okay. Let's get lunch before we go that route. If we're going to force May to visit, we need to be fueled up and ready for a lengthy diatribe. She hates being told what to do."

25

TWENTY-FIVE

Planning my first séance was exciting … and nerve-wracking. My stomach was a mess of worry worms that squirmed and made me uncomfortable as I paged through an instructional book in the living room while Galen worked his phone for information on Henry and Barbie's movements the past few days.

I'd read the passages on séances at least five times – and called for backup in the form of Lilac and Booker – but I was having trouble concentrating.

"Oh, who am I kidding?" I slammed the book shut and got to my feet to pace. "I can't do this. I'm not a witch. I'm an … idiot."

Galen remained calmly talking into his phone as he watched me. "That's right, Roscoe. I want you to find out where Henry and Barbie are, and when you do, keep them close. But don't arrest them. I want to talk to them myself." He was quiet as he listened and then nodded. "That's it exactly. I'll be in touch."

I did my best to tamp down my agitation. "Did you hear me? I can't do this."

"I heard you." Galen placed his cell phone on the coffee table and snagged me around the waist when I returned to my pacing.

"Stop it!" I slapped at his hands as he tugged me to his lap.

"Shh." He kissed my cheek.

"I can't do this," I repeated, frustration building up. "I don't know how. I mean … am I really supposed to read a book and then magically call a ghost and make her come to me? I don't think that's how it works."

"You're freaking yourself out for nothing." Galen's voice was soothing as he rocked me back and forth. "You can do this. I have faith."

I hated that he was so ridiculously supportive. "You could freak out with me occasionally," I suggested. "You know, just to prove we're on the same wavelength or something."

Galen chuckled as he rubbed his cheek against mine. "I don't think you really want that."

"Oh, no." I vehemently shook my head. "I want you to freak out with me. It can be a couple's thing."

Galen's smile was so wide it was almost contagious. "Actually, if you want to know the truth, I think we should make a rule that only one of us is allowed to freak out at a time. I think the world would tilt on its axis if we both did. It's safer if we take turns."

I didn't want to laugh because it would only encourage him, but I couldn't stop myself. "I guess that sounds like a plan." I leaned my head against his shoulder. "What if I can't do it?"

"Then you can't do it." Galen sounded entirely too reasonable. "No one expects you to do more than you're capable of but you. The rest of us will be okay if this fails. It's just an attempt, Hadley. It's not the end of the world."

"Right." I shifted a bit so I could stare into his eyes. "You're kind of reassuring when you want to be."

"I do my best." Galen gave me a soft kiss. "It's going to be okay. In fact … ." He furrowed his brow when he heard the weak sound of a horn in the driveway. "What the heck is that?"

I shrugged and got to my feet, making a face when Galen cut in front of me before I reached the door.

“Let me look first,” Galen cautioned, his eyes somber. “If it’s trouble, you be ready to run.”

“It could be Booker and Lilac,” I reminded him. “I called them for the séance because we needed bodies.”

“It could be,” Galen readily agreed. “Except Booker’s van sounds nothing like that and Lilac doesn’t have a vehicle of any sort.”

“Oh, well … .” I licked my lips. “If it’s Barbie or Henry, what are you going to do?”

“Start shooting.”

Galen was so businesslike all I could do was gape. “You’re full of it.”

Galen cracked a smile. “Maybe. But you stay behind me. It’s probably nothing, but … I want to be sure.”

“I’ll stay behind you for now,” I conceded. “We’re going to talk about this macho thing you insist on doing later.”

“I can’t wait.”

Galen was leery as he opened the front door a crack, his brow furrowing as he caught sight of something in the driveway.

“What is it?” I asked, my patience wearing thin. “Are we about to be attacked?”

Galen shook his head. “No. I believe this visitor is for you, though.” He was smiling when he stepped away from the door.

“This is my lighthouse,” I reminded him as I shuffled forward. “All the visitors should be for me.”

“Duly noted.”

I peered through the screen door, my mouth dropping open when I realized who was standing in the driveway. I immediately jerked open the weathered screen frame and stepped outside. “Wesley?”

My grandfather looked nervous, his hands stuffed in his jean pockets as he shifted from one foot to the other. “Hey, Hadley.” He chuckled hoarsely. “Um … I thought I might stop in for a quick visit.”

His timing was interesting – to say the least – and I couldn’t help feeling a quick tug of shame because of what we were planning. He loved May beyond reason even though they were divorced. I planned to force her to me, in essence control her movements, whether she wanted to visit or not. He probably wouldn’t like that.

"Oh, well … ."

Galen placed a reassuring hand on my shoulder as he moved to my left, fixing Wesley with a smirk as he shook his head. "Nice ride."

"What? Oh." Wesley shook his head and focused on the peach-colored golf cart – complete with storage bins and an awning. "I bought this as a gift for Hadley."

The admission threw me for a loop. "What?"

"I figured you did," Galen said, descending the steps and moving closer to the golf cart. I barely noticed it at first because I was so surprised to see Wesley that I didn't look beyond him. Now that I focused on the cart, I wasn't sure how I'd missed it. The color was … loud. That was the best word to describe it.

"You bought that for me?" I was dumbfounded as I followed Galen. "Why?"

"You need a vehicle if you're going to visit me," Wesley replied without hesitation. "I won't have you being ripped off by the taxi hacks – who are lucky I haven't put a boot in a behind as of yet. This way you'll be able to drive your groceries back without renting one of those carts."

I was touched he even thought of something like this. Peach-coloring aside, it was a beautiful gesture. "This is too much." I felt ridiculous as I finally met my grandfather's steady gaze. "You must have spent a fortune on this. It's not necessary. I … um … should write you a check. Yeah." I started to retreat toward the lighthouse, but Galen grabbed my arm before I could disappear inside.

"This is a gift, Hadley," he said pointedly. "Your grandfather bought it as a gift. He doesn't want a check."

I looked to Wesley for confirmation. "You don't want a check?"

He shook his head, his lips curving. "I don't want a check," he confirmed. "Your boyfriend is right. I bought this as a gift."

"But … it's too much."

"It's not enough," Wesley fired back, his tone gruff. "I haven't bought you anything since you were born. Your grandmother bought you a lot of stuff right before your mother was due, but then when we heard what happened … ." He broke off, clearly uncomfortable.

My heart went out to him. "Well, this is just the best gift ever." I meant it. "I wanted a golf cart of my own really badly when I was a teenager. My father thought it was a terrible idea and never bought me one. Now I can mark that item off my bucket list because I actually have a golf cart."

Galen snickered, genuinely amused. "You do indeed." He moved closer to the cart and ran his hands over the seat. "This is in pretty good shape. Where did you get it?"

Wesley was blasé. "Florida."

Galen arched an eyebrow. "Florida? How did you get it here so fast?"

"I'm a man of means," Wesley replied. "I have a farm that keeps most of the island in beef and chicken. That means I have special privileges."

Galen wasn't convinced. "But a golf cart?"

"I said I needed it for getting around and nobody questioned it." Wesley ran his hand over the shiny hood. "I picked peach because … well … I have no idea. You can have it painted here if you want. Booker can do it. I know he's painted some for the golf course a time or two."

I knit my eyebrows. "We have a golf course?"

Galen chuckled. "I really need to take you on a more formal tour. Once we figure out if Henry or Barbie is a murderer, how about we take a day and I'll drive you all over the island? We'll turn it into a picnic."

"That sounds nice."

"That sounds like you plan to get handsy," Wesley corrected, his eyes dark as they locked with Galen's more amused orbs. "Do you plan on getting handsy?"

Galen bobbed his head. "Absolutely."

Wesley scowled. "You're not supposed to own up to that. I'm her grandfather. You're supposed to be frightened of me."

"Oh, I'm frightened of you," Galen drawled as he sat in the driver's seat of the cart. "I find you absolutely terrifying. This is kind of neat, by the way. How far can she drive this thing between re-fuelings?"

"Only twenty-five miles," Wesley replied. "That means she'll have to fill up in town and at my place before leaving."

"Still, this will be easier for you to get around town," Galen said. "We can get Booker to paint flames on it or something."

I made a face. "Is this my golf cart or your golf cart?"

"I'm going to be in it occasionally," Galen argued. "I just want to make sure you're safe. In fact … ." He broke off and checked the ignition.

"If you're looking for these, I have them." Wesley gave the keys in his hand a good jangle. "I had to drive it here because it was the only way to deliver it. It's too big to fit in any of the trucks I had available."

Galen held his hand out. "Toss them here."

"No." Wesley made a face. "It's not your golf cart. It's Hadley's golf cart. She gets to drive it first."

Galen scowled. "Shouldn't I at least check out the safety features first? I mean … I am her boyfriend. That's part of the job description."

"I'm not giving you the keys." Wesley's annoyance was obvious. "You just said you wanted to take her on a trip so you can get handsy. I'm not rewarding that sort of behavior."

Galen snorted out a laugh. "I'll have you know that she's the handsy one. She can't keep her hands off me. It's quite invasive, if you want to know the truth."

My mouth dropped open. "Oh, you're done sleeping here, buddy. That is a filthy lie."

Galen was clearly enjoying himself, because his shoulders shook with silent laughter.

"Why has he been sleeping here?" Wesley asked, confused. "He has his own house."

"Oh, well … ." I wasn't sure how to answer. I'd never had a grandparent ask me that question. My father was careful to completely ignore the topic from the time I hit sixteen onward. It was as if I no longer had a bed in his world.

"I've been spending the night to make sure Hadley is safe," Galen replied smoothly, turning serious. "You're aware of what happened on the beach yesterday, right?"

Wesley furrowed his brow and shook his head. "What happened on the beach?"

Galen exchanged a quick look with me before sliding out from behind the steering wheel. "You're not going to like it." He launched into the tale with a detached tone that I envied. He didn't get worked up. He didn't let his anger – which was clearly still close to the surface – come out. He merely reported the facts.

When he was done, Wesley was flummoxed. "I don't understand any of this."

"It's a mess," Galen agreed. "We're working on the assumption that whoever killed Gus is responsible for Trish's death. It doesn't make sense otherwise. I ran Maureen's alibi this afternoon and she's clear for Trish's death. She still could be guilty of Gus's death, but there's no motive as far as I can tell."

Wesley was speculative. "Money?"

Galen shook his head. "Maureen was cut out of both wills. She gets nothing."

Wesley thoughtfully stroked his chin. "I can't see a motive here either. I don't know what to make of it."

"I don't think Maureen is our culprit," Galen admitted. "I was keen to tear her apart earlier, but she didn't act guilty. I mean … I know that she could be putting on a show, but it didn't feel that way."

"Who does that leave you with?"

"Barbie and Henry," I automatically answered. "If we're voting, by the way, I think Barbie is clearly the guilty party."

Galen's lips curved. "I think that's only because you disliked her so much when you went over there."

"Her face doesn't move," I argued. "That's a clear sign that a person is not to be trusted. A face should move."

Wesley chuckled, amused. "You can't argue with her logic."

"No, you can't," Galen agreed. "The thing is, Barbie is mean and nasty, but she's never struck me as one of the great thinkers of our time. Whoever did this had to plan it out. I'm not sure Barbie is capable of that."

"You think it was Henry, don't you?" I searched my heart for a reaction when he nodded, but came up empty. "He was a main participant in the feud. I guess that makes sense."

"It's not just that," Galen said. "Whoever killed Trish had to shove a knife in her throat. That takes a sort of cold calculation that I'm not sure many women have."

"That's sexist," I argued. "A woman could easily stab another woman in the throat."

"I don't discount that. But a woman might not like the mess associated with that. You heard the crime scene tech while he was there. Trish lost a lot of blood in a short amount of time. The killer would likely have been splattered with blood. Can you see Barbie taking it well if she was covered in blood?"

He had a point ... which I hated. "Still, she's more evil than Henry." I was certain of that. "You should've heard the things she said to me. The things I saw were even worse. She's not a good person."

"The things you saw?" Wesley leaned forward, intrigued.

I had no choice, so I told him about the vision I'd experienced while leaving Barbie's house. "She clearly had a secret with Henry and it's not something she wanted Ashley to know. She's a horrible woman. Henry seemed more resigned, as if the feud and carrying around so much anger had sucked the life out of him. Barbie wanted to control things. That's why I think this is right up her alley."

"Do you think she's capable of hiding in the trees and firing a bullet over a long distance and hitting her target?" Galen challenged.

"Um ... ." Crap. He had me there. "I don't know. Maybe she hired someone."

"Like who?"

"Madame Selena." It was the first name that came to mind. "We both agree that she had something to do with the spell that paralyzed me yesterday."

Wesley was still behind. "Wait ... what spell?"

I related that part of the story to him, and when I was done the look on his face promised mayhem. "I really am fine," I added hurriedly. "I wasn't grazed or anything."

"She was in shock when I got to her," Galen volunteered. "She had no idea what was going on. Once she explained about the spell, I felt a little better. She managed to shake the aftereffects fairly quickly."

"Well, that's good." Wesley brightened, although only marginally. "It's impressive you managed to break free from a spell of that magnitude with no training. Was May proud when you told her?"

The question caught me off guard. "She hasn't been around. I mean ... not for days. I'm starting to get a little worried."

"We're going to hold a séance," Galen volunteered, slipping his arm around my waist and anchoring me to his side. "Hadley has been reading up. It's not just that we're worried about May. It's also that we're worried about Hadley. We want to know if May has seen anything."

"Sounds fairly practical to me," Wesley said. "When are you doing it?"

I wrinkled my nose, worry coursing through me. "Now. We're just waiting for Booker and Lilac to get here so they can help."

Wesley's expression turned grim. "Now?"

I nodded. "I'm sorry. I had no idea you were heading over here ... and with, like, the best gift ever."

"No, it's okay." Wesley waved off my apology. "It makes sense what you're trying to do. In fact, it makes a lot of sense." He moved his jaw back and forth, his mind clearly busy. "You know what? I'm in. Let's do this."

I was beyond surprised by his reaction. "You want to do the séance with us?"

Wesley nodded. "Believe it or not, I've participated in similar efforts a time or two. I told you I had some wizard in me, right? That will come in handy today."

I glanced at Galen for his reaction. He was smiling.

"That's a great idea," Galen offered before I had a chance to answer. "Hadley is worried about doing this. It will be good for her to a have a family member close when it comes time."

"I'm glad to be that family member." Wesley said the words, but there wasn't much energy behind them. "We should probably gather some supplies." He looked up to the third-floor window. "That means I'll have to go inside."

My heart went out to him. "Just tell me what you want and I'll collect it."

"No." Wesley was firm when he shook his head. "It's time. I want to see May. I want to help you. We'll do this together."

I was relieved beyond measure. "Thank you ... for this and the really cool cart."

Wesley's expression softened. "Just think of it as a lifetime of missed Christmas and birthday gifts all rolled together."

"It's more than that." I smiled at him, my eyes suddenly burning with tears. "I really do appreciate it."

"Oh, now, none of that!" Wesley looked panicked as he focused on Galen. "Can't you do something to make her stop that?"

Galen shrugged, noncommittal. "Maybe, but you've forbidden me from being handsy."

Wesley rolled his eyes. "You're going to be trouble, aren't you, boy?"

Galen snickered. "I certainly hope so."

26

TWENTY-SIX

Wesley gave me a list of ingredients to gather. Thankfully May had them all in stock on the third floor. When I came downstairs, I heard Galen and Wesley talking in the kitchen, their voices hushed.

"She seems worried," Wesley noted. "I'm not sure what to make of it."

"Why do you have to make anything of it?" Galen was calm as he brewed coffee. "This is her first séance. Of course she's worried."

"Emma was thrilled the first time she held a séance," Wesley argued. "She was eight, hosting a slumber party, and her mother was ticked off because she tried to call for Bloody Mary, which thankfully didn't work. May made her settle for a nice and sweet spirit, which Emma hated."

"Hadley is not Emma," Galen pointed out.

I could see Wesley through the crack between the door and the frame. He bristled at Galen's words. "I know she's not Emma. Did I say she was Emma?"

Galen refused to back down. "No, but you're treating her as if she grew up in the same manner as Emma."

"I am not." Wesley was clearly annoyed, although his anger lasted only a moment. "What do you mean by that?"

Galen, who I often thought had infinite patience, looked tired as he regarded my grandfather. "Hadley is her own person. She's a pretty great person."

"I happen to like her, too," Wesley argued. "She's a mixture of things. Of May … of me … most importantly, of Emma. I see Emma in her whenever she smiles."

"Which is great, and I'm happy for you." Galen's tone was even. "But she's not Emma, and it's unfair to hold her to that standard."

I was both impressed and worried by his words. What if Wesley didn't like what he had to say and took off? It wasn't just that I needed my grandfather for the séance. I wanted to get to know him better.

"I'm not holding her to any standard," Wesley shot back. "I'm not pushing her to be something she's not."

"I know, but … it's hard for her." Galen was somber. "She belongs here, but she feels like an outsider. Comparing her to Emma won't make that better. She's brave, but she's also afraid of failing at being a witch because all she hears is the amazing things that May could do."

"That's not fair." Wesley's expression twisted. "Honestly, that's not fair at all. Hadley was raised on the mainland. She didn't know about any of this. No one expects her to be May."

"Except for Jareth, who couldn't glamour May," Galen argued. "He managed to glamour Hadley at the funeral home the other day and then pointed out that May couldn't be glamoured, which I'm sure didn't make Hadley feel good."

"I've always hated that bloodsucker," Wesley muttered as he rubbed the back of his neck. "I'll handle him."

"You'll stay away from him," Galen shot back, extending a finger. "I already had a talk with him. Sometimes he forgets his manners, but he's basically a good guy. He and Hadley made up on their own. Let her decide how she wants to deal with him."

"But … she's my granddaughter."

"And you should celebrate that by getting to know her. She's pretty funny … and entertaining … and sometimes a bit of a spaz. She's great, though. She deserves for you to get to know her as she is, not as you think she should be."

Wesley rolled his eyes. "I'm not sure I should be taking advice from the guy who has been sharing a bed with my granddaughter for the past week despite barely knowing her. What's up with that, by the way? I hear the gossip from my workers, and I don't like it."

Galen's eyes lit with mirth as I bit the inside of my cheek to keep from laughing at Wesley's outrage. "Are you asking my intentions toward Hadley?"

"I guess. I want her with an honorable man."

"I try very hard to be an honorable man."

"Honorable men don't sleep in the same bed with single women," Wesley argued.

"Really?" Galen didn't appear bothered by Wesley's statement. "Last time I checked, you and May divorced a long time ago, yet you shared the same bed quite often. Does that make you a dishonorable man? I mean ... she was a single woman once divorced, after all."

Wesley's scowl was so pronounced it made him look like a cartoon character. "You think you're funny, don't you?"

"No." Galen's face remained impassive. "I think I care about Hadley. I think I care about her a great deal, so much that I think about her half the day when I should be working."

Oh, that was kind of sweet. My cheeks flushed with pleasure, but I was careful to keep myself hidden from view because I didn't want to be caught eavesdropping. That would be embarrassing.

"That doesn't mean you have to spend the night," Wesley argued.

Galen sighed. "Things are different now. It's not like when you and May started dating. I don't know why I'm even telling you this because it's not your business, but nothing has happened. We've only slept."

"Oh, right. Nothing has happened." Wesley adopted a mocking voice. "I didn't just fall off the turnip truck. I know what happens when two people share a bed."

"Yes. They sleep."

Wesley wrinkled his nose. "I don't believe you."

"I don't care." Galen was firm. "Things aren't going to change between us. We're happy together. We're having a good time. If people would stop dying around us we'd be even happier. I won't let you derail this."

"I don't want to derail this." Wesley let out a heavy sigh. "She's all I have left. She's ... my legacy."

"And I'm hoping she's my future," Galen supplied. "You're doing right by her, Wesley. The golf cart was a nice touch, and she'll remember her first gift from her grandfather forever. That doesn't mean you can exert yourself on her life. She's an adult.

"She doesn't know you," he continued, "but she wants to. Don't ruin things by being you."

"I'm pretty sure that was an insult," Wesley grumbled, folding his arms over his chest.

"And I'm pretty sure you can take it," Galen fired back, growling when his phone dinged. He reached for it on the counter, his jaw tightening as he read the message on his screen. "Apparently Henry has been seen by the Elks lodge. Two people are reporting it."

Wesley turned serious, all frustration from their earlier conversation evaporating. "Go. I know it's important. I'll stay here and do the séance with Hadley."

"Booker and Lilac are coming, too."

"Why?"

"Because I want Hadley protected just in case."

Wesley furrowed his brow. "Do you think she's in danger?"

"I think someone has broken into this lighthouse at least once, probably twice," Galen replied. "I think Hadley's senses told her someone was watching her at the cemetery the other day. I think someone tried to frame her for murder yesterday. I think she could've easily been killed yesterday. I'm not taking any chances."

Wesley sighed. "See, I want to dislike you because I'm convinced you're a pervert, but you're too good of a man to allow me to do it. I hate that."

Galen grinned. "You'll live. I need to tell Hadley I'm running out."

"I can do that," Wesley protested. "She'll be fine. I promise."

"I know she will." Galen pushed himself away from the counter. "It doesn't matter. She already knows. She's been eavesdropping through that door for at least five minutes. I still want to say goodbye."

I scowled as his words registered. Crap. And here I thought I was being so stealthy.

I was still stewing when Galen strolled out of the kitchen and tapped my chin. "Give me a kiss."

"I wasn't eavesdropping," I said hurriedly, brushing the front of my shirt to give me something to do with my hands. "I was just … listening."

"That is eavesdropping." Galen didn't seem bothered by my actions. "I have to follow the lead on Henry. I'm sorry. I'd like to be here for you, but … ."

"You have a job to do," I finished, sulking. "It's okay. Booker and Lilac will be here."

"They will be. I'll be back as soon as I can."

"Okay."

"Great." Galen gave me a quick kiss. "When I get back I'll give you a few pointers on eavesdropping without getting caught."

I glared at his back. "You're not nearly as smart as you think you are."

"Oh, I'm plenty smart. I think you're plenty smart, too. I'll be back as soon as I can. Be safe."

"I'll be fine."

"You'd better be."

WESLEY SET UP FOR the séance. I watched closely, barely glancing at Booker and Lilac when they joined us. I was interested in the process and eager for it to get underway.

"We're ready," Wesley said when he was sure the candles were in the right positions. "Everyone gather on the floor and hold hands."

I sat to his right and Lilac settled across from me. Booker took his spot across from Wesley and didn't complain when I gripped his hand a little more tightly than necessary. He gave me a knowing look and an easy smile, but remained silent.

This was Wesley's show, so I watched as he closed his eyes and began to speak.

"May Belladonna Potter," he intoned. "We call to you in the great beyond. We demand your presence. Right now!"

I gaped. "Oh, well, that's not going to work."

I couldn't have been more wrong. May, her ghostly face determined, appeared in the center of the circle. She glanced between faces as she got her bearings, ultimately focusing on Wesley.

"Well, it's about time."

Wesley snickered. "It's good to see you, too." He sounded almost reverent as he gazed upon her. "You look … good."

May rolled her eyes. "I'm sure I look stretched, because that's the way I feel. We have to be quick. I'm not sure how much time I have."

Now it was my turn to make a face. "I thought you were a ghost. Don't you have all the time in the world?"

"That's not what I mean." I could tell May was feigning patience when we snagged gazes. "Something has happened the last few days. I'm not sure how to explain it."

"I know how to explain it. You haven't been visiting even though I desperately needed someone to talk to. Do you even know what happened to me yesterday?"

May looked exasperated. "We're talking about me right now, dear. We can talk about you when my problem is fixed."

I was taken aback. "What's your problem?"

"Someone has built a barrier of sorts," May replied. "I can't control my comings and goings. In fact, I haven't been able to enter the lighthouse since … well … I can't keep track of my days. When was the last time you saw me?"

"The night you saw the person break into the lighthouse," I answered automatically, my mind buzzing with possibilities. "You scared him or her off. Galen searched the lighthouse and came up empty. That was it."

"And when was that?"

I shrugged. "Days ago. You haven't been back since."

"Not for lack of trying." May's eyes landed on Wesley. "The only reason I managed to break through now is because Wesley used magic to call to me. Even now I can feel something trying to push me out."

"You should've come to me," Wesley groused. "You should've visited the ranch and told me what was going on. We could've fixed this days ago."

"I tried," May said simply. "I don't think I'm strong enough to visit other places … at least not yet. I'm anchored to the lighthouse. It was my home. Maybe eventually, but … for now I can't."

Wesley clenched his jaw. "Then we'll fix it so you can come here whenever you want. This is your home."

"It's Hadley's home now," May corrected. "I would love to be able to visit from time to time. I can't even do that. Someone is working against me."

"It has to be Madame Selena," I supplied, twitching my nose because it itched. I was too afraid to release Booker and Wesley's hands to give it a scratch. "She's behind all of this, including what happened on the beach."

May made a face. "Selena? What does that old hag have to do with anything?"

"That's what I'd like to know." Wesley shifted to get more comfortable. "I'm confused."

I related the story of Gus's death again, keeping it quick and succinct. When I finished, Wesley was more furious than the first time he heard the story and May was flabbergasted.

"Why didn't anyone tell me about Selena's part in this sooner?" Wesley barked. "I heard about the shooting, and you mentioned it briefly a few minutes ago. I naturally assumed Gus was the target."

"He was the target," Booker interjected. "He was always meant to die. Hadley was meant to serve as a distraction to Galen because whoever did this didn't want Galen to clear Ashley. This all began when he started asking hard questions of others."

"But … what does Selena have to do with it?" May asked, still confused. "How could she have ties to either of them?"

I shrugged. "I don't know. Would she take money to cast a spell?"

May nodded without hesitation. "She was known for it. That's why we didn't get along."

"But that rift was started on your end," Wesley pointed out. "She wanted to be friends, but you wouldn't allow it. She was always bitter about the way you were regarded in town, as if you were the expert and she was a fraud."

"She was a fraud." May was unemotional. "She had access to a lot of magic, but never bothered to learn how to properly wield it. She wanted me to give her the secrets of the trade, but I couldn't do that if she was going to be lazy about it."

"She obviously picked up on something," Booker pointed out. "She was strong enough to try to curse Hadley to forget."

"Hadley was strong enough to break free." Wesley puffed out his chest, pride evident. "She didn't need any help to do it. Her instincts took over."

"And she's lucky for it." May looked thoughtful. "Where is Selena now?"

"We don't know. Her golf cart was found tipped over on the main highway this morning. Galen had his men out looking for her last night, but they never found her."

"There was blood on the cart seat," Booker added. "It wasn't enough to make me think she died there, but it was enough to cause concern. The working theory is that someone forced her off the road – perhaps the same person who shot Gus – and then took her from the accident scene to make sure she couldn't talk."

"I guess that makes sense." May continued floating in the center of the small circle, but took on a far-off expression. "Does Galen think she's dead?"

"He said she was either dead or about to wish she was," I answered. "We don't know. He thought maybe Maureen was behind everything, but she has no motive. Even with both Gus and Trish dead, she inherits nothing. Also, she apparently has an alibi that holds up for Trish's death."

"She could've hired someone," Lilac pointed out. "Maybe she didn't know she wasn't in the wills."

"She's the one who told us she wasn't," I countered. "I really don't think it's her."

"Then who does that leave us with?" May asked. "Who else could've done this?"

"Henry and Barbie are Galen's top suspects," Booker supplied. "Henry was sighted at the Elks lodge and Galen headed out there to see if he could track him down. If it's not Henry or Barbie, I don't think we have any ideas on culprits."

"And we believe Selena cast a spell to keep me out of the lighthouse," May mused. "That sounds about right. She would want to visit and knew I would pop up and tell you to kick her out if I realized she was here."

"Could she have been the one who broke in the last time we saw you?" I asked.

"I don't know. I don't know what to make of any of it."

"She came here under the guise of helping me," I offered. "She was far more interested in looking at your books, though. Then, when I came back here yesterday to research cupids, I felt certain that someone had moved things around on the third floor."

Booker scowled. "You researched cupids?"

"You bet your diaper-covered posterior I did." I winked at him, causing Wesley and Lilac to snicker. "I'm nowhere near done either."

"Ugh. I knew I shouldn't have told you. This is going to be the worst thing ever."

"Oh, stop being a baby." I pursed my lips. "You don't know what kind of spell Selena cast, do you, May? Wesley might be able to put something together to counter it if you do."

"I have no idea. The thing is … if Selena cast the spell and she really is dead, it should've lifted when her soul was released from her body," May explained. "The spell is still active. In fact, I can't stay much longer. I'm weakening. I think that means Selena is still alive."

I didn't know whether to be relieved or annoyed. "Okay, well … ." I didn't get a chance to finish because the sound of someone banging on the front door drew my attention. "Who could that be?"

"I don't know," Wesley said grimly, his expression a mixture of fury and disappointment. "May just disappeared. We need to figure this out … and fast. I don't like the idea of knowing she can't visit her own home."

I released his hand and stood. "We'll figure it out … right after I see who's at the door. We're not done here. We're just getting started."

27

TWENTY-SEVEN

I was frustrated when I made it to the door.

"I'm going to start throwing punches at whoever this is," I muttered. "I mean … it's like the worst timing ever."

Wesley, his expression forlorn, stared at the spot May had hovered in only moments before. "We'll fix it so May comes back. I'll … we'll fix it."

Sympathy washed over me. "Of course we'll fix it." I meant it with all my heart, for his benefit as well as my own. "We'll figure out what's going on. I'll do research and then you can … do whatever needs to be done."

I was frustrated when Wesley didn't meet my gaze. Lilac, as if sensing my distress, made a tsking sound with her tongue and rested her hand on Wesley's forearm.

"We'll find a way to make sure May can be here," she said. "Don't be sad. We'll figure it out."

Whoever was outside pounded the door again. Hard.

"I'm coming," I grumbled, stomping my feet to make my irritation known as I reached the door. "There's no need to get your panties in a bunch, for crying out loud. I mean … ." I was about to say something really mean, but it died on my lips when I saw the person standing on the other side of the threshold. "You've got to be kidding me."

Booker immediately keyed in on my demeanor and jumped to his feet, his eyes going wide when he saw the disheveled woman standing on the front porch. "Hadley … ."

He was going to warn me to step away. I was already doing it when Madame Selena swooped into the room, her gray hair poking out from beneath a messy turban. I was keen to keep distance between us, so much so that I almost tripped over the coffee table (which we'd moved to make room for the séance) and banged my knee hard against the corner.

"Ow!" I dropped to the ground on the other side, grimacing as I held my knee tight.

"You're so graceful," Booker drawled, causing me to scowl.

"You have to save me," Madame Selena announced. "I'm in danger of losing my life."

"I'll say," Lilac drawled. "We might all kill you now that we know what you did to May."

Madame Selena blinked several times in rapid succession and I could practically see the gears in her mind grinding. When she spoke, I wasn't surprised by her words. "Whatever do you mean? I think there must have been some sort of mistake."

I rolled my eyes so hard I would've probably tipped over if I hadn't already been on the ground thanks to my throbbing knee. "Don't bother denying it."

"Really," Wesley growled, slowly getting to his feet. His eyes blazed as he focused on Madame Selena. "Why would you do something so terrible to May?"

Madame Selena balked. "I have no idea what you're talking about. Whatever she told you … well, it's a lie. She never was very truthful. I guess she carried her lying ways into death with her."

Wesley moved to lunge at her, but Booker was clearly expecting an act of aggression because he caught Wesley around the waist and kept him from closing the distance … and potentially committing murder.

"Simmer down, Wesley," Booker ordered, his eyes keen and thoughtful as they landed on Madame Selena. "She's not worth it."

"I don't care if she's worth it," Wesley spat. "It won't take long, and I bet I don't even break a sweat. I'm not a proponent of hurting women, but she has it coming."

I decided to be practical as I rubbed my knee. "Wesley, you can't kill her. We might need her to help bring May back."

"Oh, I'm not bringing back May." Madame Selena's face remained impassive even as she wiped her sweaty brow. "I didn't spend two days coming up with the perfect spell to keep her gone just to bring her back."

I was floored. "What?"

"Let me go, Booker!" Wesley growled as he doubled his efforts to escape.

"I can't bring her back." Madame Selena was straightforward. "I mean … I just can't. If she's here she'll try to stop me, and there's nothing more annoying than a ghost who tries to act as your conscience."

"I'm guessing you don't have a conscience," I shot back. "You knew I wanted to spend time with my grandmother, learn from her, and then you cast a spell to keep her away."

Madame Selena didn't bother to deny it. "I needed time to work without May breathing down my neck. If she knew I was in here she would've told you, and that would've made accessing the lighthouse all the more difficult."

Something occurred to me. "You're the one who broke in." I wanted to get to my feet so I could look Madame Selena in the eye, but my knee was throbbing. "You let yourself into the lighthouse but hid your features under a hoodie so May couldn't recognize you. Then, when she made noise, you bolted."

"I heard she was hanging around," Madame Selena said, making a face. "It didn't surprise me. I mean … the woman never recognized when it was her turn to step back and let someone else shine. This is my island now. She's gone. She won't let me have my moment to shine."

"Ugh." Now I was sorry Booker didn't let Wesley kill her. "Why did you even come here? I don't understand. If your goal is to be more famous than May, why not just perform some magic and worry about yourself?"

"Because I don't know how to perform magic," Madame Selena shot back. "I'm not a born witch. I'm a learned witch. Everything I can do I had to train myself to do ... and it took a long time."

I had no idea what that meant and looked to Lilac for help. Her expression had turned thoughtful as she looked Madame Selena up and down, but she didn't look particularly worried.

"Some witches are born with magic, like May, Emma and you," Lilac supplied. "Others have to learn from books."

Books? Hmm. "Like the ones on the third floor?"

Lilac nodded, her eyes never leaving Madame Selena's face. "Exactly like that. But not all power can be taught."

"No, it can't," Madame Selena agreed, her cheeks flushing with embarrassment under Lilac's glare. "Can you please not stare at me like that?"

Lilac ignored the request. "You came here because you thought there was a secret in the books to boost your powers. You thought May might know a cheat, didn't you?"

Madame Selena, refusing to show embarrassment, merely shrugged. "She was always keeping things from me. I tried to learn from her, but she told me I was limited. I didn't believe that. I knew I wasn't limited and that she only wanted to keep me down. That's when I knew she was an enemy rather than a friend."

"You didn't tell her that, did you?" Wesley challenged. I swear he looked as if his eyes were about to catch fire and shoot laser bolts in Madame Selena's direction. His fury was palpable, taking over the room to the point it felt hot enough to infringe on breathing. "You kept pretending you were a faithful student even as you plotted against May. She knew you'd turn on her, by the way. She knew what you were. She tried to help anyway, believed she could change you. That was one of the few things she was wrong about."

"She lied to me!" Madame Selena barked. "I am not limited. I'm just as powerful as May."

"If that's true, you wouldn't need May's books and supplies," I pointed out. "You were in the attic moving things around. You changed the order of the herbs and looked through the Book of Shadows."

"I was certain she was hiding a spell that could help me." Madame Selena didn't even bother looking at anyone else. She focused on me, probably because she thought she could snow me. That was my guess, anyway. "The problem is, May cursed the book so it can't leave the lighthouse. I wanted to grab it and go, but I couldn't break the spell. I had to read it here."

"Is that why you cast the spell on the beach?" I asked, my frustration growing with every word the woman uttered. "Did you want to distract me so you could find a way to steal the book?"

Madame Selena narrowed her eyes. "What do you mean?" She wasn't a particularly good actress, so I could tell right away that she was thrown regarding how much we knew.

"Oh, don't do that." Lilac wagged a finger as she slowly stood. I'd never seen her look as angry as she did now. "We know it was you on the beach. We know you wanted to distract Hadley to the point she wouldn't remember what happened, so when she was accused of killing Gus ... well ... she really wouldn't know if it was true."

"You tried to glamour her from afar," Wesley supplied. "You thought because she was a new witch you'd be able to control her. She's stronger than you, even though she doesn't realize it. She slipped the spell before you could get what you wanted."

"Is that what you really wanted?" I couldn't help being confused. "It was the book all this time? Gus died for a book?" That made absolutely no sense to me.

"Oh, good grief." Madame Selena tilted her head back and pinched her nose as she stared at the ceiling. "I can't even believe we're having this conversation. I mean ... how did you even know?"

"About the spell?" I shrugged. That was a good question. "The world turned shimmery. I realized something was very wrong."

"But how did you break the spell?"

"I don't know." That wasn't a lie. I'd given it a lot of thought, but I had no answers. "I just did."

"Hadley is gifted," Wesley said. "She's May's granddaughter, so she would have to be. She's a born witch who had no idea what she was until two weeks ago – and she's still stronger than you."

Madame Selena made a face. "Yes, well, that won't be true if she's dead, will it?" Madame Selena drew a small handgun from her pocket and pointed it in my direction. "Everyone back up." Her voice turned deadly cold. "I'm not kidding. If you don't give me some room, I'll blow Hadley's brains out."

Wesley was furious as my breath caught in my throat. For once, I believed every word that came out of Madame Selena's mouth. She wasn't kidding. She had no qualms about killing me.

"What are you doing?" I was dumbfounded. "How do you think this is going to work?"

"I have no idea how it's going to work but I have to try," Madame Selena replied. "I'm in real trouble here. You're right. I did cast the spell on the beach. I didn't do it to steal the book. I wanted the book – don't get me wrong – but I didn't intend to steal it right away. I had other things on my mind that day."

I furrowed my brow. "You were helping someone all along," I surmised. "Galen was right. You were working with Henry or Barbie, though I have no idea which one."

Madame Selena narrowed her eyes to glittery slits. "What does Galen know? Don't mince words. Don't lie. I'll know if you lie. What exactly does he know?"

"He knows enough to lock you away," Booker answered. He remained calm, his face unreadable, but I could sense the anger radiating from him. We were separated by a coffee table and a crazy woman with a gun, but I had no doubt he'd make both disappear in an instant if he thought it was necessary. "He's out at the beach looking for Henry right now. Someone saw him near the Elks lodge."

"Oh, that would be Mary Dardin," Madame Selena said. "I put a suggestion in her head and told her to call. I thought that would leave

Hadley here alone. I had no idea she'd have so much company. There are no vehicles in the driveway."

"I drove the cart," Wesley said. "I need to call for a ride from one of my men when I leave."

"And I left the van down the beach," Booker added. "She's right. It looks as if no one is here."

"But I didn't get that lucky, did I?" Madame Selena's frustration was obvious as she heaved out a sigh. "I'm in trouble here, people. It's your job to get me out of it. I know you didn't sign up for this task, but if you want Hadley to live you have no choice." She waved the gun in my direction. "Figure out a way for me to get off Moonstone Bay within the next hour or I'll start shooting."

"You won't do that," Booker shot back. "If you kill Hadley, you have absolutely no leverage."

"Don't push her, Booker," Wesley warned, fear apparent. "You have no idea what she's capable of."

"I know what she's not capable of," Booker argued. "She's not capable of killing all of us. If she hurts Hadley, there's nothing that will stop the rest of us from tearing her apart. She knows that."

Wesley glanced to me and swallowed hard. "I'm not willing to risk Hadley's life on a hunch."

I pursed my lips and then offered a small smile. "Thanks. But you don't have to worry about me. I'll be fine."

"Did you hear that?" Madame Selena's eyebrows migrated north. "She'll be fine. She's got stones the size of … um … boulders. She's going to help me figure a way off this island and then everyone will be able to return to their regularly scheduled lives. Doesn't that sound terrific?"

It sounded unlikely, but I kept it to myself. I was a much better liar than Madame Selena, and she didn't know me well enough to realize I was about to start telling tall tales. I only hoped Booker, Wesley and Lilac realized what I was doing and didn't contradict me when it started happening.

"First, we have to know who you're running from," I prompted, doing my best to appear outwardly calm even as my heart rate ratcheted up a notch. "We can't help unless we know which enemy we're fighting."

"Enemy?" Now it was Lilac's turn to be confused. "Which enemy are you talking about?"

I remained where I was, basically sitting on the coffee table as I continued to rub my sore knee. I had two choices, but one made much more sense than the other. "Barbie Conner," I said finally. "She hired Madame Selena to help her cover up two murders."

Madame Selena flicked her eyes to me, something dark lurking in the depths as she stared. "How can you possibly know that?"

"Because Barbie is keeping a secret," I replied calmly. "She has something she doesn't want anyone else to know. I'm pretty sure I know what that something is." That was a lie. I was guessing.

"Oh, really?" Madame Selena drawled. "Why don't you enlighten the class?"

"It doesn't really matter." I meant it. "She killed Trish. I'm guessing because Trish found out the truth and confronted her. Barbie needed to keep her quiet, so she killed her. The mistake she made was using a knife from a set that probably got dispersed among her family throughout the years. She also had the rotten luck to pick a day when Ashley and Trish fought, which was unusual. She probably had no idea her daughter would be the prime suspect."

Madame Selena forced out a hollow snort. "No. She definitely didn't think that would happen." Her look turned appraising. "How did you figure it out?"

"It wasn't hard once I really looked at the facts."

"Well, she's essentially crazy," Madame Selena supplied. "Once I realized that the spell didn't work on you at the beach, I knew she'd be coming for me. I was a loose end she needed to tie up. I was the only one who knew everything she'd done."

"You faked your death, didn't you?" Booker asked. "That's why the scene was so perfectly set on the road."

"I faked my disappearance," Madame Selena corrected. "I wanted people to talk about my disappearance for years to come, lift me to lofty mythological heights. I'm not sure that's still possible but I'm going to try. To make it happen, you need to get me off the island. You have to start thinking."

I could do nothing but stare at her. "We don't have control of the ferries and planes. We can't get you off the island, for crying out loud. Why would you possibly think we could?"

Instead of answering me, she turned her gaze to Wesley. "Because your grandfather has ways on and off the island the rest of us don't have access to. How do you think he managed to get you that fancy new cart in the driveway? That's divine, by the way. I'd be totally jealous if I were staying here."

I rolled my eyes. "Whatever. Smuggling a person is different than importing a golf cart."

"Wesley can do it," Madame Selena pressed. "He'll have to if he wants to keep you alive."

Wesley glared at her. "Don't threaten my granddaughter."

"I'll do what I want," Madame Selena fired back. "This is my last chance."

I sensed a new player entering the room from the kitchen before I saw her, my internal danger alarm going completely wonky at the exact moment Barbie Conner appeared behind Booker. She, too, was armed. Her gun was three times as big as Madame Selena's weapon.

"You're out of chances, Selena," Barbie drawled. "You gave it a good try, but there's no way out of this for you. I'm sorry. That's simply the way it is."

And just like that, I realized the game was about to shift again.

28

TWENTY-EIGHT

Barbie looked calm. Too calm, really. I'd expect someone in her position to be fearful. She didn't look that way at all, though. Of course, her face never moved, so it was hard to grasp what she was feeling. All that stared back was a blank mask of human flesh.

"How did you get in here?" Wesley asked, glaring at Barbie.

"The back door was open."

Wesley shot me a look. "Why was the back door open?"

That was a good question. "I … don't know. I didn't really think about it. The house is full of people."

"And now there are two more," Booker pointed out. "They even brought guns for their visits."

"It was an accident," I muttered. "I really didn't give it much thought."

"Next time, huh?" Lilac was unnaturally bright as she snagged my gaze. I didn't understand how she could remain perky under this particular set of conditions. "I bet you won't forget again."

"Definitely not," I agreed, my fingers busy as they massaged my knee. "How did you even know to come here, Barbie? I mean …

Madame Selena faked her death. How could you possibly know she was coming here?"

"I faked my disappearance," Madame Selena snapped. "Disappearance! Get it right."

"Yes, because that's what's important," Booker drawled. "Still, Hadley has a point. How did you know to come here, Barbie?"

Barbie shifted to give Booker a weighted look. "I'm a genius."

"Why really?" Lilac challenged. I couldn't help being surprised at her bombastic attitude. She should be quaking with fear at being caught between two delusional women, but she didn't look worried in the least. That was odd, right? "You had to be tipped off somehow."

"It wasn't as difficult as you might think," Barbie said breezily. "Like I said, I'm a genius."

For some reason I could see the truth in her head. Whether from magic or an inherent ability to read people, I knew exactly how this occurred. "You were watching the lighthouse. You knew Madame Selena would come back because she can't stay away from the book. She thinks that book will make her powerful, and you knew she'd come back at least once more in an effort to get her hands on it."

Barbie smirked. "Maybe."

"No, she's right," Wesley said. "That's exactly what you did. Everyone assumed Selena was hurt in the golf cart crash, that someone went after her and dragged her away. The assumption was she was already dead or injured. You were her partner, so you knew that wasn't the case because you didn't have her. That meant you had to watch for her to show herself, and the lighthouse made the most sense."

Barbie pursed her lips. "Maybe I'm not the only genius here, huh?"

"That wasn't genius deduction," I countered. "It was common sense."

"You say potato."

Ugh. She might fancy herself a genius, but she was obviously a moron. I had to distract her until I could come up with a plan. I didn't think Madame Selena was half the threat that Barbie was. That didn't mean Madame Selena wouldn't start shooting if she thought it could serve as a distraction and she could make her escape. I had to be wary and careful, two things at which I wasn't very good.

Thankfully Booker seemed to be thinking along the same lines, because he put his full focus on Barbie. "Why did you kill Trish?"

Barbie snorted. "Oh, don't act like you care. We all know you didn't love Trish."

"I never said I loved her." Booker remained calm. "But I didn't want to see her die. She was a good person, a bit rough around the edges. She didn't deserve what happened to her."

"Then she should've thought better about threatening me."

I knew it! When I mentioned to Madame Selena earlier that I'd grasped what was going on, that wasn't an exaggeration. I'd figured it out ... although how was anyone's guess. "Trish found out that Ashley wasn't Henry's daughter, didn't she?" The question was out of my mouth before I thought better about uttering it.

Barbie pinned me with a hateful expression. "I have no idea what you mean."

"There's no sense denying it at this point." I opted to be pragmatic. "We're all in this together. I think we'd all like to understand exactly why we're here."

"And I think you should shut your hole," Barbie snapped. "You're the reason we're in this situation. If you'd simply let things go, not used your feminine wiles on Galen to keep him investigating, we wouldn't be here."

Feminine wiles? Good grief.

"No, but your daughter would still be in jail for something she didn't do," Lilac pointed out.

"That can't be my concern." Barbie turned icy. "It's Ashley's fault for remaining friends with that girl. I told her from the start that it was a mistake, but she refused to listen. She said ending the feud was the most important thing."

"She didn't realize she was partially at the center of the ongoing feud, did she?" I challenged. "She didn't realize Gus was her father. I guess he lied about you guys having an affair. And here I thought we were having a moment at the bar."

"It was a very long time ago, and I wouldn't call it an affair," Barbie sneered. "It was at a party at the Elks lodge and there was some drinking going on."

"Man, these Elks people must party like it's the eighties," I groused. "It seems like all they do is drink and have affairs."

"That's not all they do," Booker said. "That's only the tip of the iceberg. You don't want to know the rest of it."

He was probably right. I licked my lips as I regarded Barbie. "When did you find out Ashley was Gus's daughter?"

"When I saw the results of some blood work when she was a teenager," Barbie replied. "I believe she was getting her routine exam before her freshman year of high school. The doctor insisted that we all get tested again because something wasn't right. He thought it was a clerical error. I talked him out of it and convinced him to fix the chart."

"Fix it, huh?" I felt mildly sick to my stomach. "I'm sure that would've gone over well if Ashley had a medical emergency down the road."

"Oh, don't worry. I had the doctor alter Henry's chart. It didn't even cost that much. Five-hundred bucks and the possibility Henry might get the wrong blood if he was ever in an accident. It was well worth it."

Yup. Now I definitely felt sick. "How did Trish find out?"

"She and Ashley gave blood together at one of those drives they hold downtown every few months," Barbie replied. "They found out they had the same blood type – or I guess it was the same Rh-negative factor, which is rare – and thought it was weird. Apparently Trish thought it was weirder than Ashley and did some digging. She found out Henry's real blood type – I'm still not sure how – and confronted me."

"Ashley was her sister. That would've been a big deal to her."

"Ashley was her half-sister in blood only," Barbie countered. "They weren't sisters. They never should've been friends."

Something about the story didn't sit right with me. "Why did you even care after the divorce? I mean … once you got your settlement from Henry, a guy you obviously don't like, why not tell the truth?"

Barbie turned haughty. "What makes you think he doesn't know the truth?"

I was dumbfounded … but then I remembered the vision I had when leaving her house. "You told him at some point."

"I did. We were in a fight and I blurted it out. By then he loved her. She was a teenager, after all. He said blood didn't mean anything."

"And then he turned around and had an affair with Maureen," I deduced.

"Pretty much. It was payback."

"He conveniently left that part out of his story," I muttered. "It might've saved us some time if he'd simply told the truth."

"Oh, he would've never done that," Barbie intoned. "He didn't want Ashley to think of him as anything other than her doting father. He wanted her to live her entire life in the dark."

"Did he know Trish had found out the truth?"

Barbie shrugged. "I don't believe so. She came straight to me. She was too sympathetic to approach Henry in case he didn't know. She wouldn't want to break apart his world."

I swallowed the lump in my throat. "What about Gus? Why did you kill him?"

"Wait … forget the why of it." Booker held up his hand to draw Barbie's attention. "We know the why. Hadley was pressing for further information. You believed she was pushing Galen to keep digging, and you didn't want that. You were more than willing to sacrifice your own daughter if it meant you got away with it."

"Pretty much," Barbie agreed. "Ashley has been insufferable since her teenage years. I really don't have much love for the girl. I wanted to protect her a bit, make sure she didn't find out the truth because it would've resulted in a lot of whining. And Henry would have demanded some of his money back from the divorce because he made sure I got more than I deserved in exchange for keeping the secret. But I'm willing to sacrifice her to keep myself safe."

"You thought killing Gus would distract Galen, didn't you?"

Booker pressed. "You enticed Madame Selena to help you pull it off. You wanted Hadley confused so she wouldn't know if she somehow killed Gus, and you wanted Galen focused on her above everything else. If Hadley was in trouble, he'd stop looking into Trish's death."

"Basically." Barbie was blasé. "It didn't even have to be Gus. I just needed someone to get Hadley out in the open. I saw Gus down the beach and approached him. He was a wreck, sunburned and crying. He was broken-hearted ... showed me his gun. I saw my opportunity then and sent him in Hadley's direction with a little help from Madame Selena.

"She was supposed to control Hadley just as easily," she continued. "Unfortunately, Hadley broke from the spell before I could put the gun in her hands. She broke right before the shooting. I saw it on her face and I knew trouble would follow. Selena did, too. She ran before I was even off the beach.

"That was a big problem for me," she said. "I knew that Selena was prone to talking if she thought it would get her out of trouble. I couldn't allow that to happen. I couldn't lose everything because of her big mouth."

Madame Selena was affronted. "Hey! I don't have a big mouth. I never would've said anything. You could've trusted me."

"Even though you were Hadley's first suspect?" Barbie challenged. "Galen knew right away what had happened on the beach. He knew who to go after. He also knew that someone was breaking into the lighthouse, and it was easy enough to figure out who would have the motive for that."

Madame Selena looked like a kid caught with her mother's makeup. "They didn't know." She looked to me for confirmation. "You didn't know, right?"

"We didn't technically know, but it wouldn't have been that hard to put together," I replied. "I mean ... you were only interested in May's books when you stopped by. We performed a séance to call May, and she said someone was trying to keep her from the lighthouse. Only a few people could do that, and you're the first to jump to mind. It wouldn't have taken long to figure out."

"Oh, well … ." Madame Selena broke off and licked her lips. "Fine. You're right. I totally would've turned you in to save myself."

"See." Barbie knowingly bobbed her head. "I told you I was a genius."

We were getting off course. "So, what's your plan now?" I challenged. "We know the truth, and you're outnumbered."

"I have this." Barbie held up the gun. "I can do anything I want with this."

"Madame Selena has a gun, too," Lilac pointed out. "It's not as if she's going to sit back and watch you kill everyone – including herself – and not do a thing about it."

As if realizing for the first time that she was in a vulnerable position, Madame Selena quickly leveled her gun at Barbie. That allowed me the space to breathe a little easier, although we remained exposed.

The good news was that Barbie and Madame Selena were nowhere near as smart as they thought they were. In fact, they were both a little idiotic. Things wouldn't end well for them. They wouldn't get away no matter what. That didn't mean, however, that they wouldn't inadvertently take us along for a very bad ride.

"Don't point that thing at me!" Barbie snapped, her eyes flashing. "I'm in no mood for your games."

"This isn't a game," Madame Selena fired back. "This is my life and I want to protect it. I'm not going to fight it because you're a money-hungry B-I-T-C-H."

I looked around, genuinely confused. "Who are you spelling for?"

Madame Selena sent me a frustrated look. "I have to spell bad words when I run a tent at a festival because kids are always around. Parents don't like it when you introduce the little ones to bad words. It's become something of a habit."

"Oh, well, that's good, I guess." I really didn't know what to make of it. "You should definitely take her out if you're worried she's going to kill you. You know … be proactive."

Booker widened his eyes to comical proportions as he met my gaze. "What are you doing?"

I ignored the question and remained focused on Madame Selena.

"I'm serious." A plan had formed and I was determined to get Wesley, Booker and Lilac safely out of this situation. I was pretty keen on keeping myself safe, too. I didn't care what Madame Selena and Barbie did to each other. They were horrible individuals who had earned whatever was coming their way. "You should totally shoot her, Madame Selena."

Barbie's mouth dropped open. "What are you telling her to do?"

I refused to back down. "She has to protect herself." I was serious. "You're here to kill her and us, Barbie. Madame Selena has to be the first to go because she's armed. Even though she's a terrible person – and I do mean terrible – I don't want her to die."

"I'm not a terrible person." Madame Selena adopted a whiny tone. "I just want to be a more powerful witch. Is that too much to ask?"

"You can't be a more powerful witch," Wesley answered. "You're not a born witch. There's a ceiling that learned witches can't move beyond. I'm sorry. I don't make the rules. There's nothing any of us can do to help you."

Madame Selena wasn't ready to give up. "If I could just take the book I know it would help. May cast a spell so I can't, but I think if Hadley puts a little effort into it she could lift the spell. Then I'll take the book and be on my way. No harm done."

And leave us with crazy Barbie in the process, I thought. No thank you. "That's not going to happen." I chose my words carefully. "I don't know how to lift the spell and I'm much too worried about surviving to do it. You should be worried about surviving, too. I mean ... look at that woman." I gestured toward Barbie. "She has murder on the mind, and you'll be the first one she takes out. I promise you that."

Madame Selena balked. "How can you possibly know that? She can't make an expression – her face is frozen in time – so how do you know what she's thinking?"

Barbie beamed. "Thank you."

"I'm pretty sure she didn't mean that as a compliment," Booker offered. "You look like a science experiment gone wrong."

"I look young," Barbie shot back.

"Fine." Booker was deadpan. "You look like a young science experiment gone wrong."

Barbie made a screeching sound as Madame Selena searched my face for answers.

"How do you know?" Madame Selena asked, her voice barely a whisper. "How do you know what she's going to do?"

"Because I've seen inside her head." That was kind of true. "You're first on her list. Then she'll go for the rest of us. You have to protect yourself."

"But … ." Madame Selena broke off and chewed her bottom lip. "Maybe this situation can be salvaged. Maybe we can work together."

"She used you to bewitch the father of her daughter," I pointed out. "She killed him just to give herself some time. She's fine with her daughter going to prison for something she did. What do you think she's going to do to you?"

That was enough to break through Madame Selena's foggy brain. She widened her eyes at the words and pointed her gun directly at Barbie's chest. "She's right. I didn't even think about it."

It was time to act. I gathered my nerves and courage and tugged on the energy I could feel whipping through my body. It felt fragmented, not yet ready to come out and perform, and yet I knew I had to force the wisps into something complete and powerful.

"Don't be an idiot," Barbie said. "I don't want to hurt you, Selena. She's making that up."

"You came here to hurt her," Booker pointed out. "You don't care about us any longer. You only care about Madame Selena. She's the only one who can hurt you."

"He's right." Madame Selena was furious. "You're a murderer, and I'm next on your list. Do you think I'll allow that?"

"I don't think you're in a position to allow anything," Barbie barked. "I'm in charge."

"No, I am."

They faced each other, guns pointed at chests and eyes wild with suspicion. Wesley and Lilac realized what was about to happen and scrambled out of the way.

"You've ruined everything," Barbie screeched. "You're a complete and total idiot. I had it all figured out, but you ruined everything!"

I exchanged a quick look with Booker, hoping he'd somehow grasp what I was about to do. He simply nodded at me, ready.

"You ruined this," Madame Selena said. "You had to take things too far. You've always been like this. Even when we were in high school you took things too far. That's why everyone hated you."

"They hated you. I … ." Barbie trailed off, making a face as she stared at her gun. "What's going on here?"

"What's going on is that I'm going to shoot you and save myself," Madame Selena replied, oblivious to the power I was releasing in her direction. It seeped out of me rather than sped, but it was building quickly. "I'm the boss. Me!"

"Not that, you ninny." Barbie's eyes filled with panic. "I can't move. I'm frozen like a statue. I can't even … no, it doesn't work. I can't move."

"You're still flapping your lips," Madame Selena pointed out.

"Yes, well, I can't move my body." Barbie looked as if she was about to cry, which was impressive because I'd never seen her face move a single muscle. "Can you move?"

Madame Selena finally realized she was in the same boat and she turned screechy. "No. I'm frozen, too! I … what is happening? Are the aliens coming? Am I about to die?"

"No, but you are about to go to jail." Booker calmly got to his feet and plucked the gun from Barbie's hand. She didn't react, instead remaining rooted to her spot. "This is kind of fun." He poked his finger into her cheek. "It's like having a real-life Barbie doll. Quick, someone see if she's anatomically correct."

I scalded him with a dark look. "Don't you dare!" I reached forward and grabbed the gun from Madame Selena's hand, just to be on the safe side, and rubbed my forehead. I was weary after expending so much energy. For some reason, once I pooled the power, it was easy to form. I wasn't sure why, but I knew I would give it endless thought later. "Someone should get some rope. I'm not sure how long this will last."

"I'm on it." Lilac, eager to help, hopped to her feet. "This was a really great showing, by the way. I can't tell you how impressed I am."

"Me, too." Wesley moved to follow Lilac. "I know where May kept the rope. We'll be right back."

"Hurry." I couldn't stop rubbing my forehead. I worried I would pass out. "Hey, Booker?"

"Hmm." He was fascinated with the frozen women, so much so that he didn't even look in my direction despite my raspy voice.

"If I pass out, make sure you don't tell anyone. I want to maintain my street cred."

"What?" He finally dragged his eyes to me and frowned. "You look pale."

"I feel pale."

"Well … stop it." He was clearly agitated. "You're not allowed to pass out. You just saved the day."

"I know, but I expended too much energy. I think I might actually throw up and then pass out."

"I could show you how to fix that," Madame Selena offered, desperate. "Trust me. I'm an expert at magic."

"Shut up." Booker flicked her ear as he passed, kneeling in front of me. "Do not pass out. I'll make fun of you forever if you do."

"Galen." I barely managed to get his name out before I listed to the side. My head felt too big for my body and my torso too heavy to support. "Call Galen and get him back here. I … crap. I'm going to pass out."

Booker seemed resigned to it happening too. "It's fine. I'll take care of all this … including getting the credit." He patted the top of my head. "Nighty-night."

I wanted to smack him, but it was too late. The darkness was already upon me. "I won't forget this."

"I don't think any of us will."

Then I was gone.

29

TWENTY-NINE

I woke up to find Madame Selena and Barbie hogtied on the floor. No, really. They were face down, their hands and feet bound together behind them. They didn't look happy.

As for me, I was on the couch with a pillow under my head. Wesley, Lilac and Booker stood a few feet away, heads bent together.

"What happened?" I croaked, swiping at my face as I tried to regain the strength that had fled so quickly after the magical display I didn't even know I was capable of performing.

Wesley snapped his head in my direction, relief obvious. "See! I told you she'd be okay. She simply overexerted herself. She's fine."

"I don't think Galen will feel that way when he sees how pale she is," Booker argued. "In fact … yup, here he comes now."

As if on cue, the door swung open to allow Galen entrance. He looked annoyed more than anything. Then he got a look at what was going on in the living room. "What the … ?"

Booker filled him in quickly. He didn't meander and cut directly to the heart of matters. When he was finished, Galen was staggered. Instead of moving to the vociferously complaining women – Barbie was busy trying to blame Madame Selena for putting a spell on her that made her act out of sorts – he headed straight for me.

"Hey." He sat on the coffee table and leaned close, his hand gentle as it brushed my hair from my face. "Do you need to go to the hospital?"

There was no way that was going to happen. "No. I'm just ... a little tired. I'm fine."

Galen didn't look convinced. "You're so pale I can practically see through you."

Speaking of that, I had other things to focus on. "We need to find a way for Madame Selena to break her spell. We can't let her leave this house until she does. I don't want to risk May not being able to come for a visit. I'll need a mentor and I'm running out of options."

Galen heaved a sigh. "Fine. You don't have to go to the hospital. I'm going to be watching you closely, though, so get used to it."

I tried to hide my smile, but it was a losing effort. "I've been getting used to that since we met."

Galen grinned. "Cute." He leaned forward and gave me a kiss on the forehead. "You stay here while we handle the rest of this. Lilac, get her some water. As for these two ... I think we're going to have a long afternoon of answering questions. I'm still not sure what happened here, but I'm guessing it's a doozy of a story."

"Don't let Madame Selena leave without lifting the spell," I repeated. "I saved the day. I was the hero. That's all I want in return."

"Oh, geez!" Galen made a face. "I can already tell this hero stuff is going to go to your head."

He wasn't wrong. "By the way, you're definitely the sidekick. I'm the main character in our little partnership."

Galen barked out a laugh. "I guess you are. No, you stay right there. You are officially on lockdown for the next twelve hours at least. If you try to break from that, I'll take control and make sure my sidekick spends the night in the hospital. I'm not kidding. Not even a little."

I wasn't quite ready to let it go. "You're my sidekick. I'm going to get a button made up for you and everything."

"I'm looking forward to you trying."

EVEN THOUGH HE WASN'T keen on the idea, Galen finally relented, and allowed Lilac and Wesley to stay with me while he and Booker transported our captives to the police station. Their truce was all but eradicated as they left, both of them firing verbal jabs at one another as they herded the cursing and swearing women out of the house. Madame Selena agreed to lift the spell keeping May from the house, but I had a feeling it was only so she'd appear cooperative when it came time to cut deals.

Five minutes after the spell was lifted May was back, and she and Wesley set about hovering like … well, doting grandparents. It was kind of nice, but mostly annoying. Then they started sniping at one another, a couple with a lot of history settling into a routine. They were so loud Lilac was keen to escape. I walked her out without anyone noticing, waved as she hit the driveway, and then made my way to the loungers on the back patio.

It was interesting, I noted, as I stretched out and listened. May and Wesley kibitzed and insulted one another, but there was an underlying shimmer of love and passion that made me smile. I was glad Wesley was seemingly over his aversion to the lighthouse. I was also glad May could make regular visits. Hopefully that meant she would answer questions when I was up to asking them again.

My strength returned relatively quickly, but I remained weary. I drank a bottle of water as I watched the sun set and then fought sleep as I waited for Galen to return. By the time he found me on the back patio, takeout clutched in a bag against his chest, he looked as tired as I felt.

"I thought I told you to stay on the couch." His tone was accusatory as he placed the bag on the table and sank into the same chair as me. He used his hip to nudge me over, slipped his arm around my waist and pulled me close so he could hug me. He clearly wanted to sound bossy, but didn't have the energy to pull it off. "You're supposed to be resting."

"I am resting." That was mostly true. "It was too loud in the house to catch a catnap."

Galen tilted his head as he listened to Wesley and May fight. "Ah, it's just like old times."

"Were they like that in life?"

Galen snickered. "Worse. They used to throw things at one another. Occasionally I'd get a call because half the contents of the lighthouse were on the front lawn and the neighbors were worried someone might get hurt."

"Did anyone ever get hurt?"

"No. It was mostly for form's sake." Galen smoothed my hair. "They loved each other too much to take things that far."

I heard something that sounded suspiciously like a dish breaking from inside. "Are you sure?"

"I'm sure." Galen tightened his arms around me. "So … how much do you want to hear?"

"Just a brief rundown."

"Barbie is still claiming that Selena cast a spell on her and made her commit murder. Selena says that she's not powerful enough to do that, which means all the stories she told over the years were lies and she looks like a real idiot. The prosecutor already has a headache, but he's going to charge them both."

That was encouraging. "What about Ashley?"

"She's being released. In fact, she's probably already out. I stopped by her cell long enough to tell her what was going on. We were just waiting for the final paperwork, which I left for Roscoe to handle because I didn't want to be away from you."

"Because you were worried?"

"Because you're still pale and it's the sidekick's job to take care of the hero."

Okay, that was ridiculously cute. "Good point."

"I thought so." Galen rubbed idle circles against my back. "Ashley was upset when she heard everything, although I think she was mostly upset to find out Trish was her sister after the fact. She didn't take it well."

"Can you blame her?"

"No. I'd be upset, too. She didn't seem all that surprised that her mother was willing to let her go to jail for something she did. There's no love lost there. Henry showed up and admitted he knew that Ashley was Gus's daughter but said he loved her no matter what. They spent some time together while waiting. I think they'll get through this."

"I don't see where they have a lot of options," I pointed out. "Gus is dead. Ashley can't get to know him. Trish is dead. There's nothing there. The feud is essentially over. All Ashley and Henry will have is each other."

"And neither of them will stand by Barbie," Galen supplied. "Henry is already talking about having a freeze put on her accounts so she can't use the money he gave her to fund her defense."

"Do you think he'll be able to pull that off?"

Galen shrugged. "I have no idea. I … ." He broke off when Wesley stuck his head out of the door. "Hey. Thanks for staying. I didn't know how long you'd planned to hang around so I didn't bring enough dinner for all three of us. I should've thought ahead."

Wesley didn't seem bothered. "I can handle my own food. I was just checking on Hadley. I didn't know you were back."

"I'm fine," I offered. "I'm feeling fairly decent. I'm sure once I stuff my face with whatever is in that bag I'll feel ten times better."

"I can stay," Wesley offered. "I can sleep on the couch and make sure you're okay."

Galen cleared his throat. "That won't be necessary. I'll be staying the night."

Wesley eyed him for a long beat. "I guess that's probably the right way to go," he said finally, nodding. "But she needs her rest. She doesn't need you to get her all worked up."

Galen's grin was back. "I'm so charismatic I work up the ladies without even trying. I can't help myself."

"Oh, whatever." Wesley rolled his eyes and looked over his shoulder when May floated out to join him. "Apparently Galen is staying the night, so I don't think it's wise for me to stick too close."

May bobbed her head. "I agree. Three is not company when one of the participants is a grandfather." May giggled at her own joke. "Besides, now that the spell is lifted and I'm feeling stronger, I'll be able to pop in for a visit whenever I want. I can watch her."

Hmm. That was something I hadn't considered. "Yeah, speaking of that, maybe we should come up with some rules." I scratched my chin as May adopted an innocent expression.

"What rules could we possibly need?" May asked. "I've lived here for decades. I know how things go."

"I think she means because I'll be spending the night," Galen offered. "We should come up with rules like … I don't know … you're not allowed in the bedroom."

"Or upstairs bathroom," I added, something occurring to me. "Shower time should be private."

"Definitely," Galen agreed, smirking. "Maybe we can devise a way for you to knock before popping up. I think that would be good for both of our nerves."

"You don't live here," May pointed out. "You two haven't even done the horizontal mattress tango yet, unless I missed that when Selena was doing her evil, rotten thing. Did I miss it?"

Galen, always cool under pressure, refused to make eye contact. "I think it's time for Hadley to have her dinner. She needs some fuel. Then we're turning in early."

"Because she needs her rest," Wesley said pointedly.

"She definitely needs her rest," Galen agreed. "As for the other thing we were discussing, May, we'll sit down and talk about rules tomorrow."

"That sounds like pure torture," May complained. "I hate rules."

She wasn't the only one. "I really am starving."

Galen helped me sit up. "Me, too. How about we have dinner and take a short walk by the water? By that time, everyone should be gone from the lighthouse for the night."

"I just got back," May protested. "I don't want to leave again."

"Maybe you should try visiting the ranch," Wesley suggested. "You need to see if you can go other places, and these two are obviously fussy about their privacy." He jerked a thumb in our direction. "It might be the best thing for all of us if you can hop around."

"I totally agree with that." I was enthusiastic about the prospect. "You should practice now."

"Definitely practice," Galen agreed. "Do it inside, though. We want some time alone."

"Oh, boy." May made a clucking sound and shook her head. "This arrangement is going to be trouble. I can already feel it."

I could, too. Unfortunately for her, I was too tired to deal with it tonight.

"It will be fine." I knew that was a lie, but I didn't care. "Everything will work out as it's supposed to."

"That's cute," Wesley drawled. "I was sad I didn't get to spend time with her when she was a little kid, but she's still naïve enough that it doesn't matter. It's nice."

"It is," May agreed, shooing him toward the door. "I'm not naïve enough to know they're going to be smooching each other to high heaven when they're done out here. I don't want to see it."

"You and me both," Wesley grumbled. "I think she's too young for this."

May winked. "I think she's just right."

"I think so, too," Galen said as they disappeared inside. "If you notice, I was right. You figured all of this out on your own, just like I knew you would."

"Not all of it," I clarified. "It's just a start."

"It's a great start." Galen handed me a takeout container. "In fact, it's the best start ever. I think you'll be a legend amongst witches after this story goes public."

I couldn't help but agree ... although not about the "legend" part. The part about it being the best start ever was spot on, though. "Let's eat and take that walk. I'm feeling better."

"Good. But no more adventures until you're fully recovered. I can't take it."

"That sounds like a plan."

Unfortunately for him, adventure seemed to continuously find me since I landed on Moonstone Bay. I wasn't eager for things to change just yet.

He didn't need to know that. He deserved one night of peace – and so did I.

Made in the USA
Coppell, TX
22 April 2022